FIGHTING LOVE

NINA WHYLE

ACKNOWLEDGMENTS

Many thanks to Sarah J and Liz H for their proofreading skills, and to James B for his brilliant cover design.

CHAPTER ONE

I love being a stuntwoman. LOVE IT. One week I could be drowning. The next, throwing myself off a tall building. There's no telling where my feet might end up … if they land at all! But there are days, like today, when my brain is rattling from a fight sequence, my body all bruised and sore, that I can't help wondering if I should have chosen a more anodyne career; a librarian, or maybe a florist. Anything that requires my feet to be at ground level for a good proportion of the day. OK, perhaps not a librarian or florist, admirable career choices though they are, but I get hay fever and the temptation to karate-chop the encyclopaedia section would be too great.

'What's wrong with you two? Getting old?'

Sam, the stunt coordinator is just too funny for words. Using the little strength, I have left I haul my arse off the floor.

'When I was your age I could—'

'Wrestle lions with your bare hands,' I interrupt. 'Leap over buildings …'

Sam doesn't laugh. 'Don't get smart with me, Harriet

Quinn, and wipe that grin off your face, Matthews.'

I swear Sam has eyes in the back of his head. I wink encouragingly at my sparring partner; he returns the gesture by going cross-eyed. I snort out a laugh.

'I'm glad you two find this amusing because we still have two more hours to go.'

'WHAT!!! But … I thought … You said …' I'm spluttering.

Sam starts laughing. 'Your point, Harry?'

'I-I'll co-llapse!' And I'm not exaggerating.

'You! You're as strong as an ox.'

This isn't the response I am hoping for but exhaustion is not part of Sam's vocabulary.

At sixty-one Sam Yuen is considered one of the top ten fight choreographers in the world, a true perfectionist. He demands absolute dedication from anyone who is lucky enough to work with him and I do appreciate it, really, I do, it's just … I resist the childish urge to stamp my feet, and to think there was a time when I could twist Sam around my little finger and he would call me his little muffin puffin.

I drag my tired body to the middle of the floor and take up the fighting stance; I don't see I have much choice. Sam could run me down in a second if I decide to abscond. Besides, if I want to get out of here and into the luxury bath I've been promising myself, I would do well to keep my mouth shut. Luke, I notice, does the same.

Sam and my dad are friends, best friends in fact. They were stuntmen together back in the day, as was my mum. But when my mum died my dad gave it up. I was too young to remember much about that time although I do have one vivid memory that encapsulates the fun they all had back then; a bright summer's day in the middle of an airfield with a rickety old Boeing Stearman, each taking turns to strap themselves on the roof for a loop-the-loop – this type of escapade being in the normal parameters of a day out to me. I sat on top of the car clapping and cheering thinking it was all just for me.

My mum's death didn't occur on an airfield. Nor did it occur on a film set while performing a death-defying stunt. My mum was killed when a car jumped a red light on a pedestrian crossing. She spent two weeks in a coma before she died from her injuries. Dad at the time was intent on hiding himself from the rest of the world and shielding me from it (and at four years old I didn't have much say). He ended up buying a remote farm in the middle of Devon.

Sam was not about to let his grief-stricken best friend become a recluse and convinced him to transform the farm into a stunt school. I grew up surrounded by people being set on fire and having sword fights in my backyard, exciting stuff to an inquisitive tomboy. I guess it was inevitable that I would follow in my parents' footsteps.

As for tall, dark, handsome Luke Matthews, he popped into my life when I was twenty and perfecting my high falls. Meanwhile, he was busy perfecting his pulling technique. Ten years on and some things never change. I love him dearly but he has the most appalling track record where women are concerned. Like most men he prefers variety to be the spice of life. Not that he has ever dared to make a move on me. Actually, now I come to think about it *why* hasn't he made a move on me? I'm not sure if I should be relieved or affronted.

Relieved, of course. Definitely relieved.

One thing I can tell you about the stunt world, and this will come as no real surprise, it is a male-dominated environment. I, however, have always been considered one of the lads, a calculated decision on my part and I slavishly earned the respect I fought for, literally and twice as hard. After years of survival in this testosterone-driven micro-world I have a curious insight into the male psyche. And really, it's no wonder I'm still single.

Boys are annoying, feckless, and basic.

The film industry breeds men who are more interested

in spinning you a line then leaving as soon as someone bustier and erm … blonder comes along. OK, so I had one bad experience.

I'm just not the sort of woman men go for. I'm OK with that. I don't need them either. Apparently, I scare men away, all five feet four of me. Oh, and I come across as too aggressive, too opinionated, and my best friend tells me I seriously need to ditch the grunge teenage look. I'm twenty-nine.

Urgh. Enough of this nonsense! I can't believe I'm even thinking about the lack of decent men in the world when I have more pressing issues to contend with, such as kicking Luke's butt. Pulling my shoulders back I clench my fists in front of me and prepare to take aim, only to notice Luke has dropped his stance and is looking over my shoulders. I swivel around to see what all the fuss is about and come to an abrupt halt. The fuss comes in the delectable shape of Alex Canty.

Delectable! Now where the hell did that come from? Believe me, 'delectable' isn't a word I often use when referring to the male species.

It's the first time I have seen the actor in the flesh and not mounted on a billboard or appearing larger than life on a cinema screen somewhere. It isn't difficult to see why he tops the *Sexiest Males Alive* polls; and I always thought I was immune to good looks.

The actor strolls towards us and I notice he doesn't even bother to look in my direction. I, however, cannot take my eyes off him, merely out of curiosity, of course; with him being such a huge star it is hard not to. He is dressed in the colour favoured by the rich and famous – black. Black bomber jacket zipped up to the collar, black sweatpants, black trainers and a black woolly hat that he takes off and stuffs into his back pocket. His customary bleached-blond hair has been cut really short and I can't decide if he looks like he has stepped off the front cover of a magazine or is about to rob a bank. Oddly enough, bank robber seems more fitting. He has a dangerous aura about him, animal-like. I would prefer to say ape-like but his swagger is more that of a black panther. He walks like a hunter stalking its prey; that prey being Luke. I dart a look at Luke but far from appearing worried my friend is grinning like a goofball.

'You're an arse, Luke,' the actor says breaking into a spine-melting smile.

Spine melting! Now I'm annoying myself.

The actor turns his attention to Sam and holds his hands up in apology.

'Sorry, Sam, I got here as quick as I could.'

Yeah, sure you did I want to say, but I don't. Like a lot of stars, he thinks he can just waltz in whenever he feels like it. As if the world simply revolves around him. Sam, I know, will put him straight.

'No worries.' Sam waves away the apology and my jaw drops.

I watch as the two men shake hands with visible fondness. Sam is becoming hypocritical in his old age; there is no way he would let Matthews, or me, for that matter, waltz in several hours late.

'I would have got here sooner …' The actor shrugs his shoulders. I notice they are broad and just the right amount of muscle too … Urgh. What has got in to me? Nice arms too … Well, you know … toned. Oh crikey.

I cross my arms and raise a questioning brow because, what the hell, no one is paying me the slightest bit of attention. It's like I've become invisible.

'No sweat,' Sam says. 'Besides it's given me a chance to work with Luke and Harry.'

That's me, I nearly shout, only managing an involuntary semi salute instead. What the hell was that? Now I just look plain weird: 'Commandant F. Spencer at your service … if you please.' I'm such an un-cool buffoon. The actor continues to ignore me. Or he might as well have since the inconsequential nod of his head isn't exactly inviting. He turns his attention back to Luke and little ol' me can take a running jump. Insolent pretty boy can go and F**K himself. He's just delaying my rendezvous with a bubbly bath and a glass of vino.

'I've got a bone to pick with you, Matthews. Where the hell did you run to the other night?'

'I can explain,' Luke chuckles holding his hands up in mock surrender.

'She told me she was your biggest fan – I thought you'd be pleased.'

'Is this the lingerie model?' Sam shakes his head with amusement.

'Too right,' Luke leers, 'and what a beauty.' As if his point needs to be accentuated further he uses his hands to suggest just how beautiful.

I prop my hands on my hips and fume at the men. This has as much effect as before. OK, so I'm not exactly looking my best right now – shoot me, why don't you. I just happen to have spent five gruelling hours sweating my butt off. Give me a break. Admittedly, the grey-marl sweatpants and faded red T-shirt have seen better days and with a face free of make-up and shiny with perspiration I'm hardly going to stop traffic. But surely, I'm not totally nondescript; at the least I normally warrant a sly suggestive once over.

Long ago I accepted that I was no real beauty – not in the conventional way. My nose is way too big but I have a wide smile, which I always thought balanced it out reasonably well. If my arm was twisted and I was forced to choose one feature I liked best then I would say my eyes. They are large, wide-set, and 'the colour of melted dark chocolate framed with enviously long black lashes,' my best friend gushed after one too many chardonnays. OK, this is a drunken-female frame of reference but it is a reference. Of course, that is what best friends are for but Marissa isn't here so it's up to me to remind myself that I have a good body to boot; not Victoria Secret, but the curves I do possess are in the right places. Sure, it would be nice to have a bit more up top, bigger than a B-cup, and longer legs …

I yank at my hair tie. What is wrong with me? I'm standing here like a spare lemon that didn't quite make it into lemonade. What do I care that some dumb actor isn't bowled over by my erm … unique beauty? His loss and all that! One day I might meet a man who is … tolerable, and if that doesn't happen then I'll settle being the eccentric stunt spinster with a cat or two and a chip on my shoulder, which I can easily kick off if I choose.

I gather up my hair and pull it back into a more respectable ponytail. I'm just done when I notice six pair of eyes on me but only one pair has a peculiar effect on my knees. I hope this isn't the early stage of arthritis. I cross my arms and give the three men an impatient glower. 'Yes?'

This amuses Sam.

'When you're quite finished fiddling with your hair I want to introduce you to Alex Canty. I was just telling Alex you are doubling for Felicity Hall.'

Before I can form any appropriate niceties, Luke opens his big mouth. 'I suppose Alex has you mesmerised, huh, Harry?'

'Why is he some sort of hypnotist?' I quip, never knowing quite when to shut up. 'It will take more than some bimbo actor to turn my eye.' The words are out before I have a chance to rein them in and I hear the collective gasp just as Luke's raucous laughter kicks in.

'Oh, Harry, you're priceless.'

I have an overwhelming urge to kick Luke very hard in the shins but I refrain. Just. Bypassing his toothy grin and Sam's astonished gaze I give the actor my friendliest smile.

'No offence intended.'

'None taken.'

And he seems to mean it too.

The actor takes a step towards me and I am forced to look up; six feet two, I remember reading in a magazine once. Not that I've read much about him. Hmm, let me see. Born in Lexington, Kentucky, parents divorced when he was eight, childhood split between the UK and America, studied drama at Guildford, London, moved to California and became a huge TV star playing Dr Mel Keaton, then moved into films, solidifying his place as an A-list movie star.

What? I have this uncanny ability to remember the most useless trivia. You would too if you spent most days sitting around in make-up waiting to be called upon to dive into a freezing river or wrestle a maniac on high scaffolding, and all you have to flip through is a fashion magazine or celebrity tabloid.

The actor thrusts out his hand. 'Very nice to meet you, Harriet.'

'It's Harry, actually,' I correct. Reluctantly I slip my hand into his. It's a strong handshake, firm without being aggressive, not altogether unpleasant.

His eyes twinkle back at me – they actually twinkle. They are also incredibly blue; reminiscent of my times spent in the Persian Gulf.

'Enchanted,' he says, lifting my hand to his lips and kissing it. What is going on? Does he think this is the set of *Mad Men* and I'm interviewing for a secretarial post? I dart a glance at Sam and Luke and see them grinning.

'We haven't gone through the wardrobe into a land of enchantment,' I snap, pulling my hand from his.

'You're wasting your time if you think your charms will work on our Harry,' Sam chortles.

'Yeah, Harry will eat you for breakfast,' Luke adds for good measure.

'Is that, right?' The actor cocks his head to one side and gives me a speculative look. Now that I have his attention I wish I didn't, his eyes keep twinkling at me. 'Maybe I might like that.'

Luke and Sam laugh but I don't see anything remotely amusing in his smarmy presumptions.

'You don't look much like a stunt-woman.'

'You don't look much like an actor,' I snap back. My words amuse him –somehow, I knew they would.

'And pray tell me, what do I look like?'

'A bad excuse for a bank robber.' There I go again, speaking before thinking. This seems to have everyone in stitches; this is doing nothing to appease my mood.

'Told you Harry wouldn't be swayed by your charms,' Luke goads.

Ignoring Luke, I fix my eyes on the actor, determined to overcome this unwelcome attraction. He's the sort of man that lures foolish women and I'm not foolish – at least I like to think I'm not.

'I suppose I don't strike people as the type to fling myself out of windows onto speeding motorbikes but looks are *always* deceiving.'

'I couldn't agree more.'

Yep, he is definitely flirting with me. I scowl at him to show I'm not impressed. He gives me a devilish grin in return.

'OK, kids,' Sam interrupts, clearly wanting to get things moving again.

'Luke, you can call it a night but Harry, I need you to stay on.' I open my mouth to protest but Sam puts his hands together as if in prayer. 'I want to run over the new fight sequence – half an hour tops.' And knowing precisely what buttons to press he shrugs and says, 'Unless you don't think you're up to it?' Knowing full well that I will insist on doing it just to prove him wrong. Curse my indignant pride.

'Sure, whatever,' I shrug.

But Alex hesitates. 'You want me to throw Harry over my shoulders?'

'Er, yes,' Sam says.

'And you expect Harry to throw me over her shoulders?'

'Er, yes.' Sam smiles, 'Is there a problem?'

'I don't want to hurt her.'

I am shocked into muteness. I don't think I have ever had an actor concerned for my welfare before. Obviously, I am annoyed, after all I'm a professional stuntwoman and hurting comes with the territory, but I am also kind of flattered … What am I saying? For goodness sake stop now, he's more fake than rubber cheese.

'I wouldn't worry about our Harry,' Sam insists.

'Yeah Harry's one tough cookie.' Luke gives me a hard slap on the back, causing me to stumble forward.

Alex looks even less convinced.

'Mr Canty,' I say, finding my footing.

'Alex,' he says.

'Alex,' I grind out. 'You seem to forget that you haven't warmed up yet whereas I have been here for FIVE hours.' I emphasised that last bit for Sam but he just shakes his head as if he's heard it all before.

'But you're tiny!' His tone is incredulous. 'You couldn't possible throw a big guy like me.'

Now I'm just pissed off.

'Don't mistake tiny for being weak.' I put my hands on my hips and stare him down. He still looks unconvinced.

'She's right,' Luke says, becoming serious. 'To be honest, mate, I'd be more worried about yourself.'

'Besides, it's my job.' I almost spit the words out.

'I know but—'

Deciding to take matters into my own hands I step forward so that I'm directly facing him and grab the lapels of his jacket. With a quick swift tug, I bring him clean over my shoulders and flat onto his back. I've done it with such finesse that I take him and, judging by the deathly silence in the room, Luke and Sam too, by surprise. Well, he did ask for it!

A giggle bubbles to the surface. This I only manage to suppress by clamping both hands over my mouth. I lean over and give the A-list actor a quick once-over just to check I haven't done any serious damage. Except for a slightly dazed expression on his face he looks fine. More than fine.

'Harriet Annabel Sophia Quinn!'

I freeze. Shit! Now I'm in trouble, and quite possibly out of a job. I decide it's worth it just to see the look on the actor's face.

'What the hell was that?'

I square my shoulders and turn to face Sam's wrath. To my relief he's smiling, although he's trying hard not to.

'I was just showing Mr Can— Alex here that I'm not as fragile as I look.'

I give Sam a wide-eyed innocent look; he isn't fooled for a second. I glance at Luke and he is chuckling away softly but with Sam watching me I don't dare join in. I bite down hard on my lips and turn my attention to the floor. We all do.

Alex is still lying there but he's no longer wearing the dazed expression. Our eyes lock and suddenly I have the strangest feeling I might have bitten off more than I can chew.

I shrug the feeling away. 'You're cool, aren't you … Alex?'

'Yeah, I'm cool, Harry,' he says, mimicking my Devonian twang and pulling himself up onto his elbows. I'm not sure I like how quickly he has recovered.

'Are you going to help me up?' He thrusts out his hand. 'Well?' he persists when I continue to stare dumbly at it.

I want to tell him in no polite terms to shove it where the sun doesn't shine but the sharp look from Sam is enough to tell me that I'd better do as I am told. I smile sweetly and take his outstretched hand, ignoring the warm tingling sensation pooling in the pit of my stomach. Now that he's on his feet he's far too close for comfort. For a long uncomfortable moment, he doesn't let go of my hand. I grit my teeth and fight the impulse to look away. He flips my palm over and starts stroking the inside of my wrist with his thumb. He is being deliberately provocative.

'You really shouldn't bite your nails.'

I yank my hand free. 'So, you're up for another round shoulder trip, eh? This time I won't be so gentle.'

The actor throws back his head and laughs. It's an attractive laugh, deep, strong and sexy, just like him. Oh God shoot me now!

'I don't bite my nails. I keep them short so as not to cause any undue harm to my treasured work colleagues. I wouldn't want to scratch their scrotums, now, would I?' I throw a look at Luke.

'And very wise too,' Luke responds swiftly. 'We all know just how harmful female nails can be on the jiggly bits.'

Alex barks out an almighty guffaw. Evidently, they share the same juvenile humour. Might as well be in the prep room of an all-boys public school. I glare at them both but it has no visible effect. Sam offers me a sympathetic 'boys will be boys' shrug of the shoulders.

'I bet that's the first time a woman has swept you off your feet,' Luke sniggers.

Alex shrugs. 'I was caught off guard.'

'I take it you won't mind going over the moves with Harry now?' Sam is trying to keep the amusement out of his voice. And failing. He turns to me and wags his finger. 'Properly this time, Harry.'

I give him a sweet smile, although it is quite possible it comes across as a grimace. 'Sure.'

'And what are you still doing here?' Sam turns his attention to Luke. 'If you want to stay on I'm sure I could find …' But Luke has pulled on his jacket and flung his sports bag over his shoulder and made a hasty retreat for the door.

'Eight a.m. sharp!' Sam yells.

'Sure thing, boss!' Luke throws us all a final salute. 'Have fun, kids.'

I reluctantly drag my gaze away from the door and peek over at Alex, immediately wishing I hadn't. He has pulled his jacket and sweater over his head, which in turn has caused his T-shirt to ride up over his chest, treating me to a glimpse of his muscled torso. He's such a show-off.

'I'm … um … I'm just going to get some water.' I practically trip over myself in my eagerness to get away.

He's just a lousy actor with a good body, I tell myself. I sit down on the bench with a gloomy thud. Since when do I get all dreamy about a man's body? OK, great body, I admit grudgingly. I grab the bottled water from my bag and take a swig. Most of it escapes out of the corners of my mouth and trickles down my neck. I wipe the spills with the back of my hand and force myself to slow down and, for fuck's sake, breathe. The last thing I need is hiccups and it's not as if I'm in any particular hurry to get back. What I don't get is – why him? I have over the years seen many great bodies. It's inevitable when you work and train with some of the fittest men around. So why should his be any different? It's not, I tell myself, determined to squash whatever I'm feeling down into the pits of my grumbling stomach. I toss the bottle back into my bag and stand up. I'm a professional stuntwoman. I tug at my sweatpants, which are clinging to my bottom. If I can fling myself out of a helicopter onto a moving train then I can deal with the likes of Alex Canty. No sweat!

CHAPTER TWO

'You're enjoying this, aren't you?'

I am flat on my back with Alex sitting on top of me, my arms pinned above my head, wondering how the hell I am going to survive this. I meet his eyes and try to act cool, detached, but it's really hard when your body is having inappropriate thoughts.

'Whatever gave you that idea?'

I narrow my gaze but he just laughs and stands up. 'Want a hand?'

I eye it suspiciously. He returns my look with a beseeching smile. Last time I reached out to grab it he pulled away at the last second. I'm not about to fall for that old trick again. I pick myself off the floor, and when I look over Alex is still smiling.

Oh, how I would love to wipe that smug smile off his face. A sharp right hook to the chin should do it. I grin as the delightful picture of an unconscious Alex pops into my head.

Alex wags a finger at me as if he knows. 'Remember, Sam is watching.'

'Lucky for you.'

He starts laughing and despite myself I smile. 'Is this your idea of getting even?'

He cocks his head to one side. 'I don't know what you mean.'

'I said I was sorry.'

'You did?' His brow furrows. 'I don't remember hearing a sorry.'

'OK, perhaps I didn't use that exact word—'

Alex throws back his head and gives another short sharp laugh.

'OK let's do it one more time.'

Oh God, no, not again. I can feel myself blushing. Sam surveys me, his eyes narrowing with concern. 'Are you all right, Harry?'

I cough self-consciously. 'Sure, never better.'

So much for Sam's promised half-hour! We've been over the same sequence three times already and the first couple of times passed me by in a hazy blur but now … Oh God, now my body is alive with awareness, too much awareness.

I take up my fighting stance and fix my eyes on Alex. As soon as Sam calls 'Action' I am fighting for self-preservation. I try to catch Alex off guard but even as I aim a right punch to his face he blocks it with a flick of his arm. I punch with my left fist and he blocks that too. Block, block, punch, block, block, punch. I throw another punch to the left and he grabs my wrist and with the other hand twists me around, hauling me backwards into his body.

'Would this be an apology for throwing me over your shoulders or for calling me a bimbo actor?' His voice is soft and low.

'Both,' I gasp. I hate that my voice becomes breathless when he gets too close.

'Now why don't I believe you?' He nuzzles closer, his lips briefly touching my ear. I can barely hear him over the thump-thump-thump of my heart. His hands slide around my waist and a delicious shiver runs through my body. Luckily my reflexes respond automatically and I don't have to think about digging the heel of my foot into his shin because my foot is already there, enabling me to twist out of his embrace. I swing to a breathless stop, my hands clasping into fists in front of me.

I toss my head and smirk. 'Oh, I don't know, because you have a suspicious mind?'

He grins. I want to knock a hole through his oh-so-perfect American smile.

'You're a big boy, surely little ol' me couldn't have put a dent in your male ego?'

I bring a sudden kick to his groin. He dodges to the side. Damn! He's fast. I advance with a series of punches and kicks; he blocks them all. With his left leg, he catches the back of my calf and swings me over his shoulder. I career through the air and crash to the floor with a heavy thud. Before I can catch my breath, he jumps on top of me, grabs my wrists, and pins them above my head. Once he has me trapped his eyes bore into mine, his voice low and suggestive.

'I'm glad you noticed.'

I search frantically for a clever retort but settle with rolling my eyes because as soon as his lower body comes into contact with mine an embarrassing explosion of lustful recognition pumps through my veins. I struggle in his grip as the scene demands but each wriggle brings about a new carnal sensation. It feels good. Too GOOD, which is why it is so utterly wrong.

Get up, I silently scream. Get up. But my bones have turned to rubble and I couldn't move even if I wanted too, and I do want to, move that is, because being close to Alex and the way it makes my body feel is something I don't want to feel with a man like him. Incredibly, I find my voice.

'You can get off me now.' It comes out in a hoarse whisper.

'What if I don't want to?'

I look up and there's a predatory glint in his eyes.

'Very funny,' I mumble, but my voice is devoid of humour.

'I'm not trying to be,' he says softly.

I pale. 'If you don't get off me I'll …'

'You'll what?'

He is being deliberately provocative. 'Mr Canty!' I force assertiveness into my voice.

'Alex,' he says.

'Alex,' I hiss.

'Yes?' he says, chuckling softly.

I close my eyes in a desperate attempt to escape their powerful hold and to get myself together. But I can't keep them closed for ever and on a big breath I open them.

'You managed to throw me over your shoulders, surely getting out from under me should be a piece of cake?'

It is a direct challenge and I want nothing more than to rise to it. Lucky for me I don't have to as Sam appears. 'Good work guys. Let's call it a night.'

Ah. Music to my ears!

Alex climbs off me but not before treating me to a wicked grin. I ignore him and push myself into a sitting position, rearranging my tangled clothes. My hands I notice are trembling; I clench them into a fist.

'Harry, I know I put you through it today …'

You have no idea!

Sam holds out his hand and I gladly take it. He pulls me to my feet. 'You did well. Now see that you get an early night as we have a lot of work to do tomorrow and don't be—'

'Late, I know,' I finish for him.

I avoid looking at Alex and use the opportunity to flee to my corner of the bench. I get as far as pulling my slightly grotty but adored navy hoodie over my head when Alex strides towards me.

'You're good.'

I assume he's talking about my stunning fighting skills, because what else could he mean? I free my head from the neck of my hoodie, my hair pulling loose.

'A compliment. I'm honoured.'

'Are you always so charmingly sarcastic?'

No, but then fighting has never felt this intimate before. Neither has standing so close. I'm so acutely aware of him that I can't think straight. 'Sorry,' I say. I sweep my hair from my eyes and force myself to meet his gaze.

'How sorry?'

I flounder. 'What do you mean, how?' I narrow my gaze suspiciously.

'I'm not grovelling, if that's what you have in mind.'

'Now there's a thought.' He angles his head to the side and smiles. 'Have dinner with me?'

I blink at him. Did he just ask me out on a date?

'Dinner?' I squeak. 'With you?'

He chuckles. 'Yes.'

I look over my shoulder to see if Sam has heard but he's on the other side of the room. I drag my gaze back to Alex.

'Why?' My reluctance seems to amuse him.

'How about because I'd like to get to know you better.'

He is not the type of man that a woman simply goes out to dinner with, however charming he makes it sound. This man seduces women like it's going out of fashion, if one is to believe the gossip magazines, and I have already spent long enough in his company to know the power he possesses. If I were to go to dinner anything could happen …

Excitement surges through my veins.

Fool, I berate.

Men like him use women for as long as their amusement is satisfied then drop them like a sack of potatoes as soon as they get bored. The evidence is right there in the magazines for all to see, always out and about with a different woman on his arms and none of them lasting. I'm not about to fall for that one.

'No thank you,' I say.

'No?' He looks slightly taken back.

'You sound surprised.' I give him a cocky smile. 'Haven't you been turned down for a date before?'

'Who said it was a date?'

I feel my face go red. 'I er …'

He starts laughing. I decide I've had enough of his games. I yank my arms through my North Face puffa jacket, grab my rucksack, and turn to leave.

'Good night, Alex.'

He blocks my path. 'What about a drink then?'

I wish he wouldn't get so close.

'I told Luke and the others I'd meet them in the Snapping Turtle for a swift half. That way you don't have to be alone with me, if that's what you're worried about.'

'It has nothing to do with not wanting to be alone with you,' I say. It has everything to do with it. 'The answer is still no.'

'You're a hard lady to figure out.'

This makes me smile. 'There's nothing to figure out.' I circle around him. 'Goodnight, Alex.'

'Sweet dreams, Harry.'

'Yeah … likewise,' I say, not wanting him to get the last word in. 'Night, Sam,' I holler across the room.

'You take care out there, it's raining buckets.'

'I will,' I promise, heading for the door, all the while sensing Alex's eyes on me, making my steps feel clumsy and awkward. It's only when I close the door behind me that I let out a breath I didn't realise I was holding. And Sam wasn't kidding about the weather.

I hover uncertain in the doorway, staring at the downpour and debating whether it wouldn't be better to just sit it out. But the desire to get as far away from Alex Canty as possible and into a warm luxurious bath is all the incentive I need. Gripping the collar of my jacket I lower my head and sprint towards the hired 4x4. By the time I've unlocked the car door and jumped inside I'm drenched through.

It takes me a further hour before I have successfully navigated my way along the wet Buckinghamshire roads, checked in to the bed and breakfast, peeled myself out of my soggy clothes, and settled into the promised hot soapy bath. Ah, the joy. But I can barely lift my arms to wash myself I am so tired.

The unpacking I decide can wait until tomorrow evening.

I only arrived in England this morning. I now live in LA because that's where most of the work is. Sam had been eager for me to get started as soon as I touched down at Heathrow Airport so I drove straight to Pinewood Studios. If I'd known what was in store I might have been better prepared. But how exactly does one prepare for the likes of Alex Canty?

I close my eyes and slide under the bubbles, the water working its magic over my aching limbs, erasing the stiffness in my arms and shoulders. If only my thoughts of Alex Canty could be as swiftly dealt with, and right on cue my body begins to tingle all over as I remember what it felt like to be in his arms. Groaning, I dip lower into the bath until my face is peeping just above the surface; now is not the time to go fancying the male lead especially one with such an appalling track record.

CHAPTER THREE

I'm glad I didn't join Luke and the boys last night; it had obviously been a good night. Too good, judging by the look of them. But they were paying the price this morning; Sam was in a foul mood.

I'm not exactly bright-eyed and bushy-tailed for Sam's gruelling warm-up session either. Truth is, I hardly slept a wink last night, a combination of jet lag, the inevitable lumpy B&B mattress, and a certain swaggering actor, but at least I wasn't nursing a hangover on top.

'Right, you lot,' Sam growls. 'Shall we do that again?'

As with all fight sequences we rehearse, rehearse, rehearse until the moves become second nature and our bodies respond automatically. Each move methodically thought out and practised over and over so that the execution looks realistic enough to believe that bones are being broken. That's not to say that no one makes contact. I've certainly had my fair share of bruises and bloody noses. It goes with the territory.

Focusing on the task at hand I eye the three bad boys in front of me; Luke, O'Grady, and Marco, all sharing the same I'm-about-to-throw-up-look.

'ACTION!' Sam roars.

O'Grady runs towards me, I immediately drop to the

floor and sweep my foot out, catching the back of his leg; he crashes to the floor. I run over his body and slam a fist straight into Luke's chest, pummelling hard and fast. He collapses to the ground and before he has a chance to get up I slam my foot in his face. From behind Marco grabs my ponytail and yanks me backwards. I fall onto my bottom but force myself onto my feet. Marco comes charging forward but this time I am ready for him. I leap into the air and deliver a killer blow to his head. I step back to admire my handiwork, Sam comes over and rewards me with a hearty shiver-me-timbers pat on the back and helps me out of the body harness.

'Nice work, Harry.' When he turns his attention to the rest of the group there is no mistaking the warning message in his voice.

'In future, save the drinking session for the weekend or you needn't

bother turning up. Now take five.'

'Don't say it,' Luke warns as Sam stalks off.

Like hell I won't. 'Serves you right for going on a bender last night.' I poke him playfully in the chest.

'You're a heartless woman.' Luke grabs my offending index finger and moves in to bite it. Laughing I pull it out of his grasp but not before catching a look of astonishment flash across his face. My hand instantly goes to my hair because this is usually the source of his amusement.

'Harriet Quinn, is that make-up on your face?'

I'm in shock. 'What?'

'Make-up?'

'Don't be silly,' I say quickly, too quickly.

'It is.' His tone is amused.

'It's just a little eye-shadow.' And maybe a touch of mascara; I'm more surprised that it hasn't wiped off already.

'But you never wear make-up.'

'I do, you've just been too self-absorbed to notice.'

'Ouch! Well anyway you've smudged it,' he says,

chuckling with delight.

I wipe under my eyes with my fingertips and go to leave but Luke puts out his hand to stop me. He isn't laughing any more but I don't trust the crafty glint in his eyes.

'What?' I say brusquely.

'Doesn't matter.'

'Suit yourself.' I go to move away again but he stops me again. I slap his hand away. 'Spit it out, Matthews.'

He chuckles. 'I was just wondering why this sudden interest in make-up?' He furrows his brows as if he is giving it some serious thought. 'And it's not just the make-up, isn't that a new top? Very fetching.'

'It's a white cotton vest-top, Luke, and I've worn it dozens of times.'

'Really?'

'Yes really.' My voice is heavy with sarcasm. 'Are white vest-tops a sudden wardrobe fascination of yours or something? Hold the front page, people wear white tops … exciting stuff!' I bluster on.' (OK, it is new, but I did buy it to wear at work.)

'And there was me thinking that it is all for lover boy over there.'

The tiny hairs on the back of my neck stand up but I have no intention of following Luke's gaze because I know exactly who will be standing there.

'I thought you of all people would be immune to his charms,' Luke continues with relish.

I keep my voice calm but inside I'm sweating. 'I don't know what you are talking about.'

'Then why are you blushing?'

'I'm not.'

Luke laughs. 'But you two hit it off so brilliantly!'

'Go to hell, Matthews!' I hiss vehemently.

'I very likely will,' he concedes, his laughter petering out to a small chuckle. 'Oh, come on, Harry I'm only teasing, no need to get your knickers in a twist.'

'I'm not … wearing knickers.' I pause deliberately, waiting for the shock horror to take hold of Luke's face. 'I wear sport supports, you buffoon.' I flick him on the arm. 'Look, I just don't find what you're implying amusing that's all.'

Luke lets out a long, amused whistle. 'You really don't like him, do you?'

'I don't think he treats women well.'

Luke smiles. 'He's had no complaints so far.'

I let out an inelegant snort. 'Just the sort of remark I would expect from you. He's a spoilt chauvinistic pretty boy.'

'Oh, Alex is all right,' Luke proffers, putting his arm around my shoulders and giving me a reassuring squeeze. 'Just give him a chance. It isn't like you to believe what you read in the gossip columns. You know they print what they like regardless of the truth.'

'No smoke without fire.'

'Harry!' His tone has an edge of warning to it.

I harrumph. 'Well it's true.'

Luke sighs and shakes his head. 'And there was me thinking you and Alex had kissed and made up.' He nudges me in the ribs. 'Come on, let's go and say hello before you explode.'

'Did anyone tell you, you're a pain in the—'

Luke doesn't let me finish. 'You do, all the time.'

I smile. It's impossible to stay angry with Luke for very long. 'Only to say hello,' I warn him.

We've barely taken a few steps when Luke says, 'But I am surprised, Alex was very complimentary about you last night. I just figured he must have charmed his way into your approval.'

'You know me better than that.'

'True,' Luke says. 'But he did ask a lot of questions about you.'

I look at him but I see no display of humour. 'Nosy

parker! What kind of questions?'

Luke doesn't answer me. 'It might help if you at least try to get on with him instead of being at loggerheads. If the rest of the crew know you and him are feuding it might cause problems.'

'We're not feuding, I haven't known him long enough to feud.'

'You forget I know you, Harry.'

'And what's that supposed to mean?'

'Just because a man finds you attractive you shouldn't find it an outrageous insult undermining your feminist values.'

I stop dead in my tracks and because Luke has his arm wrapped around my shoulders he's forced to do the same, nearly taking my head off in the process. 'Watch it, Harry.'

I give him a sharp look. 'Quite the comedian today, aren't you?'

Luke shakes his head to the contrary but I can see too many white teeth to be taken in.

'You always go on the defensive if a man so much as pays you a compliment.'

'I don't.'

Luke arches a brow. 'You do it all the time.'

I open my mouth to protest but I really don't know what to say. I cross my arms. 'If I do it's only because I can sniff out ulterior motives quicker than a bloodhound.' It's not my fault they cower and disappear like fragile little kittens.

'Of course, I wouldn't recommend you stepping out with our principal star, however much I like the guy,' Luke adds.

'You're making this up.'

'He asked if you were single.'

'So?'

'And I see him watching you.'

'Us,' I correct him. 'He is watching us.'

Alex couldn't possibly fancy me. It's absurd. The most ridiculous thing I have ever heard. For starters, he can have his pick of any woman he wants, and does often; top models, actresses, singers … unless he is considering slumming it for a while. Now that sounds more like it.

'Alex fancies anything in a skirt.'

'True,' Luke says.

'And so, you see there is nothing to worry about because I never wear skirts.'

'I know.' And Luke shakes his head as if this genuinely puzzles him. 'But you should.'

'Should what?'

'Wear a skirt.'

Now I'm confused.

'Sometimes you can rebel against the sweatpants. Look at it as a double-bluff win for the feminists.'

Ha bloody ha!

'You know I would never go for a guy like him.'

Luke looks like he wants to say something then decides against it. 'True, but let him down gently, I've got to work with the guy.'

'Now I know you're pulling my leg.'

He laughs. 'Promise me you'll at least try to be nice.'

'I can't promise anything.' I grab hold of Luke's arm and give it a squeeze. 'Oh, don't look so worried, I'll be on my best behaviour. Scout's honour.'

'You were never in the scouts.'

'I know,' I pout. 'They wouldn't let me in.'

Luke grins and I grin back. We are still grinning like fools when we reach Alex.

'You looked like you enjoyed kicking Luke's butt out there.'

The sound of his voice sends a shiver of excitement through my body.

Drat! I had hoped yesterday was a moment of madness.

'Kicking Luke's butt is the highlight of my day,' I quip.

Luke rewards me with a playful punch in the arm.

'Ow!' I rub my arm as if it hurt, which actually it does a bit. Stunt people never realise their own strengths off stage; we think everyone is rock solid and ready to fight on the count of three.

'Mate, I don't know what you're grinning at, Harry will pulverise you next.'

His mouth curves into a sexy smile. 'Can't wait.'

Luke laughs and throws me an I-told-you-so look, which I skilfully ignore by diving into the pile of coats on the bench behind me so they can't see my red face. I grab a towel from my rucksack and hide behind it.

Today, Alex is unshaven and it has given him a bedraggled, slightly threatening look, the tell-tale sign that he didn't get enough sleep to bother with a razor this morning. The black uniform has been replaced with a more colourful collaboration; a faded red T-shirt with a shark and a chopper adorn his chest, and navy sweatpants. His sweatpants hang low on his hips but that's about as far as I am letting my curiosity go. Chicken, my inner voice taunts.

'How's the head, Matthews?' Alex asks.

Luke winces. 'Urghh, don't remind me. How come you're not suffering?'

'I left you to it, remember,' Alex says.

'Oh yeah, I do, now you come to mention it. A right looker too, what was her name?'

'Amanda.'

Amanda? My head shoots up, and without meaning to I clash eyes with Alex. Urgh … that wasn't very subtle. I pull the towel to my face and rub furiously. What an idiot. Of course, I should have known Luke was pulling my leg; I can be so gullible at times. So, Alex managed to get himself a dinner date after all, why am I not surprised, he probably has a long list of women on speed-dial ready to drop everything and run to his side with just a click of his fingers.

'Amanda and I went for a bite to eat,' Alex says.

And the rest!

'So, Harry, how are you this fine morning?'

Wishing I could ignore him but knowing I don't have the luxury I throw the towel onto the bench and give him a contemptuous smile. 'Actually, it's this fine afternoon.'

'So, it is!' Alex is unfazed by my hostility.

'It's so nice of you to finally grace us with your presence.'

'Why, did you miss me?'

'Hardly,' I scoff.

Luke shoots me a warning look, which I happily ignore.

'Don't mind Harry,' Luke says to Alex. 'She's in a foul mood.'

I give Luke a stony look then turn on Alex. 'Why should I wait for you lot to get up and roll in? Maybe if you put as much effort into your work as chasing skirts we might have progressed further than scene one.'

Alex throws his head back and laughs.

'I don't see what's so funny.' I turn to Luke but he is shaking his head with glee.

Men! I fume.

'I'm glad you two find this amusing but in case you hadn't noticed we start filming next week.'

Alex stops laughing but the twinkle in his eyes remains. 'I'm sure the guys are touched by your concern but we've been training for three months and have it down to a fine art.'

'And Sam shares this sentiment, does he?'

'Ah yes, well … er, perhaps we still have some fine-tuning but, Harriet …'

Who said he could call me Harriet? And, why does it have to sound so sexy coming from him?

'No one forced the beer into their hands, I didn't coax them into Satan's beer glass, they're big boys and they can do as they please.'

'Aren't you just the picture of innocence?' I cut in tartly.

'And it's Harry.'

Luke and Alex exchange looks. I'd like nothing better than to smash their heads together but I don't want to give them the satisfaction of knowing they've got to me.

'I didn't exactly hear you defending my honour when Sam was giving us a grilling,' Luke grouses.

I give him a sugary smile. 'Nothing you didn't deserve.'

Luke pouts. 'You're a heartless woman.'

I blow him a kiss. 'I love you too.'

'Now, now, children.'

I yelp with surprise. 'Sam, one of these days you're going to give me a heart attack.'

Sam laughs. 'Don't be so melodramatic.' He turns to Alex. 'Are you ready to go over the moves from last night?'

'Looks like you will get your chance to kick Alex's butt after all, Harry,' Luke chuckles.

'There'll be none of that.' Sam eyeballs me. 'Is that clear, Harry?'

'I didn't say anything,' I protest, glowering at Luke.

'See that you don't.' Sam peers down his nose at me. 'Ah good, Felicity's here.'

'Thanks a bunch, pal,' I hiss when Sam is out of carshot.

'Why, don't you want to kick Alex's butt?'

I place my hands on my hips and smirk. 'Nothing would give me greater pleasure.'

Luke chuckles and Alex gives me another one of his lazy, good-tempered grins. Does nothing faze him?

This is when Luke chooses to be the annoying brother I never had and nudges me in the ribs. 'What about kicking my butt, huh? Think you can, do ya?' He starts jogging on the spot like a boxer.

'Luke!' I warn.

'What with you being a mere woman and all.'

Right, that's it. I aim a punch at Luke's nose but it's one of those rare occasions when Luke surprises me at just how quick he can be. He darts to the side, grabs my arm and clasps my wrists together. He then begins a torturous tickling assault and I know I'm doomed. I loathe being tickled. Absolutely loathe it. It is the one sure way to have me begging for mercy and Luke knows it. If I were being interrogated it would be the way to get me to spill top secrets.

'Luke …' I gasp. 'Please!' My high-pitched squeals reverberate loudly around the room, 'Luke. I'm warnnnnnning yo-uuu!' My last words are lost in an uncontrollable fit of laughter and I collapse onto the floor.

Luke immediately jumps on top of me and pins my hands down. I am panting for breath. Tears are streaming down my face and I can barely get any words out at all.

'Luke – Pur-lease st-opp!'

Mercifully he does stop but his hand hovers in the air like a diarrhoeic bird ready to take aim. I know it's only a matter of time.

'Say Luke Matthews is the best,' he orders.

I squeeze my lips together and shake my head. Luke laughs, enjoying this rare moment of one-upmanship. 'Say it. Go on, Luke is the best.' He lowers his hand. 'Go on, Harry. SAY IT.'

Then I see it, my opportunity for escape. Luke's grip has lessened and the respite from tickling has empowered me. Without a moment's hesitation I buck my body, causing Luke to lose his grip entirely, and with all my strength I jerk away, kicking with my feet and making an impact with Luke's chest. Luke is thrown onto his backside. I scramble to my feet, pushing my hair out of my face. Now that I am standing at a safe distance I'm quite prepared for anything Luke throws at me and he knows it.

He laughs, picking himself off the floor and dusting himself down. 'Lucky escape.'

'Not luck. Talent.'

Luke strolls casually towards me and I brace myself for another attack but it doesn't come. 'Be nice,' he says and turns and walks in the other direction.

Damn. He's gone and left me alone with Alex. I take a deep breath and stomp back to the bench. I notice Alex scowling.

'You and Luke are close.'

I'm in no mood to exchange polite small talk. 'He's an irritation, the constant thorn in my side. Are you always late for everything?' Peculiarly, his face muscles relax into a smile.

'Sounds like someone got out of the wrong side of the bed this morning.'

I give Alex an insolent smile. 'At least I remember whose bed I got out of!'

He chuckles. 'I suppose you're never late for anything?'

'The human race has developed a few techniques. It's really ground-breaking stuff – you should see the inventions. First there were sundials, now alarm clocks, speaking clock, wake-up calls, phone apps ...' I smile sweetly. 'You should try one sometime.'

'If you were sharing my bed I wouldn't need one,' he replies with equal sweetness.

And that's exactly the kind of remark I could well do without. I glance around to see if anyone overheard but they're all preoccupied with what they're doing.

'Well that's a most improbable event to think about.'

'Not even if I were the last man on earth?' he says, batting his thick eyelashes at me.

'Not even the last in the universe would sway me,' I fling at him. I wish I knew what he found so damn funny.

I suppose I should be relieved that he does. I can't imagine talking to another A-lister in quite the same way. In fact, I'm pretty sure I would have been fired by now (such temperamental delicate egos they usually possess). I suppose there's still time.

He draws his thumb lazily across his jaw, appraising me with a slow smile. 'I had a lovely meal but I would have preferred it if you had joined me.'

'I'm sure Amanda – that is her name? – would have been delighted with that.'

'Amanda would have been fine.'

Is he trying to tell me that he and Amanda had some kind of open relationship? Maybe this works for some people but I find the whole notion distasteful.

'Have dinner with me tonight?'

His invitation doesn't surprise me; it just proves what a total arsehole he really is.

'What about Amanda?'

'She flew out for a modelling assignment this morning.'

I shoot him a scathing look. If ever a man needed to be taken down a peg or two.

He chuckles softly. 'If looks could kill.'

If it were not for a room full of people I would give him a piece of my mind. Instead I settle with lowering my voice to a well-controlled hiss. 'Why don't you take a mirror instead?'

'So that's a no then?'

'Nothing gets past you, does it?'

'You don't like me very much.' It's a statement rather than a question and he doesn't seem too bothered – in fact he seems more amused than ever.

'Sorry to break up this tête-à-tête.' Felicity giggles and I swing round in guilty surprise.

'Felicity!' I slap a big, fat smile on my face as she pulls me into a hug.

By rights I should hate Felicity because she's so beautiful and talented but she also happens to be one of the nicest people I've had the pleasure of working with.

'How are you, my darling?'

'Fabulous,' I reply. 'You?'

'Likewise, and what about you, Alex?' Felicity reaches up onto her tiptoes and pecks him on the cheek. 'Have you been behaving yourself?'

'Don't I always?'

Felicity giggles. 'Hardly ever.'

I wonder if it's true what the magazines said about their fling last year?

'So, you two know each other?' Felicity asks.

'NO!' I say, at the same time Alex answers, 'Yes.'

This contradictory reply causes Felicity's brows to arch ever so slightly.

'We met yesterday,' I explain. 'We sparred together but we hadn't met until … well, yesterday …' I trail off, aware that I'm babbling.

Felicity looks at me then to Alex and back again.

'Right, I, uh … I'd better go and limber up in the corner.' I give Felicity and Alex a cheery smile and head over to my fellow teammates who are stretching out at the other side of the room.

How can a man who is completely wrong for me have such a powerful hold? I rotate my neck and shoulders to loosen the tension his presence has caused and bring my left heel behind me, stretching my quadriceps. He isn't interested in me, he just gets a kick out of goading me.

'Very sexy, isn't he?'

I wobble on one foot. 'Have you been taking lessons from Sam?'

Felicity wrinkles her brow in confusion.

'Creeping up on people?' Felicity titters but is not easily diverted.

'Alex is one sexy man. Mind you, he's a bit of a rogue.'

Well I can hardly contest that assessment. I pull my arm over my shoulder and clasp it with the other hand.

'I bet he could teach a woman a thing or two.'

I sneak a peek at Felicity but she is staring straight ahead. So, the rumours about their alleged fling are false.

I follow her gaze; Alex and Luke are sparring in the centre of the room. I have to hand it to Alex, he is a natural athlete, picking up the moves quickly and making them his own. Some of these guys have studied martial arts for years but do not have the grace and agility that he naturally possesses. I know he has the respect of the guys and is renowned for trying to do as many of his own stunts as the insurers will allow – and some they don't. If only he wasn't the womaniser I know him to be. It would be too easy to fall for a guy like him. Join the queue, I tell myself before I can get carried away with the fantasy.

'Weren't you linked to Alex last year?'

'He's linked to just about every woman in Hollywood,' Felicity scoffs. 'In my case all untrue.' She smiles. 'But I wouldn't say no and neither should you.' She gives me a loaded wink and then with a flounce of her glossy dark mane bounces over to Alex and Luke.

I give a frustrated sigh and follow her. It's my own fault. Felicity and I started training a couple of months back; we were both working on films in Canada and Sam entrusted me to teach her to fight Kung-Fu style before she went on to finish the rest of her training in Los Angeles with him. On several occasions Felicity and I had lunched together and I made the mistake of confiding in her about my love life, or lack of one. Felicity has obviously taken it upon herself to try a spot of matchmaking; I will have to make sure to tell her I'm not interested.

'Now, Harry, be gentle with Alex,' Luke chuckles as I join the group.

There's a collective snigger. Felicity looks puzzled.

While Felicity and I share similar builds and long dark hair this is where the similarity ends. Felicity is a picture of girly perfection from her baby pink tracksuit to her neatly tied-back hair. Whereas I look like I've been dragged through a bush backwards and with a habit of a lifetime I reach up and tuck a loose strand of hair behind my ear. It isn't just the clothes, although I could never imagine wearing baby pink. I suspect Felicity would look good in a bin bag, she has a way about her that leaves men drooling and I wouldn't mind knowing how she learnt to bat her eyelashes. My dad taught me many things but he wasn't able to teach me that. I give myself a mental shake and bring my attention to where it should be, and not a moment too soon.

Sam commands everyone's ears, 'Harry. Alex. Why don't you go over the new moves we worked on last night?'

'Are you sure you are up for this, Alex?' someone in the group pipes up. I think it's O'Grady.

'Not worried you might hurt Harry?' chimes Marco.

Everyone breaks into laughter. Only Felicity continues to look perplexed until Luke takes it upon himself to enlighten her and once he does Felicity gives me another speculative look. I bring my hand to my temple and circle my finger, indicating that they are all crazy; the room erupts into laughter.

'Right, that's enough,' Sam says, and the room becomes respectfully silent.

I join Alex in the centre and immediately my heart starts to pound. I wipe my clammy palms against my tracksuit bottoms and bring them into a fist.

Focus, Harry. Focus.

It isn't easy. As soon as I look into Alex's baby blue eyes my heart slams into my ribcage. Not wanting to make things any more difficult I refocus my gaze to his chin. It's a good chin, strong, dominant. I blink a few times. Come on, Harry, now is not the time to lose it.

It's not nearly so bad second time around. Once I am over the initial shock of being up close and personal I feel none of the earth-shattering intimacy that threatened to engulf me yesterday, although I wonder if it has more to do with the roomful of people watching our every move than any loss of physical attraction. But whatever the reason, I'm grateful. It's still a relief when Felicity finally takes my place.

It is easy to see why she is predicted for big things in Hollywood and I watch with genuine admiration as she dazzles everyone with her athleticism and elegance – and all this without a hair out of place, how does she do it?

She could still do with putting more power behind her punches but for the most part her executions are precise and well timed. Of course, as her double – believe me, the irony isn't lost on me! – I'll be required to take the hits and any stunt considered too dangerous.

The rest of the day flies by and I find it easier to step into Felicity's shoes, especially when Alex isn't given the chance to taunt me. It will probably be a few more days before I feel completely comfortable in his company but at least my legs aren't turning to jelly every time he gets close.

CHAPTER FOUR

Beep beep beep!
Beep beEP BEEP!
BEEP *BEEP BEEP!*

Jolted awake by the persistent ringing in my ear I kick back the duvet and leap out of bed. Waking up like I'm expecting an ambush has freaked out a few boyfriends in the past but it has always got me to work on time. Like on the count of three: if you don't jump on three you're screwed.

Of course, an unrelenting loud alarm tone helps too.

I grab my iPhone and switch off the piercing noise. Dropping it onto the bed I pad over to the bathroom. Once I'm under the warm jet sprays the water pummels me into a state of consciousness promptly followed by the memory of the incredibly hot steamy sex I enjoyed last night.

What!?!

My eyes fly open and panic stutters my chest. Not content in driving me crazy by day Alex is disturbing me in sleep too. I press my hand to steady my heart. It was just a dream, a wildly sensuous dream but just a dream.

The dream consisted of our eyes meeting across an empty studio floor, a short exchange of witty dialogue where I said all the right things and managed to sound sexy, smart, and funny all at the same time. The next thing there's no more talking as we tear at each other's clothes. Then he is pushing me against the wall, my jogging pants and knickers bunched around my ankles and he waits until our eyes meet then thrusts deep inside me.

I let out a loud despairing groan. I know what this is – LUST. One hundred per cent lust. It's been a long time since I've lusted over a man quite like this. I'm not sure what to make of this mania.

Nothing.

It's only a dream and we all know dreams make no sense at all.

Half an hour later I'm standing in front of the full-length mirror, one hand on my hip, a critical brow raised, contemplating whether my fashion-conscious friend will approve. Swinging to the left I check out my bottom in my skinny black jeans (checking for stains) and inspect my white vest top (hmm, I really do need to invest in some new tops). I pull on a long grey cashmere V-neck cardigan – pity there's a hole in the armpit but if I don't lift my arm up you wouldn't know. I add a couple of colourful bangles and a long gold locket necklace. The necklace belonged to my mother; it is my most treasured possession. It has a photo of my mum and dad together holding me as a baby. I'm pretty sure Marissa will approve.

I look down at my battered Converses …

Or possibly not!

There's nothing I can do about it now, I need to get moving if I'm going to get any shopping done at all.

I've decided to bite the bullet and revamp my wardrobe. It's been a long time coming and with my thirtieth birthday looming it's about time I started to look like a woman and not a grungy teenager. It certainly does *not* have anything to do with a certain swaggering actor. I just think there comes a time in a woman's life when she needs to make an effort.

I tug my purple woolly hat over my wet hair, grab the train timetable from the table, check my puffa pocket for keys and leave for the train station.

Cream wool sweater with a beaded black bow (Paul Smith)

Grey woollen trousers (Chloé)

Gold satin blouse (Malene Birger)

Black patent three-inch (Manolo Blahnik) heels.

Chloé 'Cyndi' pale grey shoulder bag. (I've already transferred everything from my rucksack).

Considering I'm a jeans and T-shirt kinda girl, like you hadn't guessed already, I'm not a complete ignoramus when it comes to fashion. It helps that I have two fashion-crazed half-sisters and a best friend who thinks Net-a-Porter is the best thing since sliced bread. It's just I tend to have more pressing things to spend my money on, like adventure holidays, and furnishing my LA apartment. But I confess I'm quite enjoying venturing off the beaten denim track and splurging on some designer togs. I dread to think what it is doing to my bank balance. Oddly, though, I don't feel the slightest bit guilty. It could be, I suspect, a delayed reaction and the horror will come later when I pour over my credit card bill, but right now I am having fun.

I'm not done either. I'm on my way to the mothership of all department stores – Selfridges. I'm on a hunt for a smart winter coat, something chic and sophisticated, and maybe a dress; I need something for the wrap party.

I half jog, half skip across Regent Street, buckling under the weight of all my bags yet feeling wildly giddy as I head down a side street to avoid the heaving crowds on Oxford Street. I hurry along, eager to get to the store before I have to meet Marissa, when something out of the corner of my eye catches my attention. I stumble to an abrupt stop. And my mouth drops to the floor with a clang. I literally have to bend over to pick it up off the ground.

No, it can't be.

Oh, but it is.

Of all the places, in all the world …

Standing just a few feet away and looking as gorgeous as ever is Alex Canty. What were the odds!

He is huddled in a doorway looking at his iPhone, making derisive snorting sounds. His baseball cap is pulled down over his face but I know it's definitely him. It's as if my body has some kind of built-in antennae alerting me to his presence. If only it had alerted me minutes earlier I would have gone another way. I probably still can, he hasn't seen me yet. I could cross the road and dart up the alley … but what if he sees me? Then he would know I was avoiding him and I don't want that. Drat. Not knowing what to do, I just stand there. This is not good because if I want to avoid being detected I need to act now. But my legs have locked together and aren't budging. Then last night's erotic dream furiously suffocates any practical escape plans circling in my head and a sizzling wave of heated embarrassment flows through my body and up to my cheeks.

I tell myself over and over again that Alex Canty is as ill-suited as they come and needs to be avoided at all cost. The next time I get involved with a man there has to be some sort of future in it. Even if it is only a few months of guaranteed dinner dates and obligatory phone calls; well, at least once a week, nothing too clingy. With someone like Alex you would never know if you were just called in as temporary maintenance in the lull times whilst his busy carousel of overlapping women gets oiled and fully operational again. Quite plainly a booty-call scenario at best, a bit cheap really.

So, what would be the point?

Sex.

Sex is starting to engulf all my thoughts.

Overrated! I retaliate against my wandering, dirty mind.

Not if it's done right.

The cheek of my subconscious for even flirting with the idea!

I shake the totally silly notion from my head and tell myself that no woman in her right mind would be standing in the freezing cold staring at a man who picks women like Del Monte picks fruit. Sanity and coldness winning through pulls me out of my daze and onto the kerb, which is precisely when Alex chooses to look up. Damn! He immediately spots me and zooms in with his big periscopic blues. I have one foot on the kerb, the other hovering over the road.

'Harry, is that you?' I turn and act surprised. He stuffs his phone in his pocket and smiles. 'Of all the places, in all the world …'

'You had to walk into mine.' I give him a weak smile. 'Hello, Alex.'

'For a moment, I thought you were going to cross the road without saying hello.'

'I didn't see you,' I lie.

'Or were you stalking me?'

'Hardly,' I scoff.

'Wishful thinking on my part then.'

I roll my eyes. If I could just stop focusing on how gorgeous he is then maybe I'll survive this unexpected encounter. I bounce from one foot to the other, as much from nerves as from the cold.

'I suppose this is the part where we start to fight again?' he says, taking in my grim face. 'But really, what's the chance of us bumping into each other like this?'

'What can I say? The Gods have it in for me.'

He flashes me a grin. 'So, what brings you into London, or need I ask?' He gestures to my bags. 'What is it with women and shopping?'

'Didn't you know it's better than sex? If you're not satisfied after shopping at least you can make an exchange for something you really like.'

He barks out a laugh, and I'm delighted. Fool.

'What about you, what brings you to London Town?' I ask.

'The same, shopping.'

I stare at his empty hands.

'But clearly not as adept.'

'Hmm, London is difficult – there's so little in the way of shops here.'

'Droll, Harriet, very droll.'

I smile.

'I'm supposed to be looking for a birthday present for my mother,' he tells me.

'When's her birthday?'

'Tomorrow, and before you say it, yes I know I've left it to the last minute. I've spent the last few months trying to find out what she wants but what do you get someone who insists they have everything?'

'Hmm, a tough one. Does she have a penthouse in Chelsea?'

'I would if I thought she'd like it but she hates cities and she always knows if my PA has bought it, saying it's more to an American taste. So here I am, hoping bright and early inspiration will strike. It's not going well.' He seems seriously glum-faced about it.

'What time did you get here?'

'Nine. You?'

'Around the same time.'

'And before that you fitted in a ten-mile jog?'

Who does he think I am, Wonder Woman?

'No, it's the weekend – I did fifteen and a triathlon. Works wonders on alcohol remnants from the night before, shakes them all up.'

He looks decidedly queasy.

'So, you have you been spying on me,' he says.

'More of a guess.'

'I know I have a reputation as a bit of a party animal but that isn't really me.'

I let out an inelegant snort of laughter. 'Yeah, right!'

'Contrary to popular belief, even I need my sleep now and again.'

'But the vampire look is so fashionable these days.'

His lips suddenly tighten and I get the impression I've hit a nerve.

'And what a surprise you don't believe me. You have me down as a debauched playboy and you won't let me defend myself.'

I plant my bags by my feet because I've got a feeling this could take some time.

'It does annoy me when people I've never met judge me based on what they've read in one tabloid or another. It comes with the territory but it doesn't mean I like it.'

That told me!

'I admit I did my fair share of partying,' he continues. 'When I was first starting out I had to be seen at the right party. It was all about networking and yes, I like a good time, who doesn't?'

I squint at him; why is he telling me any of this?

'If I really did as much partying as the press report I wouldn't get anything done and my liver would be bigger than my head.'

'Are you telling me you're a little home body and don't party?'

'Not as much as the tabloids have you believe.'

'I see.'

'I don't think you do. Don't worry, I'm not offended even when you do look down your surreptitious nose at me.'

'Are you saying I have a big nose?'

'No, that's not what I am saying,' he says in frustration, stopping when he notices the half smile on my face. He shakes his head as if I could be driving him crazy.

'I happen to think you have a very … charming nose – regal.'

I laugh. Regal indeed. I haven't heard that one before. 'Oh yeah, bow to the nose.'

He doesn't laugh.

'Don't you mean big?' I say.

'No,' he says, his gaze serious and penetrating.

I find myself squirming a little. 'Flattery will get you nowhere!'

'Damn and I was always told it would.'

I laugh, which sounds a lot like flirting to me. Have I totally lost my mind? I clear my throat. 'Right, well I best be off.' Except that I don't move because it's hard to do anything when he looks at me as if he wants to ravish me on the spot.

'And you have stunning eyes.' And he clearly doesn't know when to stop.

I draw in an unsteady breath. 'Bravo, Alex, you're very good at this.'

'What?'

'Being charming.'

'So, it's working? I had my doubts.' The corner of his mouth curves up.

I look away and thump my gloved hands together. 'Cold, isn't it?' I say.

'So, have I changed your mind?' he asks, ignoring my attempt to change the subject.

'About what?'

'Liking me?'

'You're passable.' I can't stop fantasising about you.

He leans forward, his expression grave. 'But sometimes I annoy you?'

'You're a predictable wind-up merchant.'

He leans back and tucks his hands into his coat pocket. 'So, is it true you've jumped out of a helicopter and onto a moving train?'

If I didn't know better I would think he didn't want me to leave. 'Um … yes, and then hit by a pick-up truck.' I can't help the grin forming on my face when I see the look of stunned horror on his face. 'And thrown through forty windows. It sounds more dangerous than it is,' I reassure him.

He doesn't look at all convinced. 'I guess that makes you a thrill-seeker?'

I think for a moment, urging my ironic tendencies to stay silent. 'There definitely is an element of the adrenalin rush on completing a particularly dangerous stunt but there's more to it than that: a feeling of accomplishment, seeing how much your body can do and take. Truth is, I was never any good at sewing or cooking, so what's a girl to do?' Can't keep that wicked tongue at bay. Alex seems unaffected by my jibe.

'Don't you ever get scared?'

I could think of something far scarier – like the way my body responds even when he isn't touching me. He just has to look at me then all sense and purpose rushes out of my head. I tell myself to get a grip; this is becoming somewhat of a mantra. 'Not scared, exactly, but I think fear is a good thing. It keeps you on your toes.'

'And you specialise in …?'

I tilt my head to one side. What is it with the twenty questions?

'I'm interested,' he says, as if he can read my mind.

'Martial arts, kick-boxing, kung-fu.' I tick them off with my finger. 'My dad taught me.'

'Remind me not to get on his wrong side.'

He looks genuinely impressed and I find myself fizzing inside with pleasure. 'I'm also a professional stunt rider and have mastered swords and firearms.'

'A proper little Rambo.'

'Less of the *little*, thank you.'

'How tall are you, anyway?'

'Five feet four.' I pull my shoulders back and lift my head up as if this somehow makes me taller.

'Sorry, I didn't realise I was in the company of such a giant,' he teases.

'Size isn't everything.' Now who's flirting?

Alex looks delighted. 'It's what you do with the size that matters.'

I can feel myself blushing.

'What about injuries?'

Gee, he's really Mr Chatty today.

'I've had my fair share. Let's see; I broke my left foot, right toe, dislocated my shoulder, tore a ligament in my right knee, and suffered severe whiplash.'

Again, he looks suitably horrified.

'Oh, and this,' I grin, lifting my head and pointing to the scar under my chin. 'Eight years old, fell off the top of a slide and cut it open.'

Alex leans in for a closer inspection.

'Did it hurt?'

'I can't remember, it was a long time ago.' My voice wobbles because he reaches out and cups my chin. Quite honestly, I'm surprised I can talk at all. I hadn't expected him to touch me and I have this sudden sensation that I'm freefalling.

I tell myself to breathe but with his eyes boring into mine it's difficult to grasp this very natural act. Ever so gently Alex moves closer, as if he's testing my reaction. I stand there, putty in his hands. He draws a finger lightly across my scar.

'I suppose when I list the injuries like that it does seem a lot.' Perhaps if I keep talking, pretend nothing out of the ordinary is happening, I will survive whatever this is. 'I did a lot of work in Japan in the early years,' I tell him, a nervous chuckle escaping from my throat. It's just as well he has hold of me because my knees have gone weak and I think I might fall; no, not fall – swoon, like a nineteen thirties damsel.

'I've played plenty of drug lords' girlfriends and villains, oh, and vampires too.' His eyes bore into mine with total fascination. I step backwards, breaking his hold before I do something stupid, like kiss him. 'I must be boring you rigid.' I let out a self-deprecating laugh.

Alex shakes his head. 'On the contrary, I'm just thinking how truly remarkable you are.'

Oh, he's good.

'What you do is very dangerous.'

'For a woman, you mean?'

'For anyone,' he replies.

'What about you, any bones broken?'

'Just my nose.'

I study the slight hook in his nose and I can't think of ever seeing such a perfect nose. 'Let me guess, a bar room brawl? A jealous boyfriend?'

'Much more dramatic! My cousin took me ice-skating but I didn't know how to stop and ending up smashing into the barrier nose first.'

'Ouch!'

'I'd like to say I didn't cry but I bawled like a baby.'

There's nothing more attractive than a guy who doesn't take himself too seriously and this is something I've noticed more and more about Alex.

'How old were you?'

'Ten.'

An image of an adorable little boy with lots of dark hair and a cheeky grin pops into my head.

'Ever thought of quitting?'

'What, stunt work?'

'Yes.'

'And do what?'

'Something else.'

'Something safer?'

'Well, yes.'

'This coming from the man who insists on doing his own stunts?' I wag a gloved finger at him. 'And don't you dare say but that's different because you're a man.'

'As if I'd dare – but aren't you ever afraid?'

It isn't something I think about often but I suppose there are days when I wonder just how many lives I have left. 'Not afraid, exactly, but respectful of what can go wrong. What about you, why do you do it?'

'What do you mean?'

'Why do you put yourself at risk when you don't have to?'

He shrugs. 'I guess, like you, I see it as a challenge. A chance to see what my body can do and I always think I give more to the part if I do as many of my own stunts as possible. I think the public would feel cheated if I didn't.'

'Oh, so you like being perceived as the big action hero?' I tease.

He gives me a slow, boyish grin.

'What can I say, it's the kid in me.'

'I bet you were a handful as a kid.'

'I got into a few scraps but I was very much the skinny boy back then so I always came off worse.'

'You!'

His mouth quirks up and he wags his brows. 'Hard to believe, eh?'

I nod, my mouth suddenly dry. I only just manage to stop myself from looking him up and down and studying his lower regions. Maybe I should consider a career as a leering builder.

His eyes twinkle at me. 'You know, we have to be careful, we're almost being civil to one another.'

I cross my arms and scowl. 'Now that won't do at all.'

We both start to smile as if it is the easiest thing in the world. He has a way of making me think I am the centre of his universe. It's a nice thought but I have to remember that his attentions are not exclusive: they fly about on whatever honeybee is in his proximity.

'Harry?'

'Yes?' He looks like he wants to ask me something and I can't help wondering if he's going to ask me out on a date again. I'm swaying towards a *YES*.

'I was wondering …'

I look at him expectantly. 'Yes?' My voice has taken on an anticipated breathless quality.

'Got any bright ideas on what I can buy my mother?'

'Oh, your mother … hmm, let me think.' I pucker my eyebrows into a considered frown. Fuck, I don't know. 'Um … a novelty teapot?' I blurt.

I know it's a stupid suggestion as soon as I open my mouth. The man is rich and I suggest a teapot.

'Is that what you got your mother?'

Normally this is the part when I tell people in a neutral unaffected voice that my mum died when I was very young so I never got the chance to discover the things she liked or disliked. But sometimes when I'm caught unawares like this I feel the intensity of my loss and a feeling of irrepressible sadness crushes my heart.

'Harry?'

I snap my attention back, blinking.

'Thought I'd lost you for a minute.'

'I can't remember what street it's on but there's a shop selling novelty teapots that way near Carnaby Street.' I spin away quickly, tears gathering in the corners of my eyes. I blink them back and point in the general direction. I'm being totally ridiculous. Now is not the time to dwell on sad memories. I have a wonderful stepmother and she loves tea, and that's what gave me the idea. When I'm sure I'm not going to cry I turn to face Alex. 'It's a stupid idea, forget it.'

'A novelty teapot.' He savours the idea for a moment. 'My mother drinks gallons of the stuff.' He leans closer. 'Hey, are you OK?'

'Yes,' I say quickly. 'The um … cold is making my eyes

stream. They have some wonderful teapots.' I flap my hand in the air. 'Teapots in the shape of fruits, birds, animals … well, everything really. I didn't go in but it had a lovely window display …' I am babbling, something I seem to do a lot of when I'm in his company. I force myself to take a deep breath. Alex continues to look at me and I feel a fresh bout of tears prick the back of my eyes. He is looking at me with such concern and warmth that I'm wondering if I've been wrong about him, maybe he is a decent man after all?

'Alex Canty, you utter scoundrel!'

My head snaps to the point just over Alex's shoulder where a tall glossy blonde dressed in a floor-length beige furry coat – fake, I hope – appears at his side. This must be Amanda, I realise, as my stomach plummets to the ground. Luke was right: she's a stunner.

'Alex, you're hopeless. How are we supposed to buy a present for your mother when you can't even be bothered to come into the shop with me?' she drawls languorously.

'I don't think they have anything suitable for my mother in there,' he says.

Amanda titters. 'Yes, you might be right.'

I didn't notice the shop until now. Too busy drooling over Alex Canty. But I can hardly miss it as I take in the beautiful lingerie displayed in the front window. My cheeks flush scarlet.

'But I found something absolutely perfect for me,' the tall model says with a tinkling little laugh. She holds up a small package. 'Want to see?'

'Not particularly.'

There's a hint of annoyance in his tone, which surprises me but the model seems oblivious to this.

'Spoilsport.' She turns to me and extends a tan-leather gloved hand. 'Seeing as Alex has forgotten his manners, hi, I'm Amanda.'

I take Amanda's hand. 'Hi, Amanda, I'm Harry.'

'Pleased to meet you, Harry.' She gives me a blinding

smile. 'Alex is annoyed because we haven't found a suitable present for his mother.' She turns to him and pouts.

'Not at all,' he replies coolly. 'Besides, Harry's given me the perfect idea for a present.'

Amanda claps her hands together with delight. 'Well that's fantastic.

Now you can stay for lunch after all. We can go to the Ivy, Penny and Toby will be there and—'

'No,' Alex cuts her off. 'I want to set off for the Lakes as soon as possible.'

Amanda sticks out her bottom lip. 'You're such a party-pooper. You never want to do anything fun anymore.'

'You're going to the Lake District?' I ask, still digesting the image of Alex being a party-pooper.

Amanda wrinkles her nose in disgust. 'Alex's idea of a fun weekend is to go traipsing in the mud, and it's even better if it's raining.'

'My mother and stepfather live there,' Alex explains. 'But it's Amanda's idea of living hell.'

'There's nothing to do there,' she protests.

'There's plenty to do there, you just don't like it because there isn't a Harvey Nicks nearby,' he counters.

'That's not true. I like browsing in the town shops but all you want to do is go walking and climbing up rocks and what, pray tell, is the point of that?' She quirks an eyebrow in my direction as if to say, don't you agree?

Alex chuckles. 'I think you're asking the wrong woman to side with you on that one.'

Amanda gives me a curious look.

'Have you been to the Lake District?' she asks me.

I shake my head. 'No, but I'd love to.'

'I'll take you,' Alex says.

I blink at him with surprise. 'I wasn't suggesting you take me,' I say quickly, looking apologetically at his girlfriend, but she just rolls her eyes at me, not the least bit perturbed that her boyfriend is asking another woman away with him.

'You take a girl to Paris or Venice, not to the Lake District.' She gives me a wink.

'Paris, I …' I flounder.

'You're so right, Amanda,' Alex says. 'Would you like to go to Paris with me, *Harriet*?' saying my name like's it's a term of endearment.

Well, if he is trying to make Amanda jealous it isn't working.

'Eh, no, thank you,' I say primly, although stupidly feeling a sense of disappointment that I'll never get to experience Paris with him. 'I've been to Paris, lots of times.'

'A girl can never have too much of Paris,' Amanda sighs blissfully.

'With a lover?' Alex probes, his eyes blazing with curiosity.

Chance should be a fine thing!

'None of your business,' I reply coyly, giving the impression that that's exactly what I did.

'Are you an actress too?' Amanda asks.

'Me?' I snort with laughter. Attractive Harry, very attractive!

'Harriet's a stuntwoman,' Alex informs her.

'Harry,' I remind him.

'Harry is a stuntwoman,' he tells Amanda, smiling broadly.

Amanda's tawny-coloured eyes grow big in her face and she stares at me with shock. 'Really?'

I nod. 'Yep, it is true. I'm the person that throws themselves down staircases, crashes motorcycles into walls, that sort of thing.'

Amanda's amazed look turns to one of horror.

I laugh. 'It's all perfectly safe,' I reassure her.

She doesn't look convinced. 'So, I suppose climbing up rocks is a leisurely pursuit for you.'

'In a way, yes,' I smile.

Amanda looks at me and then at Alex and back again, a smile flitting across her lips. 'Then you must get Alex to take you.'

'Oh no … I don't, I'm not, I'm not implying … Alex should take me.' If I was Alex's girlfriend I wouldn't like the idea of him taking another woman away.

'You don't want to go to the Lakes with me?'

'I'll probably end up pushing you in using your remains as footwear,' I retort.

Amanda bursts into laughter and it's not at all ladylike. In fact, it sounds a lot like a snorting pig, which makes me warm to her even more. 'Well, if you change your mind you should let Alex take you. He's very knowledgeable about the area. But enough of that, what I want to know is do you get to work with lots of hunky men?' A sensuous smile crosses her lips.

'Harriet— Harry,' he corrects himself, 'is a professional woman, Amanda. A successful member of a very small group of stuntwomen who jump, fight, ride, fall, fly, and generally defy all types of fear and gravity. And the men she works with are professionals too.'

My mouth drops open with genuine astonishment. Amanda, too, looks a little taken aback. 'I know that.' She playfully hits him on the arm then turns to me with an excited giggle. 'But I bet there are a lot of sexy men?'

I can't help it, I start to laugh. I assumed as a model she would be cool and aloof but she doesn't appear to be any of those things. Besides, I like seeing the annoyance on Alex's face that his girlfriend is lusting after other men.

'I guess there are a few,' I confide conspiratorially.

Amanda squeals with delight. 'You have the coolest job. Literally being thrown onto hot, sweaty, rippling bodies.'

I laugh but I notice Alex has lost his sense of humour altogether, my cue to leave. I give Amanda a smile. 'Lovely meeting you, Amanda.' And I mean it.

She smiles. 'Likewise.'

'Do you want to have lunch with us?' Alex suddenly asks.

'Oh goodie, so you've changed your mind?' Amanda beams at him, but I have no intention of playing gooseberry.

'I can't, I'm having lunch with a friend.'

'Anyone I know?'

'No.'

Amanda gives me a comradely smile. 'Another time then?'

'And I want to pop into Selfridges first.'

Amanda gives me an eager look. 'Ooh, I could do with—'

'I'm not going to Selfridges, Amanda,' Alex says, all but stamping his foot like a two-year-old.

She pouts beautifully. 'Well, I am freezing my butt off out here so let's at least get walking, misery guts.' She turns to me. 'I hope we meet again.'

'I'm sure we will.' I return the smile. 'Bye, Alex.' Our eyes meet briefly and he smiles. I smile back and give them both a wave then turn and walk away.

I'm glad I won't be seeing him next week. I've got a week of second unit driving shots. The more distance I put between him and myself the better.

CHAPTER FIVE

I didn't find the perfect coat but I did find the perfect black dress: a daring backless number in satin by DVF. I also found a shamelessly short red belted mini-dress (Miu Miu), and some underwear (Myla). What? I've been meaning to ditch the raggedy old knickers and bras for ages.

By the time I realised what time it was I had to ring Marissa and tell her I was running late.

'Marissa, I'm soooooooo sorry.' I hastily pull the rest of my shopping bags out of the black cab.

'Someone looks like they've been busy.' She eyes my bags enviously.

'I'm not sure what came over me,' I say over my shoulder as I pay the cabbie.

'And not a sports bag in sight. Who is this impostor and what have you done with my best friend?'

I laugh. 'I have gone a bit overboard.' I grab Marissa for a hug. 'Oh, it's soooooo good to see you.'

'You too,' she says, squeezing me back, tightly.

We pull apart and take another good look at each other before coming back for another hug. Telephone conversations, Skype and emails are all well and good but nothing like a proper catch-up face-to-face.

Marissa has been my best friend for the best part of

twenty years. We met in primary school and became instant friends when we discovered a shared passion for My Little Pony and gourmet mud pies. And when we were older we rented a flat together in London. That all changed when she met and fell head over heels in love with Tim Dawson. It then seemed like a good time for me to up sticks and move to LA.

'You look fantastic,' Marissa says.

'And so, do you.' Even with the dark circles under her eyes. From what I hear about motherhood there isn't much opportunity for sleep.

'I don't but thanks.' She takes another envious glance at my bags and sighs. 'Oh, I haven't been shopping in ages.'

'I'll probably regret it when I get my bank statement.' I'm only half joking when Marissa spots my Chloé bag. She immediately grabs it and holds it up for inspection. An immaculate plucked eyebrow rises into an arch.

'It's a Chloé,' I say proudly.

'I know.' Marissa suddenly narrows her gaze at me. 'How old were you when you broke your arm?'

'What?'

'How old were you when you broke your arm?' she repeats with the impenetrable look of an interrogator.

'Eleven.'

'Where did you get that scar under your chin?'

I giggle. 'Top of a slide.'

'What happened when Jimmy Talbot asked you out on a date?'

'I burped in his face.'

It wasn't my finest hour. I had a major crush on him but drank a full can of sugared cola and he took me by surprise. 'What's with the Spanish inquisition?' I ask.

'Just checking that it's really you and not some alien clone.'

I roll my eyes. 'You've been watching too much *Doctor Who.*'

'Yum, Matt Smith is divine.'

I laugh. 'Well I did buy you a little something ...'

'You have?' Marissa's smile instantly brightens. 'Well, in that case would you like a hand with the bags?'

'I thought you'd never ask.' I heave a grateful sigh, piling the bags into Marissa's willing arms.

Fortunately, we don't have far to go and in two shakes of a lamb's tail I have my bags stashed around me, under the table and on the seats either side of me. Marissa orders a bottle of Rioja.

'Let's make a toast,' she proposes. 'To friendship.'

'To friendship,' I smile, clinking glasses.

I take a sip, savouring the herbaceous tones, and feel myself instantly relax. I always love the first glass of wine of the day. It reminds my over-exerted body to chill the hell out.

In the early days, my body would be on high alert at the end of each day, so much so that my legs used to kick in the night and the adrenalin made my arms twitch – I once punched a shelf down in my sleep. My dad used to make me drink a martini when I came in; I think he got bored with all the DIY chores my bedroom suffered and figured it was the cheaper option.

'So I take it Tim has Harrison?'

Marissa nods. 'I wanted you all to myself, to have a proper conversation as opposed to being distracted by a ten-month-old that's set on kamikaze every second of the day. If there's danger, he's there. The other day I ran up the stairs to get something and he was already halfway up. He nearly gave me a heart attack. We really need to get the child gates up. Maybe he has an early calling for your world.'

'With his looks, he needs to be in front of the camera.'

'He is adorable, isn't he?'

'Like father like son.'

'Harrumph!' Surprised, I look at Marissa. Usually the

very mention of Tim unravels a torrent of how wonderfully he is doing, how talented, how majestic he is, a visionary to all through the power of design, the world would be a sorrier place if his pen didn't hit the drawing board, etc. … etc. But she is staring down at the tapas menu, which she insists is the best in town. I pick up my own menu and can't decide on either *gambas al ajillo* or *jamon de Jabugo*. Oh, what the hell, I'll have both. Tapas is a sharing food, after all.

'So, can I have my present now?' Marissa asks.

Laughing, I reach inside my Chloé. 'How could I forget?' I pull out a little Liberty bag and hand it over. 'Just a little something.'

My friend unwraps the tissue with the excitement of a child on Christmas day. She holds up the chunky ethnic bangle for inspection. 'Oh, it's beautiful!!' She reaches across the table and grabs my hand. 'It's perfect.'

'I'm glad you like it.' Marissa immediately slips it onto her wrist and waves her arm in the air.

'Like it, I love it. Love it.' Her eyes are sparkling and shining.

'As soon as I saw it I thought of you: colourful and bold.' I'm pleased that I got it right.

Marissa has always loved her grand accessories. It's not all about the bling with her although she does sport on her left hand the biggest diamond ring you've ever seen. She could open an Accessorize with the collection of fashion jewellery she's acquired over the years. She is one of those people who personalise well. No matter what shop she goes into she always comes out looking chic. Today she's wearing an orange and white zigzag striped dress, which she has teamed with a chunky black necklace. You read about mothers who stop making an effort when they have children, cut their hair short, live in baggy jogging pants *all day*. This certainly hasn't happened to Marissa. I inspect her manicured nails which are putting my short unvarnished nails to shame.

'Right, lunch is on me,' she proclaims.

'No.' I shake my head, 'You don't have to do that.'

'Yes, I do.'

'No really—'

'Look. Tim gives me more money than I can spend. Please let me spend it.'

'OK.' I reluctantly accept the offer knowing this is one argument I will not win. Over plates of pimientos, langostinos, deep fried squids, and spicy chorizos we down two bottles of Rioja and catch up on each other's news. Drinking over lunch is an entirely different affair from boozing it up in the pub; ladies' style is much more acceptable to me. Little hypocrite I am. I am particularly interested in how the new man in her life is doing.

'Which reminds me ...' I pull out a blue and white striped romper suit with a big fish on the front. 'This is for Harrison.'

'You shouldn't have, the monkey's got more clothes than I do.' Marissa holds up the jumpsuit. 'Oh, it's adorable.'

'Just like Harrison?'

'He is a little heart-stopper, that's for sure.'

'Like his dad, eh?' I probe, waiting for her usual gush of love, but there's nothing, just another disgruntled harrumph. With this uncharacteristic absence of worship, I glance anxiously at Marissa but she pulls out her mobile to show me the latest photos of Harrison.

'You're right, he is a heart-stopper,' I say, cooing at them. 'And how's Tim?' I ask casually.

'Fine ... working loads,' she says, then waves her hand at me. 'Oh, let's not talk about me.' She carefully wraps the romper suit in its tissue. 'How long are you here for?'

'Three months or so, depending on the weather; we have a very fussy cinematographer!'

'That's fantastic. We need to arrange a weekend where you can come and stay.'

'Try and stop me. I can't wait to see Harrison. I still can't believe he's ten months already.'

'Neither can I.'

'I feel bad that I haven't managed to get back to London sooner.' I saw Harrison at just two days old and he was tiny.

'Nonsense, you've been busy – I understand. Besides, I've emailed you a ton of photos. You must tell me to stop if it gets too much.'

'Don't be daft, I love the photos so keep them coming.' Marissa smiles.

'So, tell me more about the hunk Alex Canty, what's he like? Have you met him yet?'

It is so casually thrown into the conversation that I'm not prepared for it and I choke on a pimiento. 'Alex,' I cough, reaching for a glass of my water.

Marissa laughs. 'THAT gorgeous, eh? You know he's been voted fifth sexiest male in a recent poll.'

'Only fifth?' This amuses me.

'So, what's he like?' Marissa prods.

I shrug my shoulders in what I hope is a nonchalant manner. 'OK, I guess.'

'OK?' Marissa looks at me with outrage. 'He's more than OK, unless …?' She narrows her gaze. 'Oh God, he's not an arse, is he? If he is that would shatter my illusion.'

Not Marissa as well. Is there no woman immune to his charm?

'Oh no, nothing like that.'

'Does he smell or something?'

'NO!'

'What then?'

I shrug. 'I've only met him a couple of times.'

Marissa gives me a long steady look and I do my best not to flinch under her scrutiny. 'He's sexy though, right?'

I pick at the tablecloth. 'I suppose, if you like that sort of thing.'

Marissa lets out a shriek of laughter. 'You like him.'

I look up, startled. 'What?'

'You like him?'

'NO, I DON'T.'

But Marissa is giggling wildly.

'What makes you say that?' I force my voice to be calm.

She continues to giggle. 'You're being far too coy, which means you fancy him.'

'No!' I protest. 'Look, I agree he's attractive, successful, rich …' I try a flippant hand in the air but Marissa is shrewd. 'But sometimes you can have too much of everything.'

She roars with laughter.

'And there's more to a relationship than looks,' I grumble.

'Did he try and get into your knickers?'

'Get your mind out of the gutter, Mrs Dawson.'

She laughs. 'So, he did?'

'No … although he did ask me to out to dinner.' I take a slug of wine, enjoying my friend's open-mouthed astonishment.

'He didn't!'

'He blooming well did.'

Marissa is quiet for a moment then she lets out a loud squeal. 'Ohmigod so when … where … are you going? What are you going to wear, ohmigod OMIGOD, wait until I tell Tim.'

'Whoa there, I never said I said yes.'

Her mouth drops open. 'WHAT?'

'He's got women tripping over themselves to be with him – I'm not going to be another notch on his bedpost. He's shallow.'

'Tell me you're joking.'

'No.'

'Are you crazy?'

I laugh. 'Quite possibly.'

'I don't believe it. You've turned down a date with Alex

Canty.'

'Shusssh! Keep your voice down.'

'But …' Marissa is genuinely perplexed.

'He's not my type.'

'How would you know what your type is if you haven't had a date in years?'

'I have dated. There was Boris from the Ukraine.'

'He was your instructor and old enough to father your grandchildren, let alone your children.'

I blink at Marissa. That's a bit mean.

She shakes her head. 'Sorry, I just can't get my head around the idea you said no.'

'He's a womaniser, that's good reason enough.'

'Oh, I wouldn't believe everything you read.'

'That's what Luke said.'

'How is the gorgeous Luke?'

'Irritating as ever.'

'What he needs is to find a good woman.'

'I don't think he has any problem finding good women. Luke's problem is keeping them. Any sign they want more than a night he legs it in the opposite direction.'

'So, you really don't fancy him?'

'Who, Luke?'

'No, Alex, silly.'

I shake my head, 'No.' I hope my lie is convincing. 'He's really not interested in me – he's interested in anything in a skirt.'

Marissa shakes her head. 'I can never understand how you can't see what is so plainly obvious to everyone else. He would be interested in you because you are a beautiful woman, smart, funny …'

'Foul mouthed …'

'That too.'

'As my best friend, you're in no position to comment otherwise.'

'Crap,' Marissa cuts in. Then she sighs wistfully. 'I bet

he's wonderful in bed.'

I move the glass of wine from her grasp. She is looking a little watery-eyed. 'I think you've had too much of the red stuff.'

Marissa giggles. 'Spoilsport.'

'And you're a happily married woman with a beautiful husband and a beautiful baby …' But she isn't having any of it.

'OK, well maybe in another lifetime,' she sighs.

'Marissa!'

'Oh, indulge me. I want to talk about girly things and not just about babies and nappies. I love the monkey but …' She takes a swig of wine. 'Oh, it's so good to see you.'

There's something she's not telling me. Something that could possibly mean not all is well between her and Tim. The thought frightens me. Their relationship is my benchmark from which I measure everything else.

'Anyway, he has a girlfriend,' I tell her.

'Oh.' Marissa is disappointed.

'A model.' She pulls a face.

'Actually, she seems rather nice.'

'You've met her?'

'Briefly. Amanda Darel.'

'Wow, she's gorgeous.'

'Yes, my point precisely.'

'Well, in that case there is someone I'd like you to—'

'Oh no, no, no,' I interrupt. In my experience, friends and family should steer clear of this sort of thing.

'Oh, come on,' Marissa begs. 'It's just one date.'

'You know I don't do blind dates.' Just the thought of it brings me out in hives.

'Well maybe it's time you should. He's a friend of Tim's. They play squash together.'

'I really don't—'

'What have you got to lose?' Marissa cuts in.

I suppose she has a point. 'What does he do?'

She shrugs. 'Something big in the city but I do know he's very successful at it.'

'I don't know—'

'Oh, come on, you're always complaining you don't meet any nice men at work, although I find that hard to believe.' Marissa has a faraway look on her face.

'Don't you think it cries … desperate?'

'Not at all, unless you're chicken?' she teases, and of course I can't have her think that and maybe it's time to shake things up. My love life has been distinctively non-existent for … far too long.

'All right.'

She is taken aback.

'All right you will, or all right give it a rest?'

'All right I will.'

'Really?' She looks gobsmacked.

I nod. 'Really.'

'Wow. That was easy. I thought I would have a real argument on my hands.'

I'm just as surprised as Marissa.

'Are you quite sure you haven't been abducted by aliens?'

I laugh. 'Quite possibly.'

When we eventually leave the tapas bar, it is dark and we are both on the wrong side of tipsy. Marissa immediately hails two cabs. It's going to cost me a small fortune to get back to Buckinghamshire but there's no way I can manage a train journey with all these bags and as light-headed as I feel.

CHAPTER SIX

Holding the call sheet between my teeth I grab the zipper on my jacket and tug it up to the neck. It's freezing and I'm ravenous. Sam said he'd only be five minutes but that five minutes has become ten minutes and he's still talking to the producer.

My stomach growls in protest. I lean back against the wall, tuck the call sheet under my arm and thrust my hands deep into my pockets. It could be a long wait.

I've been out with the second-unit director all week picking up exterior driving shots. I have managed to avoid talking to Alex. I wish I could say that this has helped stop my stubborn subconscious straying into sexy scenarios at night but it hasn't. I had another racy dream about him, woke up panting like a loony nympho. Nightmare!

The few times I have spied Alex from a distance he's always being picked up or dropped off by one woman or another and none of them, I notice, is Amanda. Like now: I watch as he climbs out of a black car, the woman winds down the window and sticks her head out, laughing at something he has said. Her laughter is girlish and way over the top. She's also got a lustful look on her face and I only hope I'm not as transparent. And to think I had been close to believing the interest he was showing me was different to that of all the other women he speaks to. I let out a bitter laugh.

'What's he done now?'

I swing round, startled. Luke laughs. I don't bother to pretend I don't know who he is referring too.

'Is there no limit to the man's prowess?' I say.

Luke chuckles. 'Caroline is a designated unit driver.'

'And I suppose it's just a coincidence that she happens to be a woman. I bet he has it written in his contract.'

'Careful, Harry, anyone would think you were jealous.'

'Hardly, just an observation,' I scoff but panic lodges itself in my throat because there is more truth in his comment than I care to admit. Damn Luke. And damn Alex. No amount of trying can get him out of my head. 'He needs muzzling,' I add curtly.

'Harry, Harry, Harry.' Luke shakes his head. 'You've got Alex all wrong.'

'Like I have you all wrong, Luke?'

Luke gives me a wolfish grin. 'I have you know I'm totally upfront with the women I date.'

'Such gentlemanly attributes,' I retort, giving him a contemptuous smile. 'How do you sleep at night?'

Luke laughs. 'Very well, thank you. Why don't you run along and get something to eat? Preferably something hot to burn that catty tongue of yours.'

I fake a gun wound to my chest. 'You go. I was here first.'

'Seriously, go and get something to eat. You're always such a grouch when you're hungry. Besides, it looks like Sam is going to be some time.

My stomach gives another loud rumble.

Luke chuckles. 'Go. I'll tell Sam where you are.'

I look at him, suspicion growing by the second. 'What do you want, Matthews? I know it's not because you have my best interests at heart.'

Luke looks hurt. 'I came over to say hi to my favourite

person even though she's a bit snappy. If I'd known she was yet again possessed by another foul mood I wouldn't have bothered.'

I knew it! His arrival is not merely coincidental. 'Spit it out, Matthews.'

He sticks out his bottom lip. 'Would you like to go to dinner with me tonight?'

'Can't. Washing my hair.'

'Ah, come on, Harry, let me buy you dinner.'

'No.' Men like Luke and Alex need to be taken down a peg or two. They seem to believe the world simply waits for their next frolic and folly.

'It'll do you good.'

I arch a brow. 'Which part of no are you having trouble grasping?'

'I'll let you eat my dessert?'

'No.'

'We haven't had a proper catch-up in ages.'

'No.'

'The restaurant is Michelin star.'

'Who is she?'

Luke looks at me with fake indignant shock.

'No one,' he says, whipping my baseball cap from my head. 'OK, there is someone—'

'No,' I say, snatching the baseball cap back and tugging it into place.

'But she could be the one.'

'Yeah right, which "one" in particular? Naughty one, dirty one, fun one or naïve one?'

'Ah, Harry, don't be like that. Pur-lease.'

'Just ask her out.'

'I don't want to rush things. I want your opinion first.'

'Since when have you ever sought my opinion?'

'Pretty please with bells on top?'

'No. I don't want to be part of your sordid sex shenanigans. Get one of your Neanderthal cronies to come with you.'

'I'll give you fifty quid.'

'No.'

'And the whole cocktail menu – they're fifteen quid a pop!'

'No.'

'And could you swing around to the hotel.'

'Charming. The least you can do is pick me up.'

'So you'll come?'

'No.'

'And wear something feminine.'

I tut loudly. 'This is the last time, Matthews.' I wag a finger at him.

Luke grins. 'You're an angel, Harry.'

'A fool, more like,' I grumble, stomping away.

Luke has an uncanny way of getting me to do things I said I didn't want to do. I wouldn't mind if he was actually serious with the women he dates but none of them last. It's all about the chase with him.

I duck my head against the sharp wind and hurry towards the canteen, my stomach grumbling with anticipation.

As I get closer my steps falter. Alex is blocking the entrance.

'You going in or out?' I say with barely concealed irritation. His face surrenders a wholesome grin, engaging me like a glimpse of sunshine, not the least perturbed by my mood. He pops his iPhone into his pocket. 'After you,' he says, holding the door open.

'Thanks,' I mumble a little insincerely.

'I've missed you this week,' he says as I brush past him.

'Yeah, wasn't it chronic, the pain, the angst, how did you survive?'

The canteen is buzzing with activity. It also feels like walking into an oven – somebody's obviously seen fit to turn the heating to full blast. I also can't help noticing the wave of excitement sweep across the room and I know it has nothing to do with my arrival. Quite funny really, a Mexican wave of heads turning to see who's arrived (looking straight through me) then pretending to be looking elsewhere whilst following Alex's every move. I take my cap and jacket off and tuck them under my arm and grab a tray. I don't bother to see what Alex is doing but when he slides his tray next to mine and his arm brushes lightly against my bare arm I have to concentrate very hard on remembering what exactly I am doing here.

Ah yes, food.

Tempted by the chicken curry but deciding on the healthier option I select a chicken salad, a large portion of pecan pie – a girl has to treat herself once in a while – and a black coffee.

I look around, searching for an empty table.

The range of people scattered about the room makes for an arresting sight: fearsome vampires making short work of their curries, a seven-foot werewolf biting into a strawberry cheesecake, and a body of people with half-eaten faces sipping drinks through straws. Spotting an empty table in the far corner I weave my way through and plonk myself down. Alex arrives shortly after.

'Mind if I join you?'

'If you want.'

'Bad day?' Alex asks.

'No,' I say, almost biting his head off. Then, realising how horrible I'm being, 'I just get grumpy when I haven't eaten.'

'Only when you haven't eaten?'

OK, he's got me there and a smile tugs at my lips.

'That's better,' he says. 'For a minute, I thought I had fallen out of favour.' He shovels a forkful of chicken curry into his mouth.

'You were never in favour,' I retort breaking into another smile.

Damn. I wish I'd gone for the curry, it smells wonderful. I tuck into my chicken salad with a little less enthusiasm. 'Wanna try?'

I look up and Alex is holding out a forkful of curry. 'Go on, you know you want to.'

So, I do what any self-respecting, starving woman would do in this situation: I lean over and open my mouth. He feeds me, and our eyes briefly lock. This is way too intimate. I'm also conscious how this might look to an outsider. I lean back in my chair. 'Yum, quite nice,' I say, covering my hand over my mouth as I chew.

I swear I can feel everyone's eyes on us.

'I love the black rubber number, by the way,' he says, a wicked glint entering his eyes.

A bubble of air trips down my windpipes and goes down the wrong way. I cough. Alex chuckles.

I take a hasty sip of my coffee. 'Likewise,' I say, once I've cleared my throat. 'The depraved vampire suits you.' I give him a small suggestive smile.

'I hear the second-unit stuff went well,' he says, coughing. 'Heard you got to run from an exploding car?'

'Yep, and did a bike lay-down yesterday. The rest of the week was just driving shots through busy traffic.'

'You get to do all the fun stuff.'

'Haven't you got to run from an exploding building next week?'

He starts to grin. 'Yeah, I do.'

We both grin like fools then turn to our food. We eat in silence but then curiosity gets the better of me.

'Did you have a nice time in the Lake District?'

'I did, thanks. Nothing like filling your lungs with clean healthy air.'

'Of course, I forgot you're a rambler in between the rare parties!' I hadn't meant to sound sarcastic; my tongue is too quick for my head sometimes.

His brows draw together in a frown. 'That's right.'

'So that wasn't you at the Q awards the other night?'

'I suppose the newspapers said I was out partying into the early hours of the morning?'

'Weren't you?'

'If you want to know anything about me you only have to ask.'

'I don't … it's none of my business, just making conversation.' I snatch my coffee cup up; it sloshes over the table. 'You're just a bit difficult to ignore when you happen to be in every single newspaper, that's all.'

'Every single one, eh. You have been busy.'

I groan. 'You know what I mean.'

Smiling, Alex shakes his head. 'I don't read them.'

This surprises me. 'You don't read anything that's written about you?'

'Not if I can help it. I suppose you're going to tell me what it said though?'

'I don't know, I didn't read them,' I lie. 'But the photos told their own story.' I doubt Amanda would be too happy to see him in the arms of a blonde beauty.

'And the camera never lies?' His mouth turns down as if I've disappointed him. 'And let me guess you disapprove?'

'I'm not the church committee. It's up to you what you get up to.'

'That's right, it is.' His words sting and I suppose I asked for it.

I watch him swivel his food around with his fork. I want to apologise but that would mean I have to admit I am wrong and I've never been good at admitting I am wrong at the best of times. We eat in silence for a few seconds, until I can bear it no longer.

'Did you get your mum a teapot for her birthday?'

Alex looks at me as if considering whether to talk to me and then puts me out of my misery. 'I did. She loved it.'

'What did you get?'

'A top hat. You know, if I thought you would have

come with me to the awards ceremony I would have asked,' he says.

I stare at him. He looks as if he is being serious. I would have loved to have gone too, which is annoying because I'm supposed to be blocking out my flights of fancy. I haven't even managed to dampen my lust levels yet.

'I'm sure there were plenty of women to keep you company,' I reply coolly.

He laughs but there is no humour in it. 'How did I know you were going to say that?'

'Well … it's true.'

'Would there be any point in me denying this?' A hard edge has entered his voice. 'You have it in your head that I have a harem on speed dial.'

'Don't you?'

He looks me straight in the eye. 'I didn't ask because I knew you would say no. Just because I enjoy female company doesn't mean I must be sleeping with them too. There's nothing wrong with two people of the opposite sex spending time together or having dinner together. And here's an outrageous notion – even have a laugh together.'

'I know that!' I feel the blood rush to my face.

'Do you only ever have dinner with the same sex?'

'Of course not.' I clear my throat. 'Actually, I'm going out with Luke tonight.'

He stares at me. 'You're going out with Matthews?'

'The one and only.'

'So, you'll go out with Luke Matthews but not with me.'

'That's different.'

Alex rubs his jaw. 'How so?'

I grin. 'I *like* Luke.'

This time when he smiles it actually reaches his eyes. 'Luke is trying to make some poor woman jealous.' I shake my head, realising how annoyed I am. 'Why he can't just be honest with her beats me.' I blow out a puff of hot air, calming myself.

'It's not always so easy.'

'I might have known you'd take Luke's side.'

'What if the woman in question keeps turning you down?' He leans towards me, elbows resting on the table, staring intently. 'Sometimes the person you really want to get to know makes it impossible for you to get to know them.'

'Still haven't convinced Amanda to give up her Jimmy Choo's for hiking boots then?'

'Amanda?' He frowns and leans back. 'Amanda has no desire to go to the Lake District.'

'How is she?'

'Fine, I think.'

'You mean you haven't spoken to her?'

'Not since London, no.'

'She must be a very understanding girlfriend.'

'Amanda isn't my girlfriend.'

'But the newspapers …'

'So, you have been reading about me?'

'No.' My face grows hot. I shrug. 'Just snippets here and there …'

'Amanda is a very beautiful, very desirable women but she also happens to be totally devoted to her boyfriend who happens to be a good friend of mine.'

'She has a boyfriend?' She has a boyfriend!

'Yes. But the gossip columns choose to ignore that bit of information – but then they've never been particularly interested in the truth.'

My cheeks grow an even deeper shade of pink. Well that told me.

Amanda may not be his girlfriend but that doesn't discount the other women he's reported to be with. Alex continues to look at me and I grab my now tepid coffee and focus on drinking it.

'Alex, we need you in costume.' The first assistant director arrives at our table. 'Hi, Harry.'

I look up. 'Hi, Mark.'

Alex pushes his seat back and gets to his feet; it's as if he can't wait to get away from me. 'See you around, Harry.' He doesn't even look at me when he says it.

I watch him go, feeling strangely dissatisfied with our conversation, with myself, but I don't get a chance to be alone with my thoughts because Sam plonks himself down in front of me. 'Good to see you and Alex getting on,' he says.

'I wouldn't say that exactly.'

'Oh, Harry, you haven't been arguing, have you?'

'No,' I reply. 'Relax, Sam, it's fine. Everything is fine. We've been perfectly civil to each other.'

'OK. Good. Now let's go over Monday's stunt.'

I snap into business mode and we talk about my fall down the stairs; it's a lot trickier than you might think.

Back at the B&B I shower, wash my hair and pour myself a large glass of wine feeling oddly morose. I pick up my mobile and dial.

'Hi, Dad, it's me.'

'Is there something wrong, sweetheart?' I lean back against the padded headboard – nothing gets past my dad.

'Does there have to be something wrong for me to ring you up?'

'Of course not.' Then after a moment, 'But you're OK, aren't you?'

'Yes. I'm fine,' I say. 'Just calling to say hi.'

'Well, that's nice. So, how's filming going?'

'Fine.'

'Sam?'

'Fine.'

'Work?'

'Fine.' If I don't stop saying fine my father is going to demand I tell him exactly what is wrong and how can I even begin to answer that?

'How's Ruby?' I ask, praying my father will indulge me.

'She's got me on some kind of detox diet,' he growls and I find myself laughing while he lists the peculiar concoctions Ruby has drawn up.

'It's no laughing matter!' he complains. 'I'm withering away.'

Dad is so lucky to have Ruby. There was a time when I worried about him: I was only eight but he worked too much and I had never known him to go on a date. When he initially hired Ruby to help deal with the administrative side of things at the stunt school it wasn't long before she was dealing with a lot more than that. That was twenty years ago and I now have two half-sisters to contend with. One looked like she was aiming for a life in the stunt world then she tried it and thought better of it. The other is the epitome of femininity: pink everything, flowers, ballet and romance. It's funny to see my dad trying to father such a sublime creature a chasm away from what he's comfortable with, searching for common ground in the realms of a pretty princess world.

'So, when you coming over to visit your old dad?'

'Soon, I promise.'

Then it is Ruby's turn to come onto the phone and she insists I describe every single clothes purchase in microscopic detail, down to the colour of the linings and cleaning instructions.

The topic of conversation inevitably turns to my love life, or lack of.

'So, is there anyone special in your life?'

'I'm going to hang up now.'

Ruby laughs. 'No, no don't go, you know we just want you to be happy.'

'I am happy.'

'You know what we mean. It would just be nice to know you're going out on a Friday night instead of ringing your folks, even though it's always lovely to hear your voice.'

'As a matter of fact, I'm going out to dinner tonight.' Glad that I do have some plans for once.

'That's lovely. Is it a date?'

'Stop fishing.' I'm certainly not going to tell her it's with Luke, she'll only be even more disappointed and start urging me to join a dating agency. I've had to sit and listen to Ruby on countless occasions about so-and-so's daughter and so-and-so's son meeting on a dating agency and now they're married with kids. Why does marriage seem to be the crusade of mothers, stepmothers, and godmothers everywhere?

We end up talking about dad's diet and I can see why he's climbing the walls; he's not even getting his evening whisky. Promising to drive down in a few weeks I hang up, feeling in a much better mood and actually looking forward to dinner and dressing up.

CHAPTER SEVEN

I'm early and Luke is late but this hardly comes as a shocking revelation to me. That man would be late for Christmas.

I strut across to the bar and order myself a beer.

Shrugging off my North Face I tug at the hemline of my Miu Miu red dress and lift myself onto the bar stool, my Chloé handbag resting by my feet. If anyone tries to nab it I'll stab him or her with a swift kick of a stiletto.

I wish I could say I feel confident and poised but really, I feel self-conscious and silly. I'm just not used to wearing short dresses or something so … bright. No way can I blend in with the wallpaper but neither am I sticking out like a sore thumb. I feel myself posing a little. The bar, like the rest of the hotel, is very cutting edge; the decor has a clever mix of ironic contrasts and clashes of eras. I pull my shoulders back and take a sip of my beer.

I could have stayed here but chose not to. I found out that most of the cast and crew would be staying here and I didn't want the pressure of socialising every single night. So, I opted for the B&B and while it might lack the panache of this place it is cosy and, more importantly, cheap. The spare cash is going to fund my trip to the Galapagos Islands, and considering the way I've been shopping recently I'm going to need every penny of it.

I take another sip. My pouting pose falls away as I marvel at the rich colour of bubbling hops.

Owing to the fact that I've travelled a lot by myself I don't have a problem drinking in a bar on my own. The first country I ever visited solo was Japan. I was nineteen years old and it was my first stunt job away. When I first arrived in Tokyo I was nervous and felt lost and lonely but there was no thought of ever turning back. I put on a brave face and learnt to quickly navigate my way around the city where the streets have no names and the subway stations are bigger than small towns. I learnt to decipher food labels and generally get through the day without committing some grave faux pas. I was there to concentrate on work (playing a hooker; nice job if you can get it). I learnt to collaborate and communicate with the Japanese cast and crew and made some good friends in the process.

Travelling the globe independently has shown me just what, and how much, I am capable of doing by myself and even though I have missed my family and friends I have become aware and fascinated by this big world of ours. Who knew there were so many ways to look at the same things! In Japan, aesthetics is very important – everything from manhole covers to traffic signs are made to be admired with their friendly naïve cartoon style. The unknown has always excited me and I was hungry to learn about the mystical east, it made such an impression on my young head.

Lost in my thoughts I only become aware of the man next to me when I feel his fingers brush against my hand. I look down at the hairy appendages. Something else travelling taught me, how to deal with unwanted advances.

'Hi.' The man leans forward and the strong whiff of beer accosts my nostrils. 'Come here often?'

You have got to be kidding!

'Are you here alone?'

'No, I'm waiting for someone.' I turn away, hoping he'll get the message for his own good.

'That's a real shame,' he croons.

Like I'd ever give you a chance! I rein in the temptation to wallop the man over his simple head.

'Can I get you a drink?'

'I have one thanks.' Indicating the full glass in front of me.

'Why don't you let me buy you another?'

When his fingers touch my hand again with the audacity to stroke my bare skin, I grab his hand and squeeze it tightly. The man winces. 'Touch me again and I'll—'

'Hello, Harry.'

My eyes swivel to Alex and my heart does a tiny flutter.

Alex prises my hand away from the drunken fool. 'Care to join us?'

The drunken man rubs his sore hand with a bewildered look on his face and then his jaw drops. 'Hey you're … you're … Alex Canty. Can I get your autograph?'

Alex puts his hand on the small of my back and leads me to his table in the corner, completely ignoring the man's request.

'You didn't need to rescue me.'

'I wasn't doing it for you. I thought you were going to deck him.'

'I was very close to it.'

'I didn't recognise you at first.'

I translate this to mean I usually look like a militant army cadet.

'Oh, just something I threw on,' I say with a casual shrug of my shoulders.

'You look gorgeous.' My cheeks warm at the compliment. 'So, what brings you to our special abode?'

'Meeting Luke.'

'Ah yes, you're on a date.'

'It's not a date.'

Alex grins. 'Can't believe he didn't pick you up.'

'It's not a date, besides I finished work before him. Anyway, he now owes me big time: he's already waived his right to a dessert.'

'A sweet tooth – I must remember that.'

We arrive at his table, which is occupied by a pretty young thing.

'This is Tania, a unit driver.'

Caroline, Tania … how many unit drivers does he need?

I smile politely. 'Harry,' I say, offering my hand to shake. 'Hi, Tania.'

She shakes it enthusiastically. 'You're doubling for Felicity Hall?' Her eyes are bright and shining and she can't be more than twenty-one, twenty-two.

'That's right.'

'That's soooo cool,' she giggles.

I smooth down the front of my dress and sit down, aware that Alex is watching me but not daring to return his gaze. I fix my eyes on Tania.

'Nice dress,' she chirps after sucking up a colourful concoction through her straw.

'I thought I'd give the tracksuit a night off.'

'And you have legs, who would have thought it,' Alex remarks.

'Covered in bruises,' I add, 'hence the opaque tights,' and I'm really glad of that because Alex looks at my legs as if he has X-ray vision. I brush at an invisible piece of fluff to conceal my embarrassment. 'I have a humdinger of a bruise right here.' I point to my thigh. 'Did it when I slid under the moving lorry.'

'Oh God, I saw that. That was amazing,' Tania gushes.

'Er, thank you. These,' I say, kicking out a high-denier clad leg, 'are vital back-up supplies when you're in my world.'

'Don't you get scared?'

'Sure, I do, but we rehearse and rehearse these things.'

'But the bike lay-down,' she shudders. 'Aren't you scared of being crushed?'

'Exactly,' Alex says.

I look at them both. 'It's all about timing. We do it like a million times to get it just right.'

'Because miss a few seconds and it could be fatal?' Alex probes.

'Well, er, yes, which is why we rehearse. To be mashed up or not to be mashed up!' I jest but they are both looking at me as if I must be insane.

'Rather you than me,' Tania says.

'I'm not sure I could watch you do that.'

I look at Alex. 'Why on earth not?'

'Couldn't bear the thought of you being hurt.'

I stare at him. He must be drunk.

'Well, on Monday I've got to fall down some stairs and that's far trickier.' I take in their disbelieving faces. 'The stairs are always nasty, a big shock to the body even though you're wearing padding. But enough about me.'

'I have to run from an exploding car next week,' Alex says, grinning.

'You two are a right pair.' Tania gets up from the table. 'If you'll excuse me.'

'Bit young, isn't she?' I say as soon as Tania has gone.

'And of course, I must be screwing her.'

'Yes! I mean no ... NO! I was just joking!'

He leans in closer. 'I think you should let me take you on a date.'

A jolt of desire runs through my veins. So, he still wants to take me out.

'I don't think that would be a good—'

'Hey, you're not trying to steal my date?' We jump apart. Luke guffaws, completely unaware to how close to the truth he is.

'You're late,' I say.

'Wow. Harry.' He lets out a low whistle. 'You look

amazing!'

I grin. 'You don't look so bad yourself.' He's wearing a pair of slim-fitted cotton-twill trousers in light blue, and a red striped shirt. Very on trend!

'Remind me why we haven't ever dated?' he asks.

'Because we don't want to ruin a beautiful tawdry friendship,' I tell him.

'Oh yeah.'

A frown forms on Alex's forehead but I haven't got time to contemplate this as Luke pulls me to my feet. Tania returns to the table and sits down.

'Hello, Tania,' Luke says. Tania's mouth drops open.

'You know my name?' she squeaks.

'I always make it my business to know a pretty face.' When she blushes, and gives him a shy smile I realises she has a crush on him. Poor girl.

I pull on my jacket.

'Are you two going on a da-date?' Poor girl can barely get the words out.

'No,' I reassure her. 'Luke's nursing several itchy STD's and I'm feeling sorry for him.'

She guffaws a laugh. Then catches herself and glances nervously at Luke. He flicks me on the arm. 'She loves me really.'

Alex remains silent throughout the exchange.

'Bye,' I say with a smile as Luke tugs me towards the door. 'See you Monday.'

'Yeah, bye,' Alex says, smiling back.

'Bye. Have fun,' says Tania.

We leave Alex and Tania at the bar and go outside, where a cab is waiting.

We've been at the restaurant for an hour and the woman of his affection is a no-show. As a result, Luke is steadily getting more agitated until I tell him that if he doesn't cheer up I'm going to leave his sorry arse. Even though I was looking forward to the caramelised duck breast with winter vegetables, chestnuts and goat's cheese.

It does the trick and after another beer Luke is back on form.

'Typical, when I actually do make a concerted effort she doesn't turn up,' he pouts.

'Well, maybe good things are worth waiting for. Not everything exciting is wham bam thank-you, ma'am!' I say, quite matronly.

The restaurant has a nice vibe about it and the food is faultless. I take a look around me and everyone has dressed according to the magnificent culinary setting. Then I spot a woman who is exactly Luke's type; blond hair, big boobs, in fact ...

'Is that her?' I say.

Luke swivels his head around and then back to me. 'Yeah, how did you know?'

'She looks like your last girlfriend.'

Luke gapes at me. 'She looks nothing like Magda.'

'And the girlfriend before.'

Luke is not happy. 'What do you know?'

'Just basic observation skills, *darling*.'

The blonde clocks us. If the trick was to make her jealous it is working. She is eyeing our table at every opportunity and eyeballing me with a look that could kill.

She sashays towards us. 'Luke, what a lovely surprise.' She ignores me completely.

'The food was so wonderful I just had to come again,' he smiles. 'Harry this is Clarissa, the proprietor of this fine establishment.'

Clarissa conjures up a fake smile. Luke seems oblivious to the frosty atmosphere. She hands Luke her card. 'You mentioned lunch – why don't you give me a call?' She curls her lip and gives him a sexy pout then struts off in her heels.

Don't mind me!

I'm not Luke's girlfriend but she doesn't know that. How tacky to give him her card in front of me – definitely below the belt. And so is arranging a date right in front of me. Where does he find them? No scruples at all, but I think that's his preference.

Luke smiles at me and I only just manage to refrain from punching him in the face. I swipe the card from his grip and see her lipstick kiss on the back of a card.

'What a cheek.'

'What?' Luke grins, oblivious.

'For all she knew I could have been your girlfriend.'

'But you're not.'

'She doesn't know that.' I roll my eyes with disgust. 'And did you see the daggers she was throwing at me? Oh no, wait, you were too busy examining her chest area to notice?'

Luke chuckles. 'Well it worked. She took one look at you and struck while she had the chance.'

'She could have been a bit more discreet about it.'

'Did I tell you she owns this restaurant? Well, she co-owns it with her father.'

'Yes, you did,' I sigh. 'Why can't you date someone with a sliver of depth or morals? What about her?' My head and eyes nod to a path behind him. Luke swivels around with the subtlety of a rhino.

'Don't make it obvious,' I hiss.

Luke turns back to me, his face a picture. 'You want me to date a waitress.'

'What's wrong? Are you so above mere mortals now?'

'Nothing's wrong with it but it's just … just …'

'For all you know she could be a struggling artist or maybe she's studying to be a doctor … or happy to be a waitress.'

'She looks too old to be a student,' Luke observes.

'She does not look old – tired, maybe, but not old. Just because she's older than the teenagers you usually date.'

'Clarissa is not a teenager.'

'No, you're definitely right there.'

Luke scowls. 'Now who's being catty? And I don't date teenagers.

Twenty, twenty-one, maybe twenty-five – that's a gaping range!'

I place my hand to my chest. 'I stand corrected.' The atmosphere between us becomes decidedly frosty and I feel I ought to make amends. 'Mind you, she probably wouldn't fancy you.'

'Of course, she would.'

'She seems far too intelligent.'

'Oh, you're funny.' But he's not laughing. 'I bet she'd jump at the chance to date me.'

We both turn to watch the waitress as she serves another customer. She is laughing at something he has said – it's an infectious laugh.

'How much do you want to bet?'

I look at Luke, not liking where this conversation is suddenly going, using women as gambling fodder.

'No, I don't want to make a bet. I'm not one of your … shush … she's coming over.'

'Can I get you anything?'

She must have seen us staring. 'Um, yes, I'll have the soufflé, thank you.'

'And you, sir?'

I look at Luke but he is staring at the waitress. Not surprisingly she seems a little nonplussed. She gnaws her bottom lip nervously, her cheeks flushing with colour. 'Sir?'

'Luke?' I kick him under the table.

He flinches. 'The same,' he says. 'I'll have the same.'

'No. You can't.' I smile apologetically at the waitress. 'Luke, you said I could have your dessert too.'

'Oh yeah.'

I turn to the waitress and beam at her and the corner of her mouth turns up into a hesitant smile. 'We'll have a soufflé and a crème brulée.'

Luke glowers at me. I snap the menu from his hand and hand it to the waitress. 'Thank you.'

As soon as she is gone I turn to him. 'What was that all about?'

'What?'

'Intimidating the poor girl.'

'I was thinking …'

'I wouldn't do that might frazzle your brain.'

'Ha bloody ha. You know I could get a date with her if I wanted.'

'Not when you glower at her, you won't.'

'She would jump at the chance to date me.'

'Wow, you can be so arrogant sometimes. Anyway, it doesn't matter because you're going on a date with Clarissa.'

'What Clarissa doesn't know won't hurt.'

'Bad idea, Luke, just stick to one date at a time.'

'Why should I take advice from a woman who never dates?'

'I do date.'

'When was the last time you went on a date?'

'Actually, I have a date.'

Luke's face is full of disbelief.

'No, you don't.'

'I do.'

'Who?'

'No one you know.'

'I don't believe you.'

'I don't care what you believe but it's true. Marissa set it up.'

'You've not met him.'

Fuck. Caught out. 'Er, no. But Marissa thinks I'll adore him.'

'You're going on a blind date?' Luke laughs cruelly.

'Lots of people go on blind dates – nothing wrong with that.'

'But you've always said you'd rather watch bacteria grow than go on a blind date.'

True. 'Well it's time to come out of my comfort zone. You should try it sometime.'

'OK, I propose a toast.' Luke suddenly gets a look in his eyes that makes me wish I could take it all back. 'A taste of something different.'

I clink his glass but I have a horrible feeling this is all going to end in tears.

CHAPTER EIGHT

I had a blind date once. It was a complete disaster. In fact, my blind date started chatting up another woman on another table while I popped off to the loo. Actually, make that two; I once went out to dinner with a guy who kept picking his teeth with every piece of cutlery, condiment, or cuisine he could lay his hands on. It was very disturbing, very unpleasant. Ironically, he left the toothpicks completely untouched. But everyone has at least one blind date from hell and as Marissa rightly pointed out I haven't been on a date in two years and I'm not getting any younger, which I think is a rather mean tactic to play but nonetheless true.

I'm back at the Dining Room, in spite of the snotty-nosed proprietor, because I can't fault the food and it's a popular place. Brett and I have already exchanged texts and he said he was very much looking forward to seeing me. We even had a bit of a text banter going on, which I think is a rather promising start.

'Can I get you a drink?'

'Oh, hi,' I say, recognising the waitress from the other night. 'Yes, I'll have …' I peruse quickly over the wine list, 'a large glass of your house Sauvignon Blanc please.'

She returns moments later with a large glass. I take an

appreciative sip.

Recently, everyone seems to have an opinion on my love life: Marissa, Ruby, even my dad has been fixated on the topic. Nearly every conversation ends with the question 'anyone special in your life?' It's as if my being single is not by choice and that I'm in a desperate state of limbo waiting to be swept off my feet. I won't deny that there are times, usually on a Sunday morning, when it would be nice to have someone to wake up to who I can send out to get the newspapers and croissants, instead of the routine, unglamorous task that entails trundling out with a coat over pyjamas, rushing to the bakers, standing there like a leper buying a selection of bread for one, please. And there might be something worthy in building a life with someone, supporting each other, making each other feel special and wanted, but it has to be the right person. And how do you know when you've met him? How can you tell beneath the dodgy haircut that he isn't Prince Charming in the making? It's not as if there's a glowing neon light above his head announcing the obvious: 'I'm the one.' The world doesn't work like that and as the days, months, years go by without so much as a whiff of him I'm not going to delude myself into thinking he's just around the corner. In the animal kingdom, it seems much simpler: breed and get on with the rest; don't breed, better luck next year. Very few species hang around each other for any great lengths of time; well, not enough time to start arguing over nests, lairs, dens, kill, prey and most importantly territory. Get what you can while you can!

I've always thought Marissa and Tim were absolutely perfect for each other but even they appear to be having trouble in paradise, and if it can't work for them what hope is there for the rest of us? Besides, I love my single life. It's my choice and I'm happy. We're not all entering Noah's Ark; we don't have to be in twos, it's not a law, just some biblical stereotype when people didn't live beyond the age of thirty.

Phew! Glad I got that off my chest.

It was Marissa's idea I get here early. That way I could have a glass of wine, relax my nerves and let him be the one to search around the room for me. I thought that was an ingenious idea but now I'm not so sure as I place my empty glass on the dimly lit bar. At this rate, I'll be drunk before he arrives. Not a way to impress a date – if he shows up. I glance at my watch. He's fifteen minutes late!

'Can I get you another?'

I look up at the waitress from the other evening.

'Sure. Why not.'

She returns with another glass of crisp, zesty heaven.

I check my mobile to see if he's texted or rung even. Nothing.

'Your boyfriend's late?'

Boyfriend? I must look confused because she elaborates.

'The gentleman from the other night.'

'You mean Luke.' I let out a tinkled laugh. 'He's not my boyfriend, neither is he a gentleman.'

She looks like she suspected as much. Well, the bit about him not being a gentleman.

'Luke's an old friend,' I add.

'Oh.'

I peer at her inquisitively. She really is pretty when you take time to look. Luke should take my advice and change the type of women he dates. He might be surprised.

'Actually, I'm on a blind date,' I whisper, unable to keep the embarrassment from my voice.

'Really?' A mixture of surprise and excitement engulfs her sweet face.

'I let my friend talk me into it but either he's late or I've been stood up. I'll give it ten minutes then I'm going. I'm filming tomorrow so I need to be up early anyway.'

'Are you an actress?'

'God, no! I'm a stuntwoman.'

'Wow. Are you working on a film right now?'

'A vampire movie.'

'The movie with Alex Canty?'

'The very same.'

'I adore Alex Canty.'

'Doesn't everyone!' I bite the inside of my cheek involuntarily.

'You know, you could give me a signal. If you don't like him you could give me call or something.'

My mind instantly thinks up a crude hand gesture but that would be too obvious. 'Hmm, that might not be such a bad idea. Are you sure? Mind you, my friend would kill me if I ran out on him.'

'I'm sure if he were a total pig she'd understand.'

I let out another laugh. 'True.'

Just then the door to the restaurant swings open and a rain-soaked man with wide shoulders on a smart black coat enters. I instantly hide behind my glass of wine – if you can hide behind a glass of wine, that is. The man shrugs out of his coat to reveal a black jumper, a lavender shirt peeking out the top and flat-front black trousers that look like they were tailored for him. The man pulls his hand from his pocket and moves toward me. I peek at the waitress and she gives me the thumbs up before scurrying off.

I take a nervous gulp of wine. He walks from his hips, all long and lean, with a purpose to each step. Not bad. Not bad at all. A part of me expected him to be small, portly and balding, don't ask me why.

I smile. 'Brett?' My voice has a wistful hopeful tone to it.

He smiles and I'm bowled over. What a first impression.

'Harry?' It comes out a bit squeaky. Bless, he must be as nervous as I am.

I smile prettily at him. 'Hi,' I say rather shyly.

He holds out his hand and I take it. His grip is strong, which I like, and he has seriously sexy hands, big with an artisan squareness about them, the fingertips smooth and manicured.

'Sorry I'm late. There was an accident on the road and I couldn't get a signal.' He pulls up a chair.

I gape at him. His voice is high-pitched and squeaky and doesn't match his otherwise ravishingly hot physique. Think David Beckham or James Blunt and you get the picture – everyone would do Beckham if he was mute! I didn't realise I was so shallow, now I know I am.

'That's OK,' I mumble.

The waitress, I never caught her name, comes to our table.

'Can I get you anything to drink, sir?'

He picks up the wine menu. 'I'll have a ... on second thoughts ...' He slaps it back on the table. 'I'll have a Manhattan. Harry, would you like another?'

'Another Sauvignon, please, make it a large one.'

I'm looking at her face and I can see a similar look of shock. She looks at me and I have a childish urge to giggle, but ever the professional she smiles sweetly. 'Right away.'

Taking a leaf out of her book I rein in my impulse to laugh. Now I know why Marissa didn't want me to speak to him on the phone. I could kill her.

'How do you know Tim?'

'We play squash together but we know each other from business.'

'What is it you do?'

'I'm a hedge-fund manager but your job is so much more interesting. You don't look like a stuntwoman.'

'What were you expecting?'

'Built like an Eastern European shot putter.'

I laugh. This date might not be so bad after all. 'And you still agreed to meet me?'

He grins. 'Glutton for punishment.'

With our food ordered and conversation flowing I find myself relaxing into the evening. Brett and I have quite a bit in common. He listens intently too, and he's a bit of a comedian – his voice becomes less of an issue as the evening progresses. He also insists on picking up the bill – at least one archaic tradition I'm happy to accept. So, it seems only fitting that we have a bit of a snog in the car park and he is every bit as manly as I hoped.

I like that his lips are soft and wet, they tease a heated response deep in the pit of my stomach.

'Mmm, you taste good,' he says, nibbling on my ear.

My hands slip deep inside his coat and I feel his hard muscles bunch as I slide my hands up and down his chest and stomach then move them around to the middle of his back.

'Oh yeah. This feels good.' Against my lower abdomen I can feel every inch of how much he likes me.

I rise onto the balls of my feet and push closer, biting his lips together, stop talking.

His hands snake around my waist, pulling me closer. 'Tiger.'

Please stop talking; it's like making out with a spaced-out porn smurf. I groan. He mistakes my groan for pleasure.

'Mmmm, you are turning me on.'

Your talking is turning me off. I silence him with another kiss but the voice is a passion killer. I don't mind a bit of talking but not when it sounds like Micky Mouse on helium. The moment is lost. I break away.

He smiles.

'I have to go.'

'Can't I persuade you to stay?'

'Sorry, no, early start tomorrow.'

'Can I see you again?'

'I …' I don't want to be rude but I really don't see the point. 'I need to check my work schedule …'

'I'll call you.'

'Er. Sure.'

CHAPTER NINE

'Harry, can you hold still?'

'I can't breathe,' I gasp.

'Tough.' Luke gives the bulletproof vest an extra sharp tug. 'Bad night?'

'NO. Great night, *actually*.' I stifle another yawn and ignore the stabbing pain in my head. 'Just got to bed late.'

Luke throws me a salacious grin. 'Oh yeah, I forgot you had a blind date. How did it go?'

Alex is standing within earshot and I really don't want to discuss last night in front of him. I fasten the blouse over my bulletproof vest and tuck it into the tight trousers. 'Your waitress was there again,' I say, trying to steer the conversation.

'Waitress?'

'The one you were going to win over with your charm.'

Luke grunts. 'Just because your friend knows you're a total fiasco at getting dates doesn't mean I need setting up.'

I thump him hard in the chest and he winces. 'Oh, I'm sorry, did I hurt you?' I pause. 'Good.'

He pulls a face. 'So, the man charmed you into his bed, did he?'

'It was a first date, Luke.'

'And?'

'And I'm not going to sleep with a man on the first date.'

'Bad date then?'

I know he is only saying this to wind me up and it's working. 'No. He's very good-looking …'

'But boring?'

'No, he's not boring. He's actually funny and smart. He works in the City, if you must know.'

'Can't quite imagine you with a high-flyer city-type.'

Neither can I but I figure if I really want to meet someone then it'll have to be someone outside this industry.

'So, what's the problem then?'

Oh God, what do I say? I can't say his voice. That will make me sound shallow, even though I am being shallow. The thing is, he is funny and I did enjoy our kiss, until he started talking, but maybe that's something I could get used to. Perhaps he'll grow on me. Like fungus. I giggle.

'So, you're seeing him again?'

'His name is Brett,' I say. 'And … er … I'm not sure yet.'

'You don't sound so excited by the prospect.'

'Unlike you, my friend, a measured approach isn't to be scoffed at. It's still early days,' I say.

'You're right.'

Luke saying I'm right; now there's a first.

'I think you should definitely see him again. Give him another chance.'

'Why bother when you know it's not right?' says Alex. Who invited him into the conversation?

My heart flutters and stops.

'Maybe,' Luke says to Alex. 'But it's about time Harry put herself out there.'

'Out and advertising the fact, more like,' pipes in Felicity.

'Do you mind, I'm standing right here.'

The three of them smile but it's Alex's grin that sends

my heart into spasm all over again.

I pull away from the group and head towards the cliff edge. I need to focus. I'm not feeling my best as it is. I really shouldn't have drunk so much but I can't do anything about it now. I've just got to get on with the scene and try not to die.

'That must be an eighty-, ninety-foot drop?' Alex peers over the edge.

I follow his gaze and my heart rams against my ribcage, as much from his close proximity as the drop itself.

'Actually, it is seventy-eight feet.' I quote from the raggedy piece of paper in my hand.

'That's OK then.' Alex's tone is amused.

I give him a wry smile. 'I've jumped from higher.'

'Of course, you have.'

Just usually not with a raging hangover.

'Are you OK? You look a bit peaky.'

'Sure, never better.' I shake the fog from my head but the movement makes me dizzy and bile stings the back of my throat.

'Sorry, would you give me a second?' I turn abruptly, putting my hand to my mouth. I notice Sam out of the corner of my eye and pull my hand away and turn back to face the cliff edge. I force myself to focus, to visualise the movements, the step back, and the position of the feet when launching … every exact detail again and again until I feel certain I'm ready.

'Harry?' The concern in Sam's voice is obvious. 'Everything OK?'

'Never better,' I cough, avoiding his hawk-like gaze.

'You're not coming down with something, are you? You look a little pale.'

'No. I'm fine.' Sam would go ballistic if he knew I had a hangover.

'Big night last night, was it?'

Shit. Shit. Shit. Nothing's secret in this place.

'No. Not really. I'm just not particularly looking forward to being submerged in ice-cold water.' That bit is true.

He continues to peer at me carefully and I return his gaze unflinching.

Donald Mann, the director renowned for his action blockbusters, joins us. 'We're going for a take, you ready?'

I nod my head. 'Absolutely.'

Luke arrives at my side and claps his hands. 'Let's do this thing.'

Donald returns to his position behind the monitor and Sam stands next to him. The atmosphere on set goes respectfully quiet as it always does whenever a stunt is involved. I'm aware that time is money so I want to get it right first time.

The adrenalin starts to pump as soon as the camera starts rolling and Donald shouts action. As the advancing vampires lunge towards us Luke grabs my hand and together we turn and step back off the cliff. The only way is down. I flail my legs as we plunge into the ice-cold water with force, my back not quite escaping its impact.

Ffff-uck! I'm winded.

The cold water is all around me, piercing my lungs, my shoes slip off my feet as I sink deeper, then I kick my legs with all my might, springing to the surface. Some of the water gets in my throat and I come up spluttering. My hair is in my eyes and my teeth are chattering. I'm so cold that I can't even feel my fingertips and it feels like wading through thick mud as I tread water.

Did we get it? Did we get it? That's all I want to know.

A speedboat turns the corner and we are helped aboard, and a warm towel is thrown around my body.

'Well, that wwww-asn't tttt-too bad,' Luke grins, his teeth and body convulsing in temperature shock.

'Ppp-iece of caa-kkke,' I grin back, then throw up everywhere.

On dry land Sam comes over. He's a happy man. With

the big wide shot in the can he starts talking about underwater shots.

'I-I-I lost mmm-my ss-shoe,' I say, my jaw almost guillotining my tongue.

'That's OK, Wardrobe have more.'

It's not so bad getting into the water after that but when it's time for Felicity to take my place for her close-ups I'm ready to get out of these wet clothes and dive under a duvet. I stand on set, dripping wet, my hair plastered to my head, towels wrapped around me tighter than a mummy's bandages. Felicity is looking terrified.

'It's nnn-not so bad rr-really,' I say, unable to stop my teeth from chattering.

'You're BLUE!'

'You should get out of your wet clothes.' Alex's words have the same effect as a hot water bottle. I attempt a smile but my jaw shudders.

Luke grabs my cold wet sleeve. 'Come on, the car's waiting for us.'

'B-b-bye,' I say, as Luke drags me by the arm. I catch a fleeting look of annoyance cross Alex's face.

CHAPTER TEN

Back at unit base I peel out of my wet clothes and jump into a hot shower then change into my dry clothes. I sigh deeply. I feel much better. I grab my bag and switch on my iPhone. I have two messages; one from Marissa checking how the date went, the other from Brett saying how much he enjoyed last night and would I like to do it again? I'm about to reply when Luke bounces up the steps and flings open the door.

'I think Alex likes you. Hey, you want to grab lunch?'

'Shut the door, it's fucking freezing.'

I don't bother to respond to his remark about Alex, I know he's just trying to goad me. My mobile goes off and I check the caller ID.

Fuck. It's Brett.

OK. I just need to be firm. Tell him that while I had a good night I don't think we should see each other again but with Luke now watching me this could be an ideal opportunity to throw him off track.

'Oh, hi, Brett.' I beam enthusiastically down the phone.

Brett seems delighted by my enthusiastic response. 'I'm glad I caught you. I was thinking you might be in mid-swing escaping from some terrifying aliens.'

Oh God, he sounds like a munchkin on the phone! 'It's

a vampire movie,' I tell him. I'm sure I told him this last night.

'Are you free tomorrow night?'

'No, I'm not. Sorry. I'm heading to Devon.' Again, I'm sure I told him this. 'I'm not back until Sunday.'

'What about Sunday night then?'

'Sunday? Oh. Er, I suppose I could meet for a quick drink.'

'I really want to see you again.'

'Er … OK.'

'Great – see you then.'

'Yes. Bye.'

I hang up, aware that Luke has been watching me the whole time.

'Is this the same Brett from last night?'

'None of your beeswax.'

'If you're going to be all cloaks and daggers about it …' He pushes open the Winnebago door and is confronted by Paul, the key grip.

'Hi, Luke.'

I zip up my puffa jacket and follow Luke out of the Winnebago.

'Hi, Paul.'

'Hi, Harry,' he beams.

'There's not a problem, is there? Please don't tell me they need me back?'

'No … no … no … There's no problem.' He looks at Luke then returns his gaze to me; he suddenly seems flustered. This is most unlike him. 'A couple of us are going rock climbing this weekend and I wondered if you'd like to go?'

'Wow, Paul, you certainly know how to win a girl over,' Luke taunts. 'Ignore him, I do,' I say.

'I've got extra ropes, cams and harnesses, so you don't need to bring anything, er … just yourself.'

'I would love to, Paul, but I can't. I'm seeing my folks

this weekend.'

'Oh, not to worry, have fun.' He quickly walks backwards and trips over his feet. Luke laughs and Paul throws him the finger.

Luke shakes his head. 'And there was me thinking you can't get a date.'

'I'm just a date magnet, didn't you know?'

He gives me a hug and out of the corner of my eye I see a car pull up and Alex step out. Tania the pretty young driver flicks her hair; Vidal Sassoon has nothing on that girl.

'Say hi to your dad and Ruby for me,' Luke says.

'I will.'

'Hey, Paul, wait up.' Luke runs over to him, slapping him on the back. Paul grabs him around the neck and they tussle before breaking away laughing. Boys!

CHAPTER ELEVEN

Despite all my protesting that I am not interested in Alex it hasn't stopped me craving for him. Why shouldn't I indulge in some uncomplicated, meaningless sex, whether it is with Alex or Brett? Although if I am going to have sex with Brett I might want to invest in some earplugs. It will at least sort out this short-term frustration.

I have listed the pros and cons of having sex with Alex.

Pros

1. He's hot.

2. He would be fantastic in bed.

3. He doesn't alert dogs with his vocal pitch.

4. He's a movie star – one to tell the grandchildren or cats!

Cons

1. He's a serial womaniser.

2. He could be selfish in bed.

3. It would inflate his ego even more.

4. He would be victorious over me.

5. He irritates me.

6. He's a cad.

I'm just getting repetitive now. I bury my hands in my

pocket and purposefully stride over to Alex.

But what about Brett? He's good-looking, funny … but the voice! I shudder. I just can't get past his high-pitched squeaky voice.

'Are you off to your parents?' Alex stops right in front of me.

'Oh no … I'm just … I've, er … just left something in my car. Erm. ALEX!' It comes out much louder and much more girly than expected … Drat!

He gives me a peculiar look. Blood starts pounding around my head and I think my smile is twitching on one side. I can't do this. Yes, you can.

'I was just er, thinking?'

'About me?' He chuckles.

'As a matter of fact, … yes.'

He groans. 'Oh God, what have I done now?'

'What makes you think you've done anything wrong?'

'You mean I haven't?'

'Am I really that bad?'

'Yes.' But he is smiling.

I return the smile. I can feel my teeth clenching like a maniac and he is staring at me … waiting. So, I cut to the chase. 'Does that invitation to the Lake District still stand?'

Did I really say that out loud? Have I gone completely mad? And if the look on Alex's face is anything to go by he thinks I'm mad too.

'I've always wanted to go to the Lake District,' I say quickly, 'and I have a spare weekend coming up …' Oh God, I really haven't thought this through properly. Alex seems to be struggling with a reply. 'Look, it was your idea in the first place.'

'You want to come to the Lake District with me?'

'Oh, never mind,' I mumble.

'Hey.' He stops me from pegging it, squaring up to me with his six-foot frame. 'Sorry, it's just you've taken me by surprise. It's not often I get propositioned by an avid Canty

Protestor.'

'It's just two work colleagues hanging out because they have a shared interest, that's all.' Now I feel foolish and I'm getting cross. 'Forget about it.'

'When?' he says.

Now it's my turn to flounder. 'Oh, I … I can't do this weekend or the next one but what about the weekend after that?'

He pulls out his iPhone and starts checking his diary. 'I can do that.'

'Er, great.'

'It's a date then.' He's wearing a familiar cocky smile.

'You mentioned your parents – will they mind me being there?'

'No, they're used to me—' He stops short. 'What I mean is, they're very happy to have guests. My mum loves to fuss and cook over us fledgling thespians. And she'll get a kick out of you being a stunt person.'

'As long as you clear it with them first,' I say, almost matronly.

'Well, Harry, I look forward to our date.'

'It's not a …' I look up and he's laughing. I gather my wits. Time to take control of the situation. I pull out my pen from my jacket pocket and write down the address of my bed and breakfast on the back of his call sheet. 'We can sort out the details later,' I say with a breezy carelessness that is all an act.

'We'll have to leave early if we're to make the most of the weekend.'

'Fine. It's not me who struggles with the early mornings.'

'I bought an alarm clock.'

My eyes spring open. 'Wow, serious stuff!'

He leans forward, a slow wolfish smile suddenly appearing. 'I promise I won't book you as my wake-up call.'

My cheeks burn. 'No, you won't. That's a service you

usually pay for.'

He chuckles, pulling himself upright. 'I better leave before I say something that will change your mind. Do you ride?'

Oh boy…

'Sure, I've got a couple of Suzukis at home.'

'I meant a bicycle.'

'Oh right, yes I do, but not here.'

'You can borrow my mum's or there's my dad's if you want something manlier.'

I roll my eyes. 'Maybe this isn't …'

'Too late to back out now.'

'I know, but just remember I'm only using you for access purposes.'

'Is that, right?' He raises his eyebrows.

'You've been hanging out with Luke too long. This is not a *Monty Python* sketch, you just don't have the range, boy-wonder.' I quickly retreat to the car before he has the last word.

It's only when I climb into my 4x4 and let my head flop against the steering wheel that I realise what I've done. I've agreed to spend a whole weekend with Alex Canty. An involuntary shiver of excitement runs through my body. Will he try to seduce me? Will, I let him?

Thud!

I leap into the air and bang my head against the roof of the car. Sam opens the door and jumps into the passenger seat.

'You've given me concussion.'

'I saw you talking to Alex.'

Straight to the point!

'Yes.'

'So, you and he weren't arguing.'

'What? Of course not! For your information, we were having an amicable chat.'

'Really, you were? That's great.' And he looks genuinely

relieved. 'I'm glad you two have finally patched things up. It's important you have a good working relationship.'

'Are you saying I haven't been professional?'

'No … no …that's not it at all. You know how people talk—'

This gets my hackles up. 'Who's been talking?'

'No one specific but you and Alex are working together so I don't want there to be any tension.'

'Sam, you have nothing to worry about and I'm quite capable of behaving myself.'

He gives me a look.

'Most of the time.'

'Look, you are a spitfire of a beauty and I can see the attraction.'

I turn and gape at Sam. 'Did you just pay me a compliment, Sam?'

'I suppose I did.'

I don't think I've ever seen him blush. 'They're not exactly forming a queue.'

'Well you can be intimidating.'

I shake my head, not quite believing I'm having this sort of conversation with him.

'And I only want the best for you,' he says. 'Don't get me wrong, I think

Alex is a great guy but he's your basic here-today-gone-tomorrow kind of guy and you deserve better than that.'

Eh? 'What has Alex got to do with this?'

'I'm not one to listen to gossip—'

'Then don't,' I cut in.

'Felicity seems to think that you and Alex would be a good match.'

'Felicity thinks she's in a Jane Austin novel.' I lean across and pat Sam on the knee.

'And Luke—'

'Is a pig.'

'He's got your best interests at heart.'

I burst out laughing. 'Luke is a wind-up merchant. Look, Sam, thank you for your concern but you needn't be – I'm well aware of the players.'

'Yes, yes.' Looking relieved that his ordeal is over. 'Your father would never forgive me if I let something happen to you.'

'You have nothing to fear. Besides, I'm saving myself for someone just like you.' I grin.

'Let's hope more handsome.'

'Not possible!' I say. 'Right then, shall we go and find Felicity?'

'Felicity, why?'

'So, I can torture her – why else?'

'Oh, you won't—'

'Just kidding. Although I might have to pull some of her extensions out.'

Sam looks horrified.

'A joke, Sam.'

CHAPTER TWELVE

It takes me five hours to drive to Devon. I'm exhausted but a reserve energy surfaces as I whiz around the quaint familiar country lanes. I'm excited to see my family and relax in the thought that there won't be any boy complications, second-guessing, or amateur psychology on the menu.

Zooming down a great big avenue lined with trees and into a sweeping gravel drive I forget how impressive the farm looks, although it hasn't been a working farm for decades.

I climb out of the car and as I approach I can see Dad in the garden. The sun is beating down and it feels like a summer's day. A far cry from the freezing temperatures of last weekend; England changes weather quicker than Jeremy Clarkson changes gearboxes. You notice these things when you don't live here.

I hurry across the unruly green lawn. They didn't hear me pull up.

'Dad,' I shout.

'Harry?' He jumps up.

'Dad! Ruby!' I fling myself into their arms and hug them both, breathing in the familiar scent of fresh sawdust – Dad's always in the fighting pit – and Ruby's perfume which makes her smell of vanilla ice cream.

I'm welling up in sentiment. It's probably just relief to be on home soil.

I haven't seen them in ages. Living in LA can be alienating sometimes; it's not as if I can just pop over the pond when I feel like a reassuring hug. It makes me appreciate the time we do have even more preciously.

'Dad, you look amazing. Detox is really working for you!' I jest, winking at Ruby. Actually, he does look a lot slimmer, he's always such a big bear of a man.

'See?' Ruby says, her face full of happiness although she's clutching Dad's arm as though he might vanish in a puff of smoke. That's a little weird. 'I told you people would see the benefit.'

Dad pulls a face over Ruby's shoulder and I laugh.

'Ruby, you look amazing too. Have you done something to your hair?'

'Oh, it's just Chrissy experimenting on a non-paying guinea pig again. "Slim haired reflective nuance intensive highlight effect" she calls it. She's trying to think up a witty acronym but was never any good at Scrabble. It took four hours; can you believe that!' she says.

'It looks stunning,' I say, admiring the pretty shining colours playing in the sunlight.

Chrissy is my eighteen-year-old half-sister who is training to be a hair stylist. She's already finished her apprenticeship in hairdressing at the tender age of seventeen. She bunked off school to work full time at fifteen, lied about her age and only got found out when a teacher came into the salon for a cut and colour. Already she is looking for her next challenge and now's she enrolled on a special-effects make-up course and is excelling at that too: slashed throats, burns, the more horrifying the better. I think she's carving out a bright future for herself. She's not afraid to take risks and has tons of initiative.

My dad looks pleased and grabs my arm, leading me

over to the roofed- terrace. 'I was wondering when you'd get here. Now we can start the barbecue.' He glances at Ruby. 'A bit of red meat won't hurt, it is a special occasion.'

'I'm off to get the veggie kebabs and couscous salad, at least you can balance it out with them.' Ruby promptly disappears inside the vast country kitchen.

There is nothing better than being at home; the warmth, the feeling of family is so cosy. I feel my whole body relax in a way it hasn't for months.

My dad sits down at the wooden table with a huge breath. I sit opposite.

'Dad, are you, all, right? You can stop the diet if it's making you feel ill. So many actresses are on these fad regimes and it makes them sick in the end.' He peers at me as if he wants to say something but Ruby interrupts the table chat from above with a huge jug of Pimm's with chunks of cucumber, orange and lemon slices swimming spectacularly in the hue of red while the mint leaves break for air at the surface. 'Here you go. Shall we say dinner in an hour?'

'OK, Stalin,' my dad jokes. Ruby rolls her eyes and heads back to her veggie kebabs.

We drink in silence for a few seconds then I start telling Dad about my upcoming fall from a tree. Dad still feels he has to mentor me, however many times I've done the stunt before.

We're in mid-argument about the fall when I hear the familiar sound of Saffy, my other half-sister. She's fifteen years old and singing along to her iPod out of her bedroom window. She's hilarious – so out of key but doesn't give two hoots. 'It's Jessie J this week. We told her to bleep the rude words and now she just sings the word bleep!' Dad chuckles. We both listen and giggle at her. I help myself to another glass and start pouring another for Dad, but he holds his hand over it.

'I'll think I'll move on to the red wine,' he says.

'Since when do you drink red wine?' I gawp at him.

'I've grown a palate for it, must be my age.' He shakes off my observation jovially. Something is not quite right, but I won't question him now. I'll wait until everyone's gone to bed.

Dad busies himself with the charcoal. Ruby keeps coming out with healthy platters of various vegetables and pulses. It's a feast for thousands.

She plonks a bottle of red wine on the table, which makes me more suspicious; she usually only drinks white. And usually my dad sips a Manhattan when he's barbecuing; it's his tradition. When I was young he let me sip it and laughed when I spat it out; it never deterred me from asking each time though. Have I come to the right house? My family have changed.

I sit back and drink more Pimm's, observing Dad and Ruby. They are communicating more with their eyes than their mouths. What is going on?

CHAPTER THIRTEEN

My dad, like most men, is fastidiously turning the meat as if he just invented a new way of cooking. It makes me smile to watch the pride grow as each slab of flesh is marinated, tenderised and cooked to perfection.

Ruby bounces out from behind me with another tray of vegetable kebabs.

'I think you need to put some of these on now, Mr Carnivore!' She moves the steaks away and plonks the tray down. Dad feebly places them on the end as if they don't deserve to be there.

Chrissy (Crystal is her full name) and Saffy (short for Sapphire) join us. Ruby immersed herself with hours of *Dallas*, *Dynasty*, and *Falcon Crest* after she was ordered to bed-rest for the last trimester of both her pregnancies due to high blood pressure. The hormones obviously got the better of her.

Chrissy helps herself to some Pimm's while Saffy continues to shuffle her iPod. I remember what it was like to be their age, struggling to find an identity as a young woman. They are not girls anymore and not yet women. I think men have it easier: a change in the voice, a bit of shaving and they're done.

I've always treated them as equals and we all get on well

enough. I've never mothered them, despite our age difference.

'Hi, Harry, I like the new look,' says Chrissy.

I'm pleased she noticed. 'It's just a little brown eyeshadow.'

'The colour suits you but the shadow is too subtle and your liner too hard. Your eyes are your biggest asset, so they shouldn't be hidden in harsh liner, they need a softer structure.' She leans closer and scans the rest of my make-up; I squirm under her scrutiny. Chrissy can't help herself, it's her passion. She's been pestering me for years to remodel my image. Whilst Saffy was busy being young and a handful, Chrissy used to walk around with her make-up bag at the ready, pouncing on me at every opportunity; she's a quicker draw than a wild-west gunslinger when it comes to an application brush.

'Perhaps you can show me later then, Miss Style Guru!'

'I think I'll get my mixing palette out and show you how to blend.' She's deadly serious about make-up.

'I'm happy to learn.'

'Excellent.' She rubs her hands together in the manner of a triumphant villain. It's not often I give her carte blanche so a bit of revelling on her part is called for.

We sit as a family, enjoying our meal, poking fun at each other, reminiscing and laughing. It's amusing to watch Dad battle the teenage strops again. Saffy clearly thinks he's prehistoric in his tastes, opinions and reluctantly shuts her iPod down. Ruby keeps taking half of Dad's meat to her own plate when there is plenty to go round. Chrissy is coming up with colour idea upon colour idea; and she desperately wants to reshape my eyebrows.

'Harry, that look went out with Madonna in the eighties, unless you want to look like Martin Scorsese!' she pleads. I'm impressed she even knows who he is – she must be broadening her horizons at last and venturing beyond the usual trite magazines she consumes.

'You can thin them out slightly but nothing drastic otherwise I'll torture you solidly over the weekend!' I laugh at her.

'Stop pestering Harry and let her enjoy her meal,' says Ruby.

'I don't know why you think everyone needs improving, it isn't a contest,' Saffy grumbles. She's a more sensitive creature. She runs away in books of fantasy and idealism but is bright enough to realise that real-life bites.

'Perfect, all my girls bickering together!' Dad relaxes back into his seat, letting the conversations run over him.

Ruby downs her glass of wine like it's nothing more than water. She seems a bit tense, maybe that's due to having two teenage daughters. It's bound to take a toll, who knows how much grievance she has to put up with every day. The girls leave as the evening draws on. Chrissy's friends pick her up for a party and Saffy goes to watch Harry Potter at the cinema with her book club. She wears an extra sparkly pink top for the occasion and ties her hair with a pink flower. It's so sweet seeing the innocent dress for a Saturday night out, nothing more to decide than is it pretty and do I wear it at school? Chrissy looks vampish, her make-up is immaculate and she has the longest legs, she gets them from Ruby because Dad certainly didn't pass that gene onto me.

'Anyone for coffee?' Ruby stretches up from her chair.

'Ruby, just relax, would you.' Dad sounds harsh, which comes as a shock; usually they are so harmonic.

'OK, you two, either you tell me what's up now or I'll be the daughter from hell. Up to you.' If they're getting divorced they might as well be upfront about it, I'm not a kid. I understand them shielding it from Chrissy and Saffy but even they deserve to know the truth.

'Harry, there's nothing up.' My dad seems genuinely surprised at the suggestion. Ruby's face tells another story.

'If you don't tell me I'll be forced to use karate!' I try

and add some humour to the mood. 'I'm not an idiot, just tell me.'

Just as my dad tries to shovel the question away yet again, Ruby's mouth runs away with her. 'Your father has angina. Nothing major …YET …' She throws him a dagger look. 'He's been advised to take care of himself, change his diet, cut down the physical work load and rest until they find the right combination of medicine for him. He's having trouble realising this even though he's been to a cardiac specialist and countless doctors have told him to take it easy.' She blurts this all out and now resembles a deflated balloon.

I stare at Ruby, still trying to digest this news.

'It's nothing really, Harry, just a small inconvenience.' Dad tries to soothe in the hope I won't make a big deal out of this upsetting revelation.

'NOTHING …' I glare at my dad, and all I can think is I don't want to lose you. 'This is your heart we're talking about and you treat it as if it's nothing more than a common cold! You have to listen to your body, for Christ's sake, Dad.'

Ruby starts tearing up and runs off to the kitchen under the guise of fetching coffee.

'Why didn't you say something on the phone?' I can't stop staring at my dad.

'Really, Harry, don't get yourself so worked up.'

'Got another heart as a spare, have you?' I'm angry. Anger is far easier than being scared or bursting into tears.

'Harry, I'm cutting out everything. No salt, no fried food, no … well hardly any red meat, no whisky … Jesus, you would think I was trying to make myself sicker. I feel fine. I am fine. Now don't start worrying about me, Ruby does enough worrying for all of us.'

'Try and see it from her point of view, she has two young daughters—'

'Now listen here, I'm doing everything the doctors have

told me, and I'm very aware of my responsibilities.'

He's just told me off as if I were ten years old again.

'Ignore him, Harry, it's the medication, makes him more volatile and emotional. He's a real snappy terrier because of it.' Ruby is level-headed in her tone and all seems normal once more. But I'm still trying to get my head around this, the fact that my dad, my hero, has a heart condition. I think I'm going to cry. Knowing these signs all too well Dad shifts around the table and tickles my chin. I've had a weak spot there since I was a little girl: every time I asked for Mummy he would tickle me as a distraction, a coping technique to hide the sheer sorrow of her untimely death and his own miserable pain.

We sit at the table for hours discussing his condition calmly, even cracking a few jokes. It gives me time to understand everything I need to know; something to live with rather than cure, his angina is manageable on medication and not as severe as needing a bypass. I come to terms with the illness and by twilight it's almost forgotten until Ruby brings out a passion fruit and banana pavlova.

My dad's eyes light up. I frown. 'I'm allowed egg whites and cream, in moderation.'

CHAPTER FOURTEEN

All too soon the weekend is over and I don't want to leave. As a little girl I wouldn't let my dad out of sight for at least the first couple of years after Mum died, the feeling of abandonment was fierce, but I grew out of this and it hasn't resurfaced until now. It's just reality catching up with me, Dad getting older, me living so far away, and so my security blanket has a frayed edge. Fallibility is sobering.

I start chuckling to myself as I remember the look of shock on Dad's face when I threw a jug of water over his head this morning. I teased him, said he wouldn't be able to catch me, knowing he would prefer to be taunted rather than tended. 'You wait until my beta blockers kick in, Harry!' he bellowed, fetching the high-pressure hose. I made a run for it but he was still able to corner me by the apple tree and drench me with icy cold water until I admitted defeat. Just like the old days.

It takes me just under five hours (again!) to get back to the B&B and the last thing I feel like doing is going out again but I grudgingly get ready for my date with Brett. A few drinks might be a good thing, help me sleep tonight and not spend it wide awake worrying about Dad. Besides, the last thing I need is earache from Marissa as to why I cancelled. She'll probably try to manoeuvre some bizarre social scenario where Brett and I accidentally bump into each other – her usual tactic is to throw an informal garden party where most of the guests mysteriously cancel at the last minute, she's so transparent.

I spruce myself up and eliminate the melancholy into the steamed-up mirror.

We've arranged to meet at a country pub which happens to be right around the corner from the crew's hotel. Not ideal, but there's not much choice in this medieval market town. I get there earlier than expected, forgetting that I'm not in the city and the only traffic hazard is getting stuck behind a tractor until the next passing spot. My 4x4 makes an unearthly sound when I park up and I'm thinking perhaps I've overworked it because something has worked its way loose. With time to spare I pop up the bonnet and have a quick nose. Nothing out of the ordinary … I look down at my oil covered hands.

Oops.

I head into the pub's toilets and wash my hands, and with only a trace of grime under the fingernails I march up to the bar and order a G&T. Just as I'm settling for a quiet moment I hear my name being called.

'Harry!' I swing round. It's Luke. If he has the dragon lady with him I can't promise to be nice. I walk over to where he's sitting and as I come closer I see the top of a brunette head – it's the waitress.

'Hi, Luke.'

Luke places his napkin on the table and stands up to greet me. I think I'm going to faint; Luke displaying etiquette as if he was Little Lord Fauntleroy.

'Harry, this is Isabel.' He looks proud and dignified.

'Hi, Isabel,' I smile. 'Nice to see you again.' We shake hands.

'Hi!' She is positively beaming which is such a nice change from the usual ice maidens with empty picnic baskets for brains that he usually dates.

'Do you want to join us?' she asks.

I know without looking at Luke that this is the last thing he wants. 'Not tonight, I have a date.'

'Don't blame you, he was hot!'

Luke glares at Isabel, bewildered. I'm positive his manhood has just shrunk out of recognition. She might actually challenge our little Don Juan, he's not used to that.

'What guy?'

'Oh … just some guy,' I say evasively. 'Nice to see you again, Isabel, I hope we meet again soon.' I glance at Luke and he's looking disgruntled. Male egos are such fragile things. I can hear her laugh at him as I head back.

I try phoning Brett when I'm outside but I'm unable to get a signal. I decide to sit in the garden under a cherry tree where the outdoor heater can keep me warm. I'd be happy if he stood me up but I don't think I'll be that lucky. Remembering my other, pay-as-you-go, UK phone in the car I fetch it to see if it fares any better in the rural setting. Frantically searching the glove compartment I locate the chunky thing only to find it's out of battery, darn it. My instincts tell me to try and start the car just in case that noise was serious. The key turns and all the warning lights flash at me, shit … I try again and it just chokes into a meagre splutter.

I down the rest of my G&T and quickly scan under the bonnet again, checking the spark plug connections, oil, water, battery and distributor. It helps growing up on a farm with disused machinery – a tinker's paradise! The trouble with modern cars is the computer controls the engine; I'm dumbfounded as to what the problem is.

I check the time and see that I'm still early so I move back into the bar and order a Manhattan … Looks like I'm getting a taxi. I silently toast my dad. Boy, that is strong … hiccup.

Two robust glasses later I check the time and I realise

he's late … again. Only twenty minutes but it still annoys me. Then I hear my name being called; I close my eyes and wish my ears had lids on them too.

'You're late.' I swing round but can barely manage a civil smile.

'So sorry but something came up.'

I wait for him to elaborate but he doesn't.

'Can I get you a drink?'

'I'll have a G&T.'

He returns with the drinks.

We sit in silence for a few seconds drinking our drinks.

'How was your weekend?'

'Good. Yours?'

'I don't know yet.'

Oh dear, I shouldn't have let him grope me last time. How can I divert his attentions? Horribly, I use Dad's condition to sober the mood. He's actually very good to talk to; I didn't expect him to be so simpatico. I thought he came down for … well, you know, to seal the deal, as it were.

We order some food and it's wholesome and tasty. Brett has a steak and I have the fisherman's pie. Nowhere in the world has the ambience of an English country pub; it's something that I miss when I'm in LA. It's so quintessentially English, you can't recreate it.

We talk about London and he asks me about LA.

'I'm going to be in Vegas next month,' he tells me. 'LA's not far though, is it?' Shit … double shit with a dollop of poo on top. I answer in the most nonchalant voice I can muster. 'Er … No, it's a short flight or about a five-hour drive.'

'Maybe we could meet up.'

'That'll be nice, but I don't know where I'll be yet, you know with work …'

'Let's see nearer the time, shall we. I'm quite often out in Vegas as our main office is there and we hold all our international conferences at the Bellagio.'

'Must be fun when you have downtime.'

'That's a luxury nowadays but when I was a junior in the company it was a different story, six guys racing to get the vice presidency and waking up in the Nevada desert with nothing on apart from our pants after a debauched evening in a Vegas stripper club.'

I giggle at that picture.

'We were set up by our boss who'd had enough of our back-stabbing attitude towards each other,' he continues. 'He got the lap dan— I mean ladies to spike our drinks. It's not a sexy Jim Morrison moment, no revelation, just a bunch of hung-over sweaty English public-school boys too shocked to react. Giles simply said, and I quote, "What an absolute rotter! The sand has played havoc with my merino sock thread and they're positively unsightly now. How's a chap supposed to stay fresh and correctly creased without one's manservant offering the delightful shade of a parasol!" I swear it was like something out of a Noel Coward play.'

I am snorting with laughter. He does a good parody.

OMG! Could he be growing on me?

He starts playing footsy with me under the table so I make the excuse of needing the toilet, I'm so confused … on one hand he's nearing perfection; on the other he's a sound engineer's nightmare. I bump into Luke on my way out.

'How's it going, stud?'

Luke looks resentfully at me. 'Harry, please … I'm not a stud, a bit of a tart sometimes … and keep your voice down.'

'OK, Prince Charming, relax. I think Isabel is very nice.'

'She's great. I haven't had a laugh like that – with a chick anyway – in ages.'

'You laugh with me all the time. And you might want to find a more appropriate way of describing the female kind if you want a second date.'

'Point taken! How's your date going?' Luke tries acting interested but I can tell he's aching to get back to Isabel.

'Fine … Oh, Luke, can you give me a lift to the B&B? My car's blown a gasket.'

'Sorry, Harry, I'm over the limit. Why don't you get lover-boy to take you back?'

'I like to arrive and leave on my own steam.' Basically to avoid the expectant, dreaded, 'Can I can come up, I could use a coffee to wake up' moment.

Luke chuckles. 'Oh, Harry, let him be gallant. You don't always have to take the reins.'

Bloody hell, Agony Aunt Luke. I'm not sure I like all this sense and sensibility spouting from the most immoral man walking this side of the Atlantic.

'Ah, Harry the wanderer returns,' Brett jokes.

'Sorry about that – I ran into someone I knew.' I purposely look down at my watch. 'I need to go.'

'OK.' Brett jumps up. 'I can give you a lift.' He has already heard about my car problem, but a lift back? I really hope he isn't expecting to stay.

'Er. OK. Thanks.'

Brett's car is gleaming in the car park; a top-of-the-range BMW coupé. None of this makes any difference to how uncomfortable I feel. Brett casually talks all the way to the B&B. He doesn't try and touch anything else apart from his gear stick, no pun intended, and I'm grateful. I know he's smart, rich, funny and has a body worth writhing on, but however palatable the visual is, the audio is seriously indigestible. So it's official – I am now the shallowest person I know. Luke has even crept up the chart from mere amoeba ranking.

We grind to a stop on the gravel drive and I take my seatbelt off ready to jump out.

'I had a nice time tonight.'

'Me too.'

'We should do it again?'

'The next few weeks are going to be really busy.'

'Oh, right, of course. Well, you have my number if you change your mind.'

'Have a safe and comparatively short journey home,' I say, brightly letting myself out of the car.

'Thanks.' He puts his car into reverse and drives off.

Wow. That was easy. He didn't even try to kiss me.

I am a two-legged female mosquito repellent.

I have this theory on dating and relationships. It's like the seasons. Let me explain. You have Winter, where you try and see if you're compatible at any level; digging the ground, as it were, laying the foundations if the ground's suitable. Spring, when you find out if you have planning permission and get excited to see the final blueprints, the architects' plans; most people's favourite season – blooms of fantasy rule here. Summer … that's easily explained in your own heads (not too lewd please, girls). You can try out all the new rooms and wallow in the exterior, maybe prod the interior and thoroughly check out the plumbing, electrics and central heating. Then Autumn: you can either have an Indian summer, so you can lie in the garden enjoying the efforts of your hard work, maybe tuning some finer details, rearrange the furniture a bit; or the leaves have changed colour, dropped and decomposed and all you're left with is a load of dead debris that needs raking up pronto.

As soon as I'm safely inside with the doors shut I ring the local garage, leaving a message for them to pick up the keys from the pub and deliver my car back to set when they're done. They are doing a few things for us already with all our equipment, motors, engines, etc. … Brett doesn't even pop into my thoughts that night. When mechanical difficulty overrides desire, you know it's not right!

CHAPTER FIFTEEN

Today's fight sequence is particularly complicated. We have twenty-three moves and thirty set-ups but mostly the moves consist of me being catapulted through the air and landing on my bum. We've rehearsed the moves and I have already tried the sequence with the harness on and the poundage dialled in.

If I'm not mistaken, Paul, our chief rigger, keeps looking over, probably checking that I don't fiddle with the ropes too much. Luke bumbles over in his padding and tries to knock me over like a sumo wrestler, without success.

'Did you let Brett drive you home in the end?'

'Yes.'

'And?'

'And nothing. You?'

Luke gives me a cheesy grin but he's so transparent.

'You didn't, did you?' I laugh.

'I wouldn't ask that of a lady unless we were thinking of a lengthy betrothal,' he jests, but I can see he's disappointed.

So Isabel snubbed the Lukey love-lunge, then, did she? 'Different going out with a grown-up, isn't it, young Skywalker?'

'Are you going to see Brett again?'

'Probably not.'

Luke grunts out his frustration. 'You protest that men are difficult to read but you women are impossible.' What's got his knickers in a twist?

'He's a nice guy. I'm just not sure he's my type.'

'Are you sure you even have a type?'

'The usual, nothing specific: nice, funny, confident, sexy but there has to be some spark, a bit of duelling, spirited … not a pushover. A challenge.' And it dawns on me that I've just described the chemistry that I have with Alex.

'No specifics! Crikey, Harry, you don't want much, do you! You'll be waiting a hell of a long time if you think that will be discovered during the course of a couple of dates. Do you give them a time clause, penalty points or what? You're tougher than a football manager.'

Luke, annoyingly, has made another valid point. It's tough listening to him when he makes sense; it's a rare phenomenon and a change of tune to his usual fun, frolics and farewell attitude. I feel like we're in role reversal. Alex is loitering behind us and I do believe he's trying to earwig on our conversation so I shut up and check the tension in my harness.

Paul walks over to me. 'Are you still on for tonight, Harry?'

'Tonight?' Shit – the wall!

'Oh, um … I …'

Now I remember Paul mentioning something about a wall-climb this morning. I think I said yes; I was half conscious at the time, nursing a coffee at six a.m.

'We could go straight from work?'

'OK. Great.'

Paul seems really happy about it for some reason. I didn't know he was such a rock-climbing enthusiast. I knew it was a hobby. Maybe he likes to share the enthusiasm.

'Just how many men have you got on the go?'

Alex's lips press against my ear; a sliver of heat runs

through my body. Calmly I turn around, my look sarcastic. 'Probably no more than the square route of what you've got on the go!'

'Brett … Paul … I think the co-director is free tonight too, shall I put in a word?'

'Yes. Why don't you do that? Can you arrange for him to see me in between my nine and ten o'clock?'

He gives a small snort of laughter.

'I'm taking part in an activity, not going on a romantic rendezvous.'

'I think Paul has other ideas.'

'This is Paul the rigger we're talking about. I've known him for years. Get your facts straight.'

Feeling like I've won this little scuttle of words I place a pompous look on my face. He can be so irritating.

'Trust me, Harry, he has the hots for you. A man knows these things.'

'Well, I will ask a man for his opinion next time I see one.'

'OK, Tyson, you win.' He shrugs his shoulders and walks away.

Oops, I think I might have really upset him. I'm just about to make amends, feeling a little harsh, when he spins his head around and winks.

'That's acting, Harry!'

Damn and blast. He won, or did I win that battle of the natter? I grumble at myself. He's so juvenile, I decide, and declare myself winner … now who's being juvenile?

Filming doesn't go as smoothly as expected. There's some digital breakdown and all the stunt people are required to stay on. It's nine o'clock when I'm called back to reshoot my fall from five different angles. My arms are heavy now and all I want to do is have a nice steamy bath and stretch out flatter than a slice of bread.

Paul keeps coming over and apologising. I'm not sure

why, it's not his fault and most of the rock-climbing daredevils are still on set, so no big deal … unless Alex was right, but that's ridiculous.

It's midnight by the time we're finished and everyone is exhausted.

'Shame about tonight, Harry,' Paul says to me as I'm fetching my things.

'I know. I was looking forward to it.'

'You were?' Paul smiles at me. Actually, it's more of a goofy grin.

Puzzled by this reaction I slowly pick up my water bottle and take a massive swig. Paul has never been flirty or shown any interest in me before. Professional and friendly – yes. Have a drink and a laugh after work with the boys down the pub type of thing, but that's it.

CHAPTER SIXTEEN

Marissa's home is situated in a leafy residential road in Battersea. It's a large three-storey Victorian house, which has been featured in *Living etc.*, *World of Interiors*, the *Guardian*, even Kevin McCloud filmed a *Grand Designs* episode when they first started renovating the dilapidated property. They begged, stole, and borrowed money to try and get the project going.

It has an amazing space-age conversion which makes the back of the house into an indoor-outdoor space; the kitchen roof and the end wall just disappear with a flick of a button. Marissa grows all manner of vegetables in there as the glass roof acts like a greenhouse and the garden is half transported into the kitchen. This dual-functioning space leads out to a courtyard garden, which has a cleverly designed Tuscan feel to it, incorporating a hidden lap pool behind a trellis of overgrown vines. I can't wait for a dip! It is an oasis in an otherwise bustling and boisterous capital city, a celebrated triumph in architectural circles.

They bought a plot of land off the adjacent neighbour and have the biggest garden on the street. Harrison's going to love growing up in his own adventure garden. They've landscaped little hills, mini valleys, secret hidey-holes and a small orchard with a fairy-tale hobby house set down a twisting fantasy path. You appreciate gardens when you live in a box on stilts. It's a dream home. Tim's small yet nearly bankrupt business flourished after all the media exposure. Marissa has worked hard for this perfect life. She always supported Tim, even in the toughest of times, never letting him give up on his dreams and aspirations.

I head briskly up the path to the wide, wooden, custom-carved front door, and press the bell. It swings opens and Marissa stands there in the sort of glamour only Elizabeth Taylor could top in her heyday, an adorable Harrison in her arms. Her face lights up when she sees me. 'You made it.'

'Bit of touch and go, the filming took longer than we thought.' I plant a

kiss on her cheeks. I look across at the little chubby fella in her arms and smile.

The last time I saw him he was a tiny pink wrinkly snuffly baby and now he's a real little person.

'He thinks everything he sees are edible treats. Maurice's tail even had a shock journey to the mouth the other day!'

'We'll have to refine your taste buds for the finer things in life … port and lobster,' I coo at the bewildered baby.

Marissa laughs, 'If only!'

I shrug off my coat and hang it up. 'God, it's been ages since I was here.'

'Just drop your bag there, Tim will take it up.'

'Where is he?' I say.

'Upstairs in the study. Had some work to rush through.'

We head straight back to the massive kitchen where she plonks Harrison down on a huge beanbag and switches the kettle on.

'Tea?'

'That would be great.'

'Or something a little bubblier?' she says cheekily.

'Oh, go on then, seeing that I'm a nomadic visitor.'

Whilst Marissa buries her head in the enormous wine cooler I fetch my bag and root around for Harrison's present.

'You didn't need to buy him anything.'

Next, I pull out a bottle of wine and plonk it on the table. 'And this is for you.'

Marissa smiles.

I unravel the drum's plastic packaging and hand it to Harrison. He dismisses the drum entirely, throwing it at Maurice the cat, who's not impressed, and puts the drumstick immediately into his mouth.

'I told you, everything is on the menu!'

On later inspection I definitely see teeth marks on the drum itself but whether those are Maurice's or Harrison's I can't quite make out.

Marissa sits down with two enormous champagne flutes and makes no hesitation in getting straight to the point. 'So, two dates with Brett, eh?'

'Oh, er … yeah.'

'So how does the land lie, how doth the wind blow? A cool breeze to the east or uphill gusts?'

'You really have missed your calling in life, ye olde matchmaker.'

Marissa laughs but wants gossip. 'I know he's really pleased to have met you. He said that he feels a real connection.'

'Really?'

'Is that all you're gonna say, Harry?'

'He's not really my type.' I put the glass of bubbly to my lips and take a sip.

'Oh, Harry. You're not going to see him again, are you?'

'It's a bit inconvenient, you know, the distance and plus I never know where I'm going to be next,' I say, hiding behind the bubbles of my glass, seeing if she believes my feeble excuses.

'He said you were getting on famously.'

Minnie Mouse might have more in common with Brett!

'He's nice and all, just not for me. There's no energy

between us … you know, electricity.'

'So it has nothing to do with his nasally girly voice?'

I look suitably affronted. 'So you knew about that bloody voice but didn't think to mention it?'

Marissa giggles. 'No, honestly I didn't. First time I spoke to him was the other day. I thought it was just a bad satellite connection! He makes David Beckham sound like one of the three tenors.'

We both try and contain our wicked grins.

'Why did he call?'

Marissa giggles. 'I think he was wondering when you'd be visiting here, Tim must have said something.'

'You didn't tell him I'd be here this weekend, did you?' Marissa starts guzzling her champagne. 'No … I didn't.' I look at her like she just committed treacherous-friend heresy.

'Marissa, if he shows up I'm off, comprende? I don't like people moving in on me when not invited.'

'I think Tim managed to deter him. I told him I hadn't heard from you so it would be a bad idea, especially as we've had this weekend planned for weeks. So was it just his voice that put you off?'

'No,' I tell her truthfully. 'Well, it wasn't the deciding factor …'

The true deciding factor, even though it's hard to admit, is Alex's constant presence in my subconscious, although I don't voice this to Marissa.

Fortunately, Harrison has crawled off his beanbag and is tugging at Mummy's leg so she has to pacify him.

I have a dreadful feeling now that Brett might turn up so I start thinking about the most courteous way I can escape. Marissa sits down with a humph at the table. 'Sometimes that boy doesn't know what he wants.'

'Who, Brett?'

'No Harrison. I think Brett knows what he wants! Look, Harry, he won't dare turn up here uninvited. Tim's not that pally with him privately, he's just a regular client that sends huge projects Tim's way. They spend a lot of time together.'

'It's OK, Marissa, I should have phoned him to say I wasn't interested but I didn't want tinnitus.'

We both start laughing. It's a contagious girly giggling fit. Each time one of us stops, the other one does an impression of Brett.

'I'd had a few drinks last time I saw him but I didn't get beer goggles, I nearly got Pimm's-plugs!'

Marissa ties her fluffy wrap around her head and I pick up a couple of

Harrison's empty yogurt pots and stuff them on my ears. Neither of us notices Tim's arrival in the kitchen while we're in mid-flow, Brett beating.

'Now, now, girls! That's not nice.' Both startled we leap out of our skins and nearly fall off our chairs in the process. Setting us off into hysterics once more. I feel like I'm thirteen all over again.

'Hi, Tim,' I guffaw. 'We, er ... I was just telling Marissa about ... er ... a Telly-Tubby thing I saw. Since when has this been so popular in England?'

Marissa chokes on her champagne at my ridiculous attempt to cover up.

'He's actually a really cool guy, Harry. Genuine too.'

'Oh, I know that. He's really nice.' I nod, sobering. Now I feel shallower than a dried-up puddle.

Tim comes over and gives me a hearty hug and I'm forgiven for ridiculing his friend.

'LA must suit you, Harry.'

I'm not sure how to take this.

'You look great.'

'I know, doesn't she?' Marissa says, wiping the tears of laughter from her face.

'Er ... thanks.'

'What time are we eating?' Tim asks and Marissa exhales loudly.

'Oh, in about an hour or so.'

'Right. I think I'll grab a sandwich and work through. You'll be able to catch up with Harry properly then.'

'Fine, OK,' she says easily but emits hostile body language. Tim gives me another hug, makes his apologies and trundles back upstairs.

I wait a moment before I ask her what that was all about.

'He's always busy working. It's just mental. He comes home and works until ten, eleven at night. We barely share the same space in the house for more than five minutes.' Sadness envelops her face.

'I expect things will get better after the job is finished,' I say.

'That's just it, Harry, the job finishes and he buries himself in the next one. I swear it's deliberate. Sometimes I feel like a single mother,' she sighs. 'Enough of my piffle – let's have dinner.'

She throws all the takeaway menus onto the table. 'You choose, Harry, you're the guest!'

After our delicious Thai takeaway Marissa takes Harrison upstairs to bed.

I have a wander around the courtyard when I hear something scuttle behind me. I look back and see Tim fighting with the coffee machine.

I am tempted to confront him but that wouldn't do Marissa any favours, so I sit down on the rustic bench. Tim comes out after a couple of minutes.

'Ah … Harry, sorry, couldn't stop for dinner, got a deadline to meet before tomorrow.'

'All work and no play makes Tim a dull boy.'

'Yeah … it is rather like that at the minute. I suppose it's the same for you: one month nothing, the next six manic!'

He has a point and I don't have any dependents. Maybe Tim's just overwhelmed with his responsibility. Of course men don't discuss it like women do.

I'll mention this to Marissa when she comes back down – that will put her mind at rest. Tim seems perfectly normal to me, we even joke about the time I turned up at their small London flat, late, drunk and still in full horror make-up.

An enormous clunk comes from the kitchen. It's Marissa dispensing an armful of baby bottles into the sink. Tim stands up and bids me goodnight.

Marissa and I settle in front of the TV ready to watch a film but rather than Marissa harassing me into watching a romantic comedy like she *always* does, she goes along with my choice for a particularly gruesome horror flick instead. I've just finished inserting the DVD when I notice she has started to cry.

'I think Tim is having an affair.'

'Tim?' I say. That can't be true. Great big tears are running down her face. 'Oh, honey.' I rush to her side and cradle her in my arms. I haven't seen Marissa cry in years. I rock her gently, patting and stroking her hair until her tears subside.

'I don't think Tim would have an affair. He loves you.'

'He's always working, and we never have any time on our own – it's always us and Harrison.'

'What you need is to get away, just the two of you, recharge the love batteries.'

Marissa takes a shaky breath. 'It's too late for that.'

I look at her incredulously. I really can't believe Tim would have an affair.

'Have you spoken to Tim about any of this?'

'God no!' She shakes her head and sighs. 'Harry, it's not just the long hours, it's always been a topsy-turvy pickle having your own business, but I swear he's become secretive. When his phone rings he immediately goes elsewhere to talk, mostly blaming it on Harrison's noise capacity, but he does it even when Harrison naps.'

'Marissa, I think you're seeing ghosts where there aren't any.'

'Harry, I may have had a baby but I'm not doolally. Well, at least not yet.'

'OK, but men can't concentrate like women can, they're singular creatures by nature.' I feel her insecurity rising and it's horrible to see my friend disillusioned by her marriage; the one couple I thought had the happy ever after.

'I've tried finding reason in the madness, but it just isn't there. I don't have the balls to confront him again either. What do I say? Er, why do you take business calls in private? You see that doesn't make any sense. Why do you avoid your family at any cost? That won't wash, he works from home and spends most of his time here too when he's not travelling. No argument, Harry, that's my problem.' She bursts into tears again. I put my arm around her but it does little comforting. Did she say she'd already confronted him? I must have misheard.

She reaches for the baby's wet wipes and blows her nose. 'Sorry, Harry, not such a great weekend for you.'

'Don't be silly, this is obviously troubling you so I think you should speak to Tim and be done with it.'

'I can't, he'll put it down to a figment of my imagination and tell me I have too much time on my hands, resent motherhood and resent not working.'

'What?'

'I have tried asking him. That's what's so hard now. He's even more distant than usual.'

I have to get my head around this. Marissa and Tim talk about everything, they are two of the most balanced and communicative people I know. They're so understanding with one another it's like they're still dating.

'Maybe pick a moment when Harrison's asleep, bring him some lunch or something special.'

'If we can't talk, Harry, a blooming gourmet lunch isn't

going to help!'

'But you can't live like this every day.'

'Oh, Harry, let's not talk about my silly suspicions any more. Let's drink some wine.' She scuttles out to the kitchen and I hear the cork pop as she slams the door to the toilet. This is bad, Marissa swigging wine in the toilet. I make my way to the kitchen only to see the bottle is still on the table. What a relief, she hasn't lost it altogether. I decide to wait for her in the courtyard – it's a mild night and fresh air might be conducive to her mood. I gather up the wine and some snacks and lay them on the table ready for her return.

I wait and wait. Marissa must need a moment, and I can hear some mumbling so I assume she and Tim are talking. I'd better stay out the way so I walk around the dream garden, then I wonder if the mumbling is coming from the hobby house. I stealthily creep closer on the other side of the decorative hedges.

Tim is talking on his mobile but why out here? Maybe he didn't manage to fall asleep and needed a break?

His voice sounds urgent, uncomfortable. I can't make out what he's saying.

In light of what Marissa just said curiosity urges me to get closer and listen in; this is so wrong of me. All I hear is the tail-end of his conversation before he hangs up with a grunt.

'Look, I can't manage it now. I'll have to talk to my lawyer. I'll call you so you can stop harassing me all hours.'

Feeling incredibly deceitful and treacherous, I don't know what to do with this information. I don't want to give Marissa more ammunition in her unfounded fear but my loyalty towards her is putting me in a conundrum. Tim's call could be totally innocent; he often has skirmishes on the legal side, unpaid builders, disgruntled unrealistic clients who dip out of the contract after the drawings are made yet find him wholly responsible when the project starts going wrong. It's part and parcel, the nature of the architects' beast.

I shouldn't go looking for drama where it doesn't exist. That call could have been one he has on an everyday basis. Of course he sounds worried, who wouldn't? I run as quietly as I can back to the courtyard and Marissa is flushing the toilet … phew, that was close.

I see Tim out of the corner of my eye, sloping back into the house via the cellar. Now that is strange!

CHAPTER SEVENTEEN

Today, I spend the morning falling from a tree. This consists of me being whipped by branches on the way down and hanging upside down with a rope tied to my ankle. It's a relief when we break for lunch as I feel like I've just done a round with Mike Tyson, and I have a really bad case of rope burn down the back of my leg.

I find a quiet spot in the catering tent, wrap a cold rag around my leg and dig into a ham salad baguette.

'That looks painful,' says a voice behind me. I look round. 'Oh, hi, Paul.' I choke over a mouthful. 'And yes, it is.'

He peels the wet rag off my leg and winces. 'I was hoping you might join me at the wall tonight.'

Luke hurdles over the table like a springbok and lands in the chair opposite. 'You're going to the wall? Great, I'll get a few of the lads together – we can place bets.'

'There's limited space,' Paul says.

'Not to worry, big boy, we can squeeze in the back of your camper van like the devious leprechauns that we are!' Luke scoffs a doughnut and starts chuckling to himself.

I have a certain amount of gratitude towards Luke's clumsy self-invite. I like Paul but I don't want to date him. Anyway, I've decided I'm not dating any more. These stupid special connections you're supposed to nurture, it's just too much like hard work. I phoned Brett the other night and said my schedule was just too packed for any further dates. He took it well, turns out he'd been dating someone else at the same time. Just as bad as the rest of them! I was too relieved to really care but Marissa was livid, seeing as she pushed me to date him in the first place. She did take great delight in telling me his new girlfriend has the voice of a foghorn. Opposites really do attract.

That reminds me, I must call Marissa later. She sent me a cryptic text earlier: *I have news.* I wonder what that's all about?

'Well,' says Paul, 'I'll let you enjoy your lunch. Catch up later.'

'See ya, big guy!' Luke spits out over his doughy mouthful. Paul turns and gives a half-hearted wave.

'Miss Congeniality, you have become a total man-magnet.'

'Shut up, Luke!' I grab my fizzy cola and start drinking through three straws. I'm terribly thirsty.

'Who's a man-magnet?' Alex whips the chair out from beside me.

I am so over-zealous with my sucking that it goes up my nose, causing me to sneeze.

'Ignore him.' I wipe my nose with the back of my hand. 'Luke is making luscious mountaintops out of barren desert dunes.'

'Hey, Alex, you up for a climb later? Paul's going to the famous wall!'

'Probably not, the insurers are prowling around today. Have to tread carefully.'

'Shame. I'd have placed a bet on me reaching the top before you.'

'I'd have placed a bet on you losing.'

Next, they'll be getting their dicks out and pissing on the flaming wall. *Sizzling wee sizzling off the burning wall… sizzle, not piss sizzle but SIZZLE.* I start speculating over Alex's member size and kick myself to my senses, bruising my ankle even more. It's going to be swollen by the end of the day … my ankle, not Alex's ****. For goodness sake!

Thankfully, Felicity comes over and balances out the male swagger swamping the table. 'What's the news, comrades?' She's greeted with an audible grumble from me and more ludicrous schoolboy antics from the clown corner.

'Really, you boys are no better than poorly drawn *Viz* caricatures!'

The conversation turns to one of the extras on set that had an unfortunate fall this morning onto Alex's blood-starved character as he collapsed in a velvet-cushioned sarcophagus. Alex remains quiet as Felicity tells the story.

'The girl didn't quite know where to put her hands next; her face was crimson. She ran off set to a gaggle of screaming virgin vampires, quite an arresting sight.'

'That must be the most sexually charged moment you've had today, old boy!' Luke guffaws.

'At least mine fall onto me, they're not bamboozled into the dirt under false pretences when I need a quick rub-a-dub!'

'I'll have you know I'm quite the gentleman these days.'

'Isabel must have you on a tight leash,' Alex smirks.

'Isabel is a lady and has no use for reins, dear man.'

'So the lashing taught you a lesson, did it?'

'Shut up, you old tart, just because you're not getting any.'

'Neither are you, wonder boy!'

These revelations are news to me. I wonder why Alex hasn't been up to his usual femme fatale seductions. I glance over at Felicity and she just groans.

'Don't you two ever stop?' She scrapes her chair out and snatches her lunch away, kicking her heel in the air and blowing me a kiss. 'See you later, Harry, I don't know how you can sit with these jokers.' I don't have a choice – my leg is killing me.

'Got any plans this weekend, Harry?' Luke asks innocently.

My eyes instantly find Alex. 'Yeah, Harry, what are you up to this weekend?' He grins.

I find myself focusing on his bottom lip, which is full, tender-looking and very sexy. I cough and recompose myself.

'Not sure I'll be doing anything with my leg the way it is.'

We haven't actually verified our arrangement to the Lake District. I was waiting for the right moment and that is not now. If Luke or anyone got even a whiff that Alex and I were going to the Lake District together they'd be lighting an effigy and celebrating it on YouTube.

Alex's gaze holds mine but I look away first.

I probably shouldn't go anyway. It's a terrible idea and in my current physical state an over-ambitious one. My guess is he likes his women fully fit and ready. I don't think he's the patient type and definitely not the nursing kind. He'll want to trek, climb, I'll be no fun.

'That was a pretty demanding scene, Harry. I haven't seen a woman do that amount of falling *ever*,' Luke says.

'Thanks, Gluteus Maximus.'

'No probs, Harry!' Alex sniggers but Luke seems to have lost the joke, puffing himself up like a peacock, convinced I've just made a comparison between him and the manly Russell Crowe, then the joke dawns.

'Oh, funny, Harry.'

'Better wire up those loose connections if you want to keep Isabel keen.' I wink.

'Yeah, she doesn't miss a thing. I made such a classic sly double entendre the other night and she duped me into thinking she didn't pick up on it. Until later when it backfired on me.' Luke spaces out once again.

I pounce to my feet, only to fall back onto my seat, my ankle giving out completely. *Shit.*

'Let me have a look at that.' Alex bends down and inspects my leg then gently pulls off my trainer and sock. I wince in pain.

'Jesus, Harry, have you seen the size of this?'

'What?' I look down at my ankle and its massive, eurgh … GROSS!!

Luke peers over. 'Shit, Harry, that's ugly.'

With a nose like a bloodhound when there's trouble Sam comes straight over. 'What do we have here?'

I sigh. 'My ankle, it won't take my weight.' Sam bends over and takes a look. 'It needs ice and complete rest.'

'But there's another scene.' I hate being incapacitated.

'No, it's been rescheduled until next week. Jean-Luc is not happy with the light; the cloud keeps ducking into the low sky interfering with the reflection on the lake. He wants glass.'

'You're not serious.'

'Oh, he is. He went mental at a tiny robin the other day,' Alex recounts. 'It swooped down and made a hairline shadow on his light reflector board.' I snort with laughter. Classy noises yet again, Harry!

If I thought my ankle was bad, when I ring Marissa I find out that things are much worse for her.

'I have something to tell you but I don't want you to worry.' Words that are guaranteed to do just that. 'I'm with my mum.'

'Eh, OK,' I say, slow on the uptake.

'Indefinitely.'

I'm stunned into muteness.

'Harry! Harry, are you there?'

'Can't you talk this over with Tim?'

'I've tried, he's just gone weird, shut himself off totally. I think he might be having a nervous breakdown, but if he can't speak to me I can't help him. I need to think what's best for Harrison. What's best for me! I've left him the number of a good shrink so he realises the gloom he's spreading over the household. He can't wallow; he hasn't that luxury when he's a father.' Marissa sounds cool and collected, the opposite of what I expected. 'I'm not going to a lawyer, yet.'

That's eerie, both of them talking about lawyers. In Tim's case it was in a separate context, I presumed, but Marissa never acts on compulsion, her words are genuinely weighty.

'Look, I've got to go now as Mum wants me to see some children's village show or something. Any chance you can come for a visit?'

'I've got a weekend with my folks coming up so I can see you then.'

'Great, it'll be like old days but make sure you tell me when so I can get Mum to babysit in between her golf tournaments. We can go out on the country razz, although I fear that'll be more of a rural rumble than sophisticated cocktails!'

Marissa is incredibly upbeat; this is not normal for someone who thinks her marriage is collapsing. She may have lapsed into a temporary sabbatical from reality. I'm not going to pull her down to earth now, it's nice to hear her de-stressed.

CHAPTER EIGHTEEN

Kathy, the owner of the B&B, caught me coming down the stairs on my bottom. Her narrow twisting staircase has no banisters and I wasn't about to chance hopping. When I told her what happened she led me to a large squishy wicker chair and table under a willow tree in the back garden, brought out a footstool and a country quilt and told me to rest. She's been bringing me out snacks, books and drinks all day. I try telling her not to fuss but she won't hear of it.

Reclining in my wicker refuge I must have fallen asleep. The sound of percolating water wakes me up. I open my bleary eyes and Kathy is carrying a coffee machine.

'This is too much, Kathy, I can hobble to the kitchen now.'

'Nonsense, you need to rest and rest you shall.'

'Thanks, you're an angel.'

''Tis no trouble, Harry, I have me very own garden gnome to tend to now, haven't I,' she laughs as she walks away then starts watering her tomatoes in the greenhouse – she is a nurturing soul.

I drift back into a doze. I'm more tired than I realised. That's the thing about a hectic schedule; it's fine when you're in the thick of it but to suddenly stop with no warning sends your body into seismic shock.

I must have fallen asleep again because next time I open my eyes the sun has dipped behind the lone great oak tree in the middle of the field.

It's a peaceful garden, surrounded by paddocks and one great cornfield. Kathy keeps a donkey, a goat and an old decrepit half-blind Shetland pony in one of the paddocks; all rescue animals. They seem to enjoy each other's company despite their varying heights, species and ailments – the three odd furry musketeers. The goat rules the roost, shoving his nose into everything with relentless nervous curiosity.

The farmer, Farmer Toad as Kathy calls him (I do believe his name is Froids, must have French ancestry), doesn't seem to mind Kathy's commandeering one of his paddocks – he just drops in for coffee and cake whenever he can. I think he has a crush on her but is too shy to act upon it.

I spy him jumping off his tractor carrying two bales of hay, and making his way to Kathy's fence. The image could be lifted straight from a Van Gogh painting: the textured field's golden light flickering its nuances and the wind eddies which sweep the corn into mini vortexes. Van Gogh could be swirling his paintbrush from heaven, it's beautiful to watch.

It's a long time since I've sat back and appreciated the nature around me. I might get my camera out this weekend; see if I can capture any of it.

Farmer Toad arrives at the fence, unlatches a gate and tosses the bales into Kathy's makeshift barn down by the paddock. She's singing obliviously in the kitchen, windows wide open while she's baking – it smells delicious.

My iPhone beeps at full volume. I lean over to pick it up but somehow misjudge the space between chair and table and fall onto the ground, tipping over the table in the process. There's an almighty crash.

I look up to see the farmer leaning down to help me up.

'Don't be tackling technology in your condition, Harry.' His eyes are worn with warmth, his skin brown-hardened from the elements, his manner kind; a country farmer at his best.

'Thanks, Farmer Toaaa— Froids.'

'I know what Kathy calls me so you needn't call me any different.'

'Oh, sorry … um … OK, then, thanks, farmer Toad!' We both laugh.

Kathy comes rushing out to investigate the noise.

'She's all right,' Farmer Toad says. 'Just 'ad a bit of a tumble, Kath.' His eyes brighten as he speaks.

'We can't have you hurting any more appendages, Harry.'

'I'm fine, I just slipped onto the grass.' I feel five years old.

'You sure?' Matronly, she picks my legs up and checks them over like a vet would livestock.

I'm giggling. 'Quite sure, Kathy.'

'What says you to a bit of my lemon drizzle, and what about you, Toad?'

'Ahhh, Kath, that'll be grand.'

'Don't think I don't know about the bales you keep sneaking into the barn, Toad. I told you I'd pay for it.'

'They'd just be thrown, Kath, from the bottom of my stack … see?'

'Bottom of your stack, my good eye. Fresh off the combine harvester more like.'

They continue like this all the way to the house, Kathy reprimanding him for pure kindness, Farmer Toad embarrassed at his apparent tomfoolery. I could be an avid spectator all weekend.

My iPhone beeps again, reminding me I have an unread text, and a missed call from Marissa, by the look of it. I pick it up and see the two messages are from Alex.

Hi, Harry, sorry haven't been in touch to see if your ankle is better, filming has been delayed and le DP has gone totally nuts about … well who knows? He's French. Didn't like the way the wind blew or the earth formation of the downs. I feel like I'm waiting for the next major tectonic plate move so he has a canyon or something French like an Alp. Alex x

Let me know if you're still up to travelling, I can give you piggy backs! Alex x

His text makes me chuckle. I text back, *As long as you don't mind my being a crutch.*

I delete 'crutch' as it's too close to 'crotch'; no point encouraging the schoolboy.

Then I press the redial button and Marissa answers.

'Hi, it's me, how are you doing?'

'I've been collecting honey all day. Think I might have over-smoked the buzzy creatures – they're more docile than Tim.'

'Any news from him?'

'He's just being difficult and ignoring the fact that we have a problem.'

'I'm sorry.'

'Don't be. If he chooses that road I'm going to start proceedings in June.'

'Marissa, don't be hasty.'

'June is hardly hasty, Harry.' I hear her giggle. 'Hasty Harry, that could be your stage name!'

'Funny!'

She giggles again. 'Oh get this! You're going to crack up. I'm a judge at the organic produce show.' She starts laughing hard and so do I.

'They must have heard about your tantalising tomatoes!'

'I think Mum's been spinning them a few porkies. She exaggerates everything. Probably told them I supply Harrods or Le Gavroche.'

I listen to the fondness in her voice as she pokes fun at her mum. A small insignificant melancholy blows over me and lingers ever so slightly on my heart. I'm glad Marissa is holding on and thankful she finds solace with her mum. I snap out of my woe and pull myself together.

'Have fun with your marrows.'

'Oh I will. I'll stuff up Mum's little parody, that's for sure!'

CHAPTER NINETEEN

Any normal, sane person nursing a swollen ankle and sore leg would have cancelled an outward-bound weekend up in the Lake District, especially with a man whose name is synonymous with – questionable – virility overload. I should have dropped out whilst I had a valid excuse.

'I thought you had all weekend to recuperate?'

Kathy enters with a full English breakfast the size of Mount Kilimanjaro.

'It feels much better now, honestly.'

She peers at me, scrutinising my face, my ankle, and the stuffed rucksack on the floor.

'Well, I hope you don't overdo it, wherever you're going.'

'Oh … I'll be careful, I promise.' I stare at my plate. 'You don't really think I can eat all this?'

'You could do with getting some more meat on those bones, cushion the falls better.'

I dubiously pick up my knife and fork and begin the demolition process.

I fill up my coffee cup and drink it slowly, methodically. I'm nervous. I tell myself there's no reason to be nervous. I'm not one of Alex's little devotees swooning all over him. I've already proven my immunity to his advances; OK, I've proven my self-control. But I do realise his game is just that, a game. So I'm going to make the most of this weekend under my rules and maybe I'll change the game-play. So why am I wearing my Myla underwear? Good question.

The thought of a one-night stand with Alex Canty has crossed my mind. In fact, it's been crossing my mind quicker than fibre-optic cables are being laid in South Korea. But I'm not someone that needs a lot of sex. I'm not a nympho; there's been drought on that front for years – well, a few oases, but nothing to brag about. But the thought of sex with Alex is getting my libido cylinders fired up. I only hope he doesn't press the turbo button, otherwise he'll be in for the shock of his life.

But I'm not going to jump his bones. It's far too complicated, we have weeks of work ahead, and I don't want any awkwardness on set for others to marvel over. He might feel the need to pretend 'a good shag' was something more. If you have a good time and that was all it was meant to be, leave it at that and get on with your life. Don't sit there pining over a romance that didn't exist in the first place. Women can be so delusional, but not me. If you don't set yourself up for limp and sketchy fairy tales then you won't fall off the storyboard. To kiss an amphibian in the raptures of love is just foolhardy. Do you know how many poisonous species there are? Girls, take heed! Right … I think my pep talk has helped my nerves.

'Morning, Harry.'

Shocked to hear another voice in the midst of early morning dew I choke on a piece of toast I'm eating. I clumsily reach for my coffee cup.

Why does he get to look so damn sexy this time of the morning?

Alex chuckles. 'You OK?'

I nod furiously, eyes watering as I slurp on coffee until the liquid dislodges the chunk of toast from my throat.

'Toast went down the wrong way.'

He sits down opposite me, not the least bit concerned I might have choked to death. 'You look radiant this morning.'

I scowl at him. Is he trying to be funny?

He smiles and I give him a wide, slightly watery grin in return. Well, I did make an effort with my appearance this morning, hair pulled back in a neat ponytail, minimal make-up, new cream Paul Smith jumper with beaded black bow over skinny well-worn jeans (I don't want to look like I tried too hard), and a pair of old sneakers (the only thing I could fit over my fat foot).

'Kathy is something, isn't she!' he says, conversationally.

Kathy! He's already on first name terms.

'She seemed pleased yet unimpressed, peering cheerily at me deciding if she'd allow me to walk you to school or not.'

'Yeah, I can't see Kathy being all that impressed with royalty or celebrity. Mildly amused, maybe.'

He laughs. 'How come you stay here and not at the hotel like the others?'

I quirk a brow. 'You really you need to ask?'

He laughs again. 'I see your point.'

I notice him eyeing up my food and I instinctively put a guarded arm around my plate.

'You're not going to share?'

'Didn't you have breakfast before you left?'

'I didn't want to be late and disappoint you.'

'Really?'

'It's true. Anyway, don't worry, I've got my own full English coming my way.'

'How did you wangle that?'

Alex wiggles his eyebrows. 'I have my ways.'

I shake my head and laugh. 'Is no woman safe from your charm?'

'Oh, I can think of one,' he says, flashing me a grin.

I scowl at him and he chuckles. 'Damn! Have I just

blown the beginnings of a beautiful relationship?'

'You'll just have to make it up to me this weekend.' Now who's flirting! Tsk!

Kathy enters with another enormous breakfast, always at her happiest when she's feeding people. I look at Alex and he flashes her a killer grin. 'Kathy, did you hurt yourself when you fell out of the sky?'

That has to be the corniest line ever but it works. Kathy looks delighted.

'Get away with you, my boy. Falling out the sky indeed. You're worse than a drunken Irishman.'

'To be compared with the most charming and able drinkers is an honour,

madam.'

Kathy giggles, 'Well, I can't sit around here chatting,' although I know she would love to do just that. 'I will leave you two lovebirds to eat in peace.'

I look at her in alarm. 'Oh no, Kathy, it's not what you think.' I can feel my cheeks growing hot. 'Alex and I are—'

'Just friends, I know.' She winks and touches the side of her nose. 'Don't worry, I can be discreet when I want to be.'

'That's because you really are an angel,' Alex croons.

'Well, you two have a great weekend, and don't do anything I wouldn't.' She leaves the room cackling delightedly to herself.

I glare at Alex. 'Why didn't you put her straight?'

He shrugs coolly. 'We know the truth, that's all that matters. Anyway, the more you try to deny these things the more people think they're true.'

Is that what it's like?

I shake my head, laughing. '"Did you fall from the sky", I mean, honestly!'

Alex laughs. 'You don't believe anything I say, do you?'

'Oh, I believe you believe what you say.' I sit back triumphantly.

'What?'

'When someone has deluded self-belief it's easy to get everyone on-board, seated for the train ride. I, however, prefer to monitor alternative transport.'

I'm in danger of growing smug. I suck in my top lip, endeavouring not to laugh.

'Harry, you won't let me get away with anything, will you?' Alex twists forward, capturing me with his gaze. He raises his coffee. 'To a cheese-free friendship.'

I'm taken aback by his choice of words but raise my glass in confidence.

'To the lactose intolerant!' We both giggle.

I'm quite impressed with the amount of food I manage to tuck away.

We stand up and I reach for my rucksack but Alex beats me to it and instead of protesting, I let him. I'm so used to doing everything it's quite nice to have someone do something for me for a change. I cautiously walk to his car, pausing a couple of times and putting more pressure on my bad foot, testing it. It definitely feels better.

CHAPTER TWENTY

I was dreading the car journey, a small confined space with nowhere to hide, wondering if we'd have anything to talk about. I needn't have worried – we had plenty to talk about and Alex even had a plump cushion for my foot waiting on the floor.

Turns out he loves travelling as much as I do so we swapped stories about the places we'd been to. We even discovered we'd been in Peru at the same time – how weird is that! And when there was silence it wasn't awkward or anything; I think I even dozed off a few times.

We arrive in record time, just under four hours.

'Let's grab a quick bite to eat then go and explore, only at a slow pace, Miss Harriet.'

I carefully step out of the warm car and into the cold air.

'Fresh air, breathe it in, lassy,' Alex bellows from his lungs and beats his chest with his fists like King Kong.

I laugh. The more I get to know him the more ridiculous he is.

I follow him up the gravel driveway. He's got my tatty rucksack on one shoulder and his smart Louis Vuitton on the other. My rucksack looks like a bird's bowel expulsion, a splattered putrid mess dripping from his coat.

I giggle, then my stomach quivers and I realise I'm

getting more nervous the closer we get to the house. I'm about to meet his parents and I really want them to like me.

The house is a picture-book seventeenth-century farmhouse. It's called Rose Petal Farm, named after his mother. Alex told me this on the car journey here. It was once the house of the only blacksmith of the village, and parts of the old forge still remain. There was a state-of-the-art (for that time) workshop, involving an odd underground furnace and slack tub. Historians think this was a primitive ventilation system fashioned by the blacksmith himself. The next owner, a farmer, made his own beer, famous in these parts for its potency and a mysterious fable that Alex promised to tell me later. They'd even turned one of the barns into a shop selling cheese, milk, horseshoes, curious iron weaponry, leathers and kegs of beer. The remnants of an ancient cottage industry right here under my feet. Alex said they still have a few artefacts and some old tools, which they found under an iron trapdoor. I love listening to the provenance of a place, I would have explored further but Alex ushers me into the house.

'Mum?' he calls, but there is no answer. 'How odd.' I follow him into the kitchen and there's a note on the table.

'I promise you I had no idea.'

'What?' I ask.

'My parents have gone to Scotland salmon fishing. Harry, I promise you I knew nothing about it – you can read the note for yourself.'

I raise an eyebrow then take the note.

Hello, my darling. We've taken Sally salmon fishing in Scotland. You know where everything is. Help yourself. Call us if you have any problems. Love. Mum & Dad.

'Sally?'

'Their boat.'

It does seem genuine enough and not some elaborate scheme to get me on my own. I've noticed he gets a certain gleam in his eyes when he's being straight up, his irises glow a milder blue. My God, can you hear me? Am I beguiled or what?

'I really wanted you to meet them too.' He shrugs.

'It's OK,' I say.

'It's just nice to get away, it chills me right out just being here.'

'I know what you mean. When I go back to my dad's farm the weight of adulthood disappears in an instant.'

'Exactly, Harry, exactly.' He looks deeply into my eyes and I feel a ripple up my leg – must be that damn ankle throbbing!

'Sit yourself down and I'll rustle up my speciality, Welsh rarebit.'

'You can cook, I am impressed.'

Alex grins. 'Cheese on toast, beans on toast … basically my repertoire is "on toast".'

'Can you stretch to a cup of tea. I'm not hungry at all.'

'Coming right up, Miss Harriet, and up here it's referred to as a "brew".'

I laugh. Sitting back I look around. The kitchen is a combination of period features, rural, rustic, and clever contemporary elements. The beautifully preserved sandstone floor is unique. I imagine the lives that trod them, what were they doing, carrying the milk, fetching the flour … My mind lapses into reverie to the old days where machines were operated by hand. The house is also full of stuff: I tend to have everything neatly tucked away behind cupboards and drawers but here everything is on show – there's stacks of magazines, old newspapers, even pieces of material. It's a house that is lived in, and used.

'My parents are complete hoarders,' Alex comments, as he raids the fridge, tossing out everything until he finds the mustard. 'They still have the first costume I wore on stage.'

'Really, what was it?'

'A Spiderman outfit. I was four.'

'I bet you looked cute in that.'

'My parents thought so. There's a photo of me in the living room.'

I promise myself I will have a look for it later.

It is strange, watching Alex busying himself in the kitchen, rustling up cheese on toast for himself and making a brew for me. If anyone had said, this time last year, that I would be spending a weekend with Alex Canty I would have laughed, but here I am and it feels totally natural. Not sure what I was expecting. No one would believe it. Sam and Luke think we're at war. I wonder what Marissa would say? What would any of my girlfriends say? Details, they would want details. Alex in a Spiderman outfit; I shake my head smiling.

He joins me at the chunky farm-style table. A massive slab of old, solid wood that's meant to be stained, chipped, scratched and used. He tucks into his Welsh rarebit. The man's appetite is insatiable.

I slurp slowly on my tea, no airs and graces, fantastic. Hate that picky sippy façade most women and men rely on at the beginning of a new ... er ... new friendship. When we've finished Alex stands up. 'Fancy a walk?

I stand up too and wobble slightly.

'We don't have to go right now, we can rest up first if you like.'

'Nonsense, it's only because I've been sitting down too long, I could do with stretching my legs.'

'Right, this way then.' He offers me his arm, which I ignore.

The stairs are rickety and uneven.

We reach a sunny spot on the upstairs hallway and my eyes are drawn to the exposed wooden beams, each one carefully restored. The corridor turns sharply into another five steps up.

'Watch your head, Harry; this passageway is Willy Wonka's medieval attempt. I'm sure of it, I have a massive lump on my skull to prove it. Deceitful perspective, you see.'

It's true, the ceiling becomes lower and the walls taper in. What a house, nooks and crannies galore. Around one more corner is a wide stable door; it feels like home. Alex unhitches the iron latch and fights the door open, revealing the most beautiful room; low, double-aspect windows reflect the sun in their many panes of warped glass. The bed is huge, modern but sympathetically styled for its surroundings.

'Harry, behind that wooden wall panel is the bathroom.'

'Wow.' I am lost for words.

'It's kinda nice here, isn't it?'

'I'd say.' I'm overjoyed. He opens the secret door by pushing the side, the most luxurious bathroom waiting to be discovered. The roof slopes in and a circular window has been custom-made for light, directly positioned above the round wooden bath. It's as if it demands its own bright satellite. I'm going to enjoy a soak in there. I'm goggling so much I might dribble. Alex grabs my bag from the hallway and places it on the bed.

I look up and see him watching me. I feel my cheeks warm and my heart begin to race. 'Ready?' I rupture the atmosphere with a newfound energy, the energy of avoidance.

In the short time I have been in the Lakes I have fallen in love with the place. We've seen all sorts of wildlife but it is a huge lake that sends a chill down my spine. 'Wow!' has become my word du jour.

Alex is pleased with my reaction. 'Beautiful, isn't it.'

'Breath-taking.' I nod in agreement, tugging at the neck of my North Face jacket. The trees had protected us in the woods but there is no cover in the open surroundings. Ducking my head against the wind I follow Alex along the pathway to take a closer look at the lake.

'This is one of the larger lakes but the Lake District has

a variety of open waters, ranging from small upland tarns, to rivers, to lakes like this,' he informs me.

'Anyone who becomes a tour guide in his syntax must definitely and absolutely love the place!'

He looks stunned for a moment then realises he's fallen into the role quite happily. He laughs, 'You sound surprised.'

'I suppose I am. I had you down for glitzy places, rocking events, champagne and lobsters,' I confess.

Standing side by side with Alex it would be easy to get lost in the romantic setting of it all. The lake gives me a sense of tranquillity and I realise I should do this more often.

Alex is so good to look at, so strong and vibrant, more masculine than testosterone itself. If I were a brave woman I would reach over and kiss him senselessly, discover for myself if it would be as good as I imagine it might be. But I'm not brave, not in this situation. Give me a mountain to free-fall down any day of the week. Alex puts his arm around my shoulders.

'How's the ankle holding up?'

I shiver but it isn't from coldness. 'It's OK,' I say, trying to sound casual. Luke often puts his arm around me. Yeah, but when Luke does it I don't have the desire to turn in his arms and press my body against his chest like I want to do right now. I hold my body rigid.

'You would say if it was hurting, wouldn't you, Harry?'

I seem to lose the power of speech.

'Harry?'

'Don't worry, if it hurts I seem to remember a back that was promised for piggying!'

'That's right, lady, and don't you forget it. That's a Canty command, you're on my turf now.'

I squiggle my nose up at him. 'Yes, sir, sorry, sir.' I continue my military chants until he concedes. It also has the bonus effect of unravelling Alex's arm from my shoulder without seeming rude. A few Benny Hill salutes can do wonders for a girl who's unsure of her next move. He peacefully resumes his stance and gets lost in the view.

I turn and look at the view.

'You forget what nature can do sometimes.'

'God, or whoever or whatever, is a pro landscape gardener.' We stand watching, both lost in our own thoughts. Mine being a mixture of confusion, desire, and tumbling back into confusing desire. I tug my woolly hat over my ears to give my hands something to do; when I next look at Alex he is watching me intently. He looks as if he is about to say something but whatever it is he decides against it and stuffs his hands in his pockets.

'Ready?'

'Lead the way.'

We cover a lot of ground. Alex is an attentive guide, pointing out areas of interest, rare birds and plants. I've nicknamed him Randy Attenborough. It's quite funny: every time he says something I reply in two ways, 'Really, Randy' which is meant to be misconstrued for the benefit of passing ramblers, or 'Is that so, Mr A.' which has a whole other connotation in America. We have our own little skit going. Alex seems to be relishing the role. He's becoming a bookish encyclopedia character; he's even made some bookworm glasses out of reeds. He just gets sillier and sillier.

We push on along the muddy pathway, through woodland, passing the occasional walker and fishermen. His enthusiasm is contagious, I can see in his face how much he loves being here. We only start making our way back when it is too dark to see any more. My watch says it's seven-thirty. Alex suggests dinner in a pub and as soon as he mentions food my stomach rumbles in agreement.

'Hungry?'

'You heard that then?'

'Your stomach rumblings woke those poor hibernating hedgehogs back there,' he says with a smile.

CHAPTER TWENTY-ONE

'My parents' local,' he says, holding the door open for me.

The pub must date back to the sixteenth or seventeenth century, again displaying the raw and age-old timber oak beams brimming with character, and a roaring open fire beckoning me over. It isn't busy, save for a few locals and tourists scattered around. Straightaway people recognise Alex but most go back to their affairs. One woman starts nudging her husband's ribs to the point of injury.

I wonder how he copes with people watching him all the time. It would drive me insane.

'Why don't you go and find a cosy corner and I'll get the drinks in. What will you have?'

'What are you having?'

'A pint of bitter.'

I wrinkle my nose. 'I'll have a glass of red wine.'

I find a table near the fire and slump down in a low comfy chair, letting out a deep sigh of contentment; my ankle is ready for a break. For a second I close my eyes and when I open them again Alex has our drinks on the table and is watching me. I sit up, feeling self-conscious, and pick up the wine gratefully.

'Thanks.'

He smiles. 'I wasn't sure if you'd fallen asleep.'

'I was just resting my eyes.' I take a sip of wine and let out another contented sigh.

Maybe it is the warm cosy atmosphere of the pub but I feel totally relaxed. Alex has proven easy company, totally different out of the male-dominant film set; kinder, gentler. I suppose he has to act all macho and Don Juan while he's around other alpha males. I didn't think he had any depth to his character but he does, and the temptation to go with the flow to see what develops is irresistible. I force myself to my feet.

He glances up, startled by my sudden movement.

'Won't be a second.' My voice sounds husky.

Once in the bathroom I place my hands on the basin and stare at my flushed reflection in the mirror. I look positively glowing, radiant even. My hair is hat-hair with windswept ends. I consider putting it up but decide to leave it loose. My hair is wild and I feel daring.

When I get back Alex has his head bent looking down at the menu. I plonk myself down and pick up my own menu.

He looks up. 'You should wear your hair down more often, it suits you.'

I blow a strand from my eyes. 'I can't be seen tumbling in this frizz, it would date the film back to the seventies!'

He laughs. 'I like a bit of seventies retro. I had massive sideburns before starting this film but they said I couldn't keep them otherwise I'd make the vampire look like Burt Reynolds making a comeback! So, what will you have?'

You! I nearly say. I cough and look quickly at the menu, undecided.

'I'd recommend the Guinness pie. Their homemade pies are excellent – each has a different ale in the pastry. They're extremely tasty.'

'OK. Sold.' I look up to find mock surprised etched across Alex's face.

'What?' I say.

'You're agreeing to do something I suggested.'

I grin. 'I trust your opinion on the small matter of a pub meal.'

'Start small, aim big,' he grins. He gets up and places our orders at the bar, bringing back a bottle of wine and another pint for himself. He's humble in his manners. I expected him to click his fingers like an A-lister A-hole.

One large pie and a bottle of wine later I lean back in my chair and pat my full stomach.

'That was delicious but I don't think I can eat another thing.'

'Not even a homemade pudding?'

'Well, now, there's always room for pudding.' My smile turns into a yawn. Oops. 'Must be all that fresh air!'

'Or the bottle of wine.' Alex is amused.

'Crikey, have I drunk the whole bottle?'

He nods.

I think I might be drunk then and hiccup in agreement with my thought. Alex laughs. Leaning back, he crosses one of his legs over his knee. If he had a pipe and a dog it would be a complete picture of country living. He links his fingers together behind his head and stares at me through half-closed eyes. 'What do you fancy?'

You is on the tip of my tongue again. Oh God, definitely drunk. I pick up the menu. 'Ummmm,' I muffle from behind the menu.

Alex takes the menu from my grasp and turns it the right way up. 'I can recommend the apple pie.'

'You do like your pies up here.'

'What's not to like? It's a three-tiered gratification trip: first the pastry all warm, sweet and crunchy, then the delectable fruity filling, soft and tangy often with a surprise, then the bonus of having something slippery, creamy, maybe vanilla, maybe almond flavoured on the side.' He's being provocative in the most hammy, corny over-the-top way.

'Crikey, Alex, did some supermarket chain offer you an endorsement for pies?'

He laughs. 'Ye of little discernment, I thought I could be the male Nigella.'

'You have to ooze sexuality. I don't think you've got what Nigella's got!'

'Interesting, Harriet, so you find Nigella attractive, do you?' He leans forward like any hot-blooded male would at this dream scenario he thinks he's getting. Strange, isn't it, women don't get all hot and bothered about gay men.

'Just because someone can recognise beauty in the same sex doesn't make them—' I stop, he's just teasing.

'Spoilsport.'

'Let's eat some fruity pie then. I hope they have peach, with its velvet covering and the sweet fragrant flesh, how I love the texture between my lips!' I taunt in my best Nigella impression, spoiling it a little by undoing the top button on my jeans to make practical room for more stodgy food. I lean back in the chair twiddling my hair for the full effect, coyly looking up to see his face.

Alex coughs. 'Is that seduction, Harry? Don't give up your day job.'

Ouch! I scowl then start to laugh. I'm not cut out for seduction. The only person getting hot and bothered is me.

He retreats to the bar to order the dessert.

'Does it ever bother you?' I ask, when he sits back down again.

'What's that?'

I lean forward, whispering. 'People staring?'

Alex leans forward and whispers, 'I haven't noticed, I only have eyes for one person in this room.'

I laugh. 'As if there isn't enough ham in the pies.'

He laughs. 'It's true though,' he says, staring into my eyes.

I find my focus making out two Alexes – two for the

price of one. I giggle.

The idea that a man like Alex could fancy me still doesn't ring true. I don't have low self-esteem, I know I'm fairly attractive, but men like Alex need more than fairly attractive. But he does make me feel like there is no other person he'd rather be with.

'Most people are respectful and leave me alone,' Alex comments. 'They know me in here so I can be myself, relatively speaking. I try not to let it bother me, otherwise I'd go insane and turn into a recluse, which happens more than you think. Why, is it bothering you then?'

'No, it's just a bit weird.' I blink to readjust my focus and the two Alexes become one. 'I've really enjoyed myself today. Thank you.'

'I sense there's a but coming on.'

'No. No but.'

'Well, in that case I'm glad you enjoyed yourself.' He leans forward. 'I have too.'

'And you are not at all what I expected.'

He arches a brow. 'How so?'

'Well, you're just ...' I search for the appropriate word but it doesn't come. 'Normal, I guess.'

'Normal? Normal? Good God, that makes me sound dull. I haven't bored you, have I?'

I laugh. 'Maybe not normal but neither are you—'

'Swinging off trees Neanderthal-style, suggesting we partake in an orgy?'

I giggle. 'So do you want to take me to bed now or later?'

Alex chokes on his bitter. 'Excuse me?'

'That's why we're here, isn't it?' *What am I saying? Have I lost my mind?*

'I've never mentioned anything about taking you to bed.'

'So you don't want to take me to bed?' I frown.

'I never said that either.'

He shakes his head, trying to get to grips with the

sudden shift of conversation. 'I think someone needs a strong coffee.'

'I don't want coffee.' I cross my arms. 'Another wine would be nice.'

Alex laughs. 'Harriet Quinn, I think you are drunk.'

'I'm not,' I protest, squinting with one eye because Alex has become two again.

'Come on, let's go.'

'So you're not going to try and seduce me?'

'No, Harriet, your virtue is safe with me.'

CHAPTER TWENTY-TWO

Outside the cold wind is instantly sobering. I step away from the light of the pub doorway and into the black of the night.

'I can't see.' I turn to Alex, giggling. I can't see him properly either and put my hands out in front of me, tentatively moving forward. It is so dark and silent, everything is strange and eerily quiet but when my ears finally tune in I can hear the air is crackling with nocturnal activity.

Alex produces a torch with a flick. 'Always be prepared, that's my motto.'

I giggle again. 'Good thinking, Batman.'

'Where's your hand?'

'I'm fine.' I say, resisting his offer of support.

'I know my way back blindfolded.' At this point he trips and I snort with laughter.

'Suit yourself,' he huffs and then I trip over. He guffaws. 'Dammit, woman.' He grabs my hand to steady me.

With his hand engulfing mine I give a shaky, breathless sigh but I don't attempt to pull away. It seems silly to protest besides, I really am quite tipsy.

It's pitch black as we stumble our way back to the house. There's a lot of giggling as we walk unsteadily along the narrow path, feeling our way through the darkness. Luckily, it doesn't take too long but I'm glad Alex has hold of my hand.

'Home, sweet home,' Alex singsongs, pushing the door open. I promptly trip over the threshold and he reaches over to steady me.

'Think someone needs their bed.'

'Well, good night, Alex,' I say, my eyes adjusting to the bright light.

'Good night, Harry.'

But neither of us moves. I look at Alex and he reaches over and touches my cheek with his fingertips.

I gasp. 'What are you doing?'

He smiles at me. 'Seducing you.'

'You said you weren't going to seduce me.'

'I lied.'

'I'm not sure this is a good idea.' Yet I lean forward for more. He draws his finger across my cheeks, his eyes never leaving mine, that slight mocking smile on his face now gone. 'So soft,' he whispers.

My skin prickles under his touch and my eyelids droop and I'm ready to be kissed. Without realising it I have placed a hand on his chest, maybe in resistance, maybe not.

His hot breath touches my forehead. 'You're right, we shouldn't. OK, to bed with you.' He holds me at arm's length.

I look at him but I can't focus. He's right, now is not the time. I tell myself to move but the message from my brain to my legs takes a long time. Finally I turn on my heels and make my way up the stairs.

CHAPTER TWENTY-THREE

I wake up still in last night's clothes. I tentatively sit myself up, testing the poundpoundpounding in my head. On a scale of one to ten it's a six – nothing I can't cope with. The pint of water before bed obviously helped.

I find the Panadol in the bottom of my bag and immediately take two. I then brush my teeth several times but can still taste the booze in my mouth. Next, I run a bath. After a long soak I feel better. I dress in my skinny jeans and a black knitted polo-neck jumper. My freshly washed hair hangs wet over my shoulders. I apply some make-up and for a morning-after I don't look too bad.

I find Alex in the kitchen, rustling up bacon and eggs.

'Morning,' I croak.

Alex turns and smiles at me. 'Morning, beautiful.'

Is he trying to be funny?

'Did you sleep well?'

'Um … Yes. You?'

'Not really.'

Oh.

He shrugs. 'I'll get over it.'

'How's the head?'

'Not too bad.'

'Coffee?'

I sit down at the table. 'Yes please.'

'Have you thought about what you want to do today?'

'I'll leave it to the man of the lakes.'

'Careful, Harry, anyone would think you trusted me.' A playful grin crosses his face.

'Very funny, movie boy.'

'How about a brisk bike ride to clear our heads, if your ankle is up to it, that is?'

'The ankle's fine.'

'Well, Lake Man can rescue you if it's not.' He uses the frying pan to animate his super powers. I laugh.

'Better take your super bike then, Lake Man!'

Any tension that might have been is well and truly extinguished by humour. Neither of us wants to bring up the near kiss and it's a relief.

After breakfast we take the bikes out and cycle for over an hour at a leisurely pace, pedalling across some rough terrain, only stopping once for a saddle adjustment along the way. The ride is invigorating and the throbbing headache is gone. I step off the bike and we settle down next to another lake.

'How's this for a view?'

'Stupendous-O, Mr Lake-O!'

'Tea?' He produces a jazzy-coloured flask.

'I'm impressed – what else have you got in there?' I lean across, trying to get a closer look. Alex's eyes dance as he roots in his rucksack and pulls out the items one by one. 'Hmm, let's see: a Snickers bar, a crusty baguette, Brie, smoked salmon, white wine, berries and an old sock, by the looks of it. I can recommend the Brie over the sock.'

I eat everything he puts in front of me.

'I can see why you love coming here, it is truly breath-taking.'

'Yes,' he agrees. I look up and find him staring. I throw him a questioning look.

'I want you, Harry,' he says in a rough drawl, 'and I think you want me?' Although he seems less certain with this admission.

I moisten my lips. This is my turn to vehemently deny I want him but the temptation to relax and go with the flow is irrepressible.

'Er … No.' I say it so forcefully that I astonish my carnal urges into submission.

'No? But last night—'

'I was drunk.'

'You want me, you know you do.'

'That might be so but we can't.'

'Why?' He almost sounds like sulking.

I sigh deeply. 'Because we don't want to ruin a beautiful friendship. Besides, what's in it for me?'

'How do you mean?'

'Say we … sleep together …'

'I'd like to think we'd do more than sleep.'

Sparks leapfrog up and down my spine.

'But then what?' I say.

'I'm not sure I follow.'

'You're offering me a bit of slap and tickle – I can get that anywhere.' Alex seems to be lost for words. 'I'm just not in the market for that.'

'So, there really is a market for that? I thought it was just say-so, I'm gonna have to look that up on satnav.'

I laugh, despite myself. 'Alex, I'm too old to be messed about.'

'Who says I'm going to mess you about? Harry, you might mess me about too, have you thought of that?'

My argument suddenly falls apart and I have no comeback.

'You blow hot and cold, it's impossible to know what you're thinking … how much proof do you need? I like you but it would be easier to advance over Afghan mountains under fire than to romance you.'

'Gee, thanks,' I say, slightly sarcastically. He's quite insulting but also funny.

'Harry, I don't know you that well, either, how do I know you won't sell your story to the papers? I have as much at stake as you do.'

Gosh, I never stopped to think of it from his point of view. 'Yeah, but Alex you have a—'

'A reputation that was written by someone else, conceived by a vicious fat balding man in his forties just so he has something to write for the next edition of his lowbrow gossip magazine … yeah, yeah … OK, Harry, enough said.'

He actually looks pissed off now. I suppose those are the paybacks for a life in the public eye but he seems genuinely distraught. I pick up the rucksack and search for a peace offering; the wine is the only thing left, and the sock. I put the sock over my hand and squeeze a blackberry to make a couple of red eyes. Armed with puppet sock and wine I tepidly venture over. 'Mr Lakes, would you care for a drop of vino?'

I'm useless at voices; it comes out all tinny and loosely cockney. Alex turns and chuckles.

'Alex, really I don't mean to be contrary. I just *probably*,' I emphasise the word to save an argument, 'want more than you can give right now and it would be wrong to begin something, not to mention the whole working together thing.'

'But I've …' He rethinks his answer and utters a different reply. 'You're right.' The words drop like lead from his lips. 'Friends then?'

'Friends, yes.'

'It would be highly unprofessional for us to form a relationship,' he says, painfully contemplating the words as each one chips away at his spirit.

'Yes, I agree.' Though neither of us sounds entirely convinced, and he used the word 'relationship'. I'm starting to regret my steadfast attitude. I never take chances with people. I've blown this opportunity into orbit. Bugger. I'm feeling a bit of a fool, a frustrated fool at that. Could I really settle for just another notch on his bedpost? God knows it would be a passionate affair while it lasted, but what about when the film is over, what then?

'Are you very angry?'

'No.'

'Irritated?' I try to coax a smile out of him before the bike-ride ends completely on a sour note.

'Let's just say you drive me to distraction.' He gets up. 'We should head back before the traffic gets really bad.' His tone says it all. This trip is at an end.

CHAPTER TWENTY-FOUR

The journey is mostly done in silence. The weather takes a turn for the worst so Alex's concentration is on the road ahead. Sometimes I feel his eyes on me but when I turn to look at him he looks away as if I have Medusa's head.

I dare not look at him again so I spend the rest of the journey staring out of the window, the uncaring weather matching my inner turmoil and the dreadful realisation that I have made a mistake.

When we eventually arrive outside my bed and breakfast I climb out with a heaviness of heart. 'Thank you for a lovely weekend, Alex. I really did have a good time.'

He gets out with me. 'Did you? Did you really have a good time?'

'Yes.' I nod enthusiastically. Any more nodding and I'll nod my head right off.

As we stand there the rain continues to pour down on us; neither of us pays much attention to it though. This feels like a scene from a movie. I just wish I could remember the outcome of it.

'Well, goodbye,' I say tentatively.

'Goodbye, Harry, see you tomorrow.'

Inside the B&B I pack away my things, scrub my face

clean, brush my teeth and pull on my old favourite flannel pyjamas. I need familiar right now. I've just climbed into bed with my book to hand when there is a knock on the door.

'Alex!' I exclaim, my hand fluttering to my throat. He's the last person I expected; I thought maybe Kathy had forgotten whether she'd put fresh towels in or not, she absent-mindedly gives me about four a day.

When he doesn't say anything I'm a bit worried. 'Alex?'

He continues to stare, and it could be my imagination but he looks suddenly unsure of himself, like he's going to be sick. 'I've come to apologise.'

I blink at him. 'What for?'

'Being moody on the drive back.'

'I thought you were concentrating.'

'I was concentrating but I was also in a mood so I've come to apologise.'

'Have you been drinking?'

'Just a whisky for Dutch courage. Can I come in?'

My stomach rolls like a happy hippo in mud. The movement is so vigorous I'm sure it's audible.

'I … er …'

'Unless you want me to repent my sins out here in the corridor?' There is a hint of a smirk I recognise.

'No. Yes. I mean come in.' It's not the first time he has caught me in a less than desirable state. I should be in full thrills, silks, and oozing with overpowering muskiness, instead I've got more plaid on than a Scottish tribe, with a puffed-up face all red and porous. Not a Sophia Loren boudoir moment to remember. I wonder if it'd be odd if I changed into something a bit more feminine. No, too obvious – he'll have to take me as I am, a raw tartan tomato.

'I've been thinking about what you said.'

Shit, what did I say?

As he shuts the door behind him I move into the centre

of the room, trying to create some distance between us. Alex seems to consume what little space there is and it's not much, three metres by four, and the bed takes up most of the floor, and you can barely stand up straight because of the sloping eaves. He appears impossibly big and the room seems to have shrunk as soon as he stepped inside. We stand in front of each other for what seems like an eternity, and I'm not sure what to do or say – I am completely thrown.

'I've brought a peace offering.' He thrusts a bottle of wine in my hand.

The wine from my peace offering, which we never got to open in the end!

'Thank you … you didn't have to …'

'It's just wine,' he says. 'Take it.'

'Er, right, OK, thanks.' Alex looks really nervous. I don't think I've ever seen him look nervous, he's usually so assured. *You and me both!*

'You're not like any woman … er, you're not like … you are … umm …' He seems tormented as he peers up into the low ceiling and catches his breath. 'Harry, you are too unusual for words.' He sounds almost angry. I am as rigid and upright as a scared meerkat, not quite believing my ears.

'Harriet, you are the most strange, sexy creature I have ever met. You're sarcastic, droll, brave and infuriating.'

I have no reaction to this. Is he paying me a compliment?

He lets out an enormous sigh as though twenty tonnes of steel have been lifted from his shoulders.

'Even in the ghastliest mismatched ill-fitting pyjamas I have ever seen you are absolutely as gorgeous as any Greek goddess ever depicted.'

I have an urge to giggle but he seems to mean every word. Again we stand with our eyes fixed on one another. I am spellbound. Alex is visibly shaking, the nerves running out his body as if he's taken adrenalin. 'Maybe I could have one drink for the road.'

'Wine?' My voice comes out in a squeak.

'Thanks.' His nerves abate and a serene expression radiates over his beautiful face.

I pad across to the dressing table, grab my Swiss penknife and pick out the corkscrew.

'Here, let me.'

I move the bottle out of his reach. 'I can manage.' I can't have him touch me. I need to keep a distance.

'I know you can.'

Gosh, he really is a jitter bags.

I pour two glasses of wine and hand one to Alex.

He sits himself down on the one single chair in the room and I have no choice but to sit on the edge of the bed. It feels like the bed is the elephant in the room: neither of us wants to look at but we can hardly avoid it.

Alex takes a massive gulp and his knee starts to twitch.

I take a careful sip of wine, letting the fragrant liquid caress its way down my throat. 'Nice wine.' I attempt to break the silence and say the first thing that pops into my head. 'I imagine this isn't the glamour you're accustomed to.' Aiming for any subject in small talk since Alex seems incapable of conversation right now.

'It's a nice room.'

'It's cheap,' I counter. 'And Kathy is lovely.'

'She is. You know she gave me a huge hug when I arrived.'

'Oh no. What must she think!'

'Weirdly expectant and pleased all at the same time. Why aren't you staying at the hotel?'

We've been over this topic already but the room is so full of tension that I don't mind repeating myself. 'I'd never get any peace; besides I save money by staying here and this will help me fund my next tropical adventure.'

There really is no flow to this strained conversation.

Alex downs his glass. He jumps up. 'No woman affects me like you do, Harry. You're far too perplexing and far too real. I shouldn't be here. I should go.'

I'm too astounded to speak.

'Of course.' I get up and follow him to the door.

He suddenly turns and grips me by the arms. 'I need to kiss you. Just to know.'

My body sizzles with the intensity of his gaze.

'I'm going to explode if I can't kiss you. Can I kiss you? I'm in danger

of going crazy if I don't.' He says this with such an animated passion that I find myself just nodding obediently.

His lips curve into a slow smile and he moves a couple of steps closer. Reaching down, he pulls me up gently but firmly. His hands control my limp body. I have run out of resistance, the hands are gliding from my neck to my waist.

He lowers his head and *whooooooaahh* … it is a very hot, passionate kiss.

His warm breath fans my lips, sending yet another cascade of shimmering sensations through my entire body. His fingers slip through my hair, cupping my head, and he deepens the kiss slowly and insistently, his arms tightening around me until I am pressed close to his hard-masculine torso. The heat of his body melts into mine, flooding my whole being. I slide my hands around the back of him and push my body closer, my hands moving to his face, pinpricks of stubble dragging on the pads of my finger as I deepen the kiss. What a kiss! He leaves no part of my mouth untouched, claiming it with a gentle aggression that sends lightning strokes of pleasure through my body. Sweet joy rushes around my limbs and a hot weakness rises from below that has my body hungry for his next touch. The uncertainty of his hand movement is driving me wild, my body clings and melts in yearning. I whimper again, the sound gets lost in his mouth, I feel the powerful muscles in his arms tensing as he pulls me closer.

Then things really start to get intense and our bodies are closing in on each other like ravenous coyotes starved of meat.

We pull apart, panting.

'Are you sure, Harry?' he rasps, looking into my soul. He is giving me a chance to say no but it's too late. From the very first day we met I have been fighting the inevitable and it's no use fighting love any more. He is able to do something to me that I can't talk or fight my way out of; I am a woman possessed. The feelings I felt from the moment I first saw him flood through me again, my toes curl inside my woolly socks and I take a step towards him and pull his head down, claiming a kiss, pressing my lips, demanding more. He draws me up into his arms and his kisses harden with speed, pushing aside my layers of hair and finding the warm spot at the base of my neck. A deep resonating sound comes from deep within my throat. It is the last thought I have as Alex brings my arms above my head, unbuttoning and peeling away my pyjama top and cupping my creamy-smooth breasts, quickly following this with his mouth as he kisses and nips his way over the soft mounds, toying with each nipple with teasing twists of his tongue. I hear another animal-like groan spill from my lips. I feel exultant.

We topple backwards onto the bed, his taut body crushing against me, the hairs on his chest acting like a trillion electrical currents as they brush against the moist, glistening tips of my breasts. We kiss again, tongues entwining, a heat-seeking kiss, all that matters is touch, and taste.

He peels off my pyjama bottoms, his eyes searing me with his approval as he teases the edge of my scarlet lacy panties (*thank heavens for one feminine item of attire*). My skin is sizzling and beaded with sweat from his touch as he gazes at my naked flesh. When he smiles with admiration my own desire breaks through the last remaining barrier. His warm fingertips encircle my leg, lightly stroking the back of my knee, trailing upwards to the enigmatic triangular shadow that sits beneath a red silk screen, along the skin inside my thighs, stroking my stomach before returning to the edge of my panties. I groan with hungry passion, lifting my body. I want to feel his fingers inside the flimsy silk fortress. Drawing my nails down his back I grab his lean, muscular buttocks then move on to cup his satiny-hot manhood. Alex growls against me. He hooks his finger under the edge of my knickers as he moves the fabric millimetre by millimetre, stopping to hear my need of him. In a sudden flurry he discards them on the floor and gently resumes his position, our hips finally touching without barricades. His throbbing grows stronger with each kiss I lay around his neck, and then he thrusts deeply into my wet, creamy depths. I fall backwards with surprised satisfaction, cupping his shoulders, my fingers slip in the sweat of his shuddering exertions as he thrusts deeper and deeper, a driving rhythm which quickens with each plunge, my arms flay in ecstasy, grabbing the headboard behind me. His hands hold mine hostage as his hips travel closer to my belly, he forces down and finds a deeper place. I can't hold on, my body is in raptures, he gauges my delight and we both explode into a mutual melody of climatic clinches. This ignited orgasm is burned into my memory forever!

CHAPTER TWENTY-FIVE

My body feels like it has travelled to celestial heights and floated down into a blissful stupor … *Ah, yawn, how wonderful … Stretch, yawn … ah.* Alex and I made love and it was magical. It was … I feel the empty space next to me. Shit! My eyes fly open and I stare disbelieving at the ruffled vacant bed.

'Sorry, I didn't mean to wake you.'

I shift my gaze to the bottom of the bed. Alex is still here; he's dressed and appears to have lost something.

'You can turn the light on if you want.'

'I can't find my trainer.'

I feel my body heat rise wildly as the erotic sensations rush into my mind, memories of what we did mushrooming all my giddy thoughts, but in the cold harsh of the day I feel weirdly vulnerable. Vulnerable is not a word that sits easily with me.

'What time is it?'

'Four-thirty.'

Four-thirty!! What's the urgency, or need I ask? Was he just going to sneak out without so much as a goodbye? Was he doing a bunk? I don't say my thoughts out loud but he reads them all the same.

'I need to get back to the hotel.'

'Right … sure.' I jump in quickly, disillusion sprouting from my voice.

God this is awkward.

'Look, I'm sorry …'

My eyes dart to his in alarm. I draw the sheets up over my naked form.

'Don't …' I say gauging the typical morning-after small talk that I want to avoid at any cost. 'Don't apologise for what happened. We both wanted it. We're both grown-ups, no need to delve into it.' It's obvious Alex is now in regret. I knew he was a smooth operator but the clichéd sneaking away … I thought he was above that. Well, I did think he would have at least a seamless tried and tested routine of escape.

'What are you talking about?'

My eyes jump to his again. 'What are you talking about?'

'I've got a car picking me up at five-thirty. I didn't think you'd want the car coming here. Knowing how you like your privacy. I thought you'd want to keep our' – he struggles for the right word – 'this, to be private.'

'Oh … right, of course.' I'm glad someone is thinking at this ridiculous hour in the morning.

'I had a great time, Harry. I'd like to see you again, if you want to … Do you want to?'

The tension in my body evaporates, to be replaced with a sudden swell of happiness. He wants to see me again. 'Yes.'

He smiles and my heart melts.

'So how do we play this?' I say with a matter-of-fact tone. He propels himself onto the bed with a speed that knocks me back against the pillow. 'Well first I kiss you …'

Laughing, I push him away. 'I think we have that sorted. I mean about work … and the nosy mob that work with us?'

'What is our business is our business. Unless …?'

'God no, they'd have a field day, it'll be impossible. Luke

will be merciless.'

Alex places his finger on my lips. 'OK, OK, it'll be our secret.'

His fingers work their way down my neck and along my collarbone. I locate my voice in the pit of my stomach. 'You know I'll have to treat you with the same contempt.'

His eyes glint with humour. 'So you agree you have been mean to me?'

'Nothing you haven't deserved,' I counter. He smiles but his thoughts are elsewhere and so are mine. He lowers his head and his lips traces a path from the hollow of my throat up to my ear. I close my eyes, letting my body languish in its own natural reaction. I can already feel him grow hard and my urgency tingles in response. I want him. I want to feel him inside me again, and he wants it too.

'I should go …' But he doesn't seem so eager to leave now so I take the initiative, clasping my hands around his neck and pulling him down on top of me.

Now that's what I call breakfast in bed!

When Alex finally leaves I roll around in bed for ages feeling deliriously happy. Everyone deserves to be this happy. It might be just great sex but oh boy, everyone should get to experience it!

I've clearly been missing out all these years.

When I finally get dressed and set off to work I am sure people will see through my glow. I'm almost disappointed when no one does. To everyone else it's just another start of a very long day ahead.

Sam and Luke are marking through a fight sequence that will be the first shot and I immediately spy Alex. My cheeks grow hot and I look down at my feet to compose myself.

'Good morning, Harry, you're looking wonderful this morning.'

I look up at Alex and I want to return a smile but Luke and Sam are watching.

'Hello, Alex, tardiness must be your middle name!' I reply, frostily. Alex chuckles. I sense Sam's disapproval glaring into my back and Luke shakes his head in sympathy but if I acted differently they would be suspicious.

'I think Harry's bed only has wrong sides to get out.' Luke, as ever, is pleased with his own jibes, and chortles away happily, knocking Sam and Alex's arms in the persona of a music hall entertainer. 'Harry needs a gallon of coffee to utter one civil word to anyone.'

'I would have thought Harry would typify that pure morning sunshine feeling.' I feel myself blushing as Alex's eyes meet mine.

'More like a gruel cloud!' Luke says.

'Luke should have his own season on Blackpool pier,' I retort.

Luke turns his attention to Alex. 'A little birdie tells me you were seen entering your digs fully clothed at the crack of dawn.' Luke is revelling in his own filthy imagination.

I'm grateful that no one is looking at me because my cheeks have reached boiling point.

'Well, Luke, strike while the iron's hot, that's my motto. Not everyone has time for the softly-softly Jane Austen approach.' This shuts Luke right up. Since he's fallen for Isabel everyone has been teasing him mercilessly.

'Harry, are you OK? You look a little flushed.' Sam's concern pools a sweat across my brow as all eyes swivel towards me.

Oh God, I inwardly groan. This is much more difficult than I thought it would be. I can feel Alex's eyes on me but I daren't look at him; if I do our secret will be out for sure. I can't hide my desire for him, my stomach flutters in excitement every time our eyes meet.

'I'm fine,' I say with a cough. 'I just had a very deep sleep, rushed to get out this morning … er …' Jeez, I'm blabbering. Acting is not one of my strongest fortes. Luke, Alex and Sam are all looking at me like red smoke is steaming out my ears. OK, things are getting far too weird around here, time to make myself scarce.

'Actually, now you come to mention it, your face does look red,' Luke says.

It requires all my hammy acting skills not to buckle. 'Are you saying I normally look like a dusty ghost? Thanks, guys … Talk about metro males – you lot are subways, metros and tubes put together.'

'Ah … sleepy Harry, can't you take a compliment?'

'I wasn't aware you were giving them out, being compared to a flushed tomato is hardly a compliment!' My tone is droll and I am relieved to hear Sam chuckle.

'Right, let's get the girl some coffee!' Luke barks his order to a circling runner. Sam and Luke start talking over the next scene leaving Alex and me alone.

'It's like being a hyena's pickings in here this morning.'

He smiles and my insides turn to mush.

'Can I see you tonight?'

I fight the impulse to grin idiotically. 'What do you have in mind?'

'A bite to eat and then back to your place?'

'Cocky, aren't you,' I say, shaking my head and laughing.

'No. Just hopeful.'

Goddammit, I want to jump his bones. 'OK, why don't we combine the two activities, saves time.' I wink suggestively.

'I love it when you get efficient, Harriet.'

CHAPTER TWENTY-SIX

The next few weeks fly by in a whirlwind of filming, romance and sex – lots of sex, more sex than I've had in years. I am so consumed by my feelings that I must try and get a hold of them for self-preservation, if nothing else. This is a dimension of living I've only dreamt about. It is a dizzy kaleidoscope of fun to travel through. There's nothing we can't discuss, there's nothing we won't do together, well, within the confines of our four walls. Kathy is the exemplar of discretion enabling us to carry out our … affair hidden from public examination. But like all good things it has to come to an end. Alex's promotion commitments start to weigh heavily on the limited free evenings we have now we're nearing the end of filming.

I do wonder if it would be better to come out? No. I couldn't bear the invasion, the scrutiny and all the questions. The fantasy of this affair might be discredited if it became a fire field for everybody to comment on. So I take what I can, when I can.

This week we have managed only one night together. We did have plans to see each other this weekend but then I remembered I'm supposed to be seeing my folks and then Marissa phoned sounding desperate. In my euphoric state I had forgotten all about her and her crisis. So I cancelled on

Alex.

I race down the M4 exiting at Newbury, cut across to Andover and hurtle down the everlasting A303; anything to avoid more chock-a-block motorway on a Friday. I've got my little route down to just over three hours. I didn't have time to eat on-set and I'm famished but I don't want to risk stopping. I need to push on otherwise I'll get there so late I'll be a walking womble. I rummage around the glove compartment, my hands touching bizarre and unexpectedly warm squishy objects. I don't know how they got in there … yuk, what was that? *AHA!* A half-finished bag of jelly babies, the sugar will keep me going. I bite a red head off in satisfaction. Small finds – big pleasures. I reach for the stagnant water bottle and swig, at least I can't taste it now. My eyes are dry, concentration is sketchy, I wind down the window … brrrrr … nippy.

Only another seventy miles … *Oh yawn.*

Luckily the drive is smooth and I pull up outside the farm. Dad is outside chopping wood. I frown – he's supposed to be taking it easy.

I wind down the window and hang my head out. 'Dad!' I yell loudly.

He stops and flashes me a smile, not a care in the world. I jump out and give him a hug.

'You should have driven down tomorrow.'

'I couldn't. I need to get up early, got to go somewhere with Marissa. In fact I thought I might drive over now.'

'We'd better get in then and try some of Ruby's anti-angina pasta. You can spare an hour, can't you? You'll need that to chew the blooming whole-wheat brown rubber she's got me on. And smuggle me a pinch of salt, Ruby keeps it under lock and key. She's taking it a little far.'

I smile and we walk arm-in-arm towards the farmhouse. The medication seems to be working for Dad. Once more I feel relaxed and at home, the stresses of the week just a fading memory.

CHAPTER TWENTY-SEVEN

It starts to rain and the track is getting sludgy. Thank heavens for my big-grip tyres. Gwen, Marissa's mum, lives up an even trickier track, way out yonder. Luckily, I know all the back roads and short cuts. It's like a trip down memory lane. There's that familiar corner again, where Marissa and I collided with the infamous hawthorn bush after our first taste of vodka. We were fifteen, precariously pelting around the country corners on rickety bikes *DOWNHILL!* Not a good idea, following an afternoon with Mr Smirnoff! I smile to myself – we certainly had fun growing up together.

Walking up to Gwen's front door brings back more memories. I can remember walking up in wellington boots that didn't quite fit, taking the rusty bucket to stand on so I could reach the brass door knocker … Ah, such innocent days where all we thought about were fairies in the woods and princesses' tree camps. Marissa would never climb up until I'd made little ruts or wooden steps, basically the easiest route up the branches for her. I was always the tomboy, she hated getting her clothes dirty. Who climbs trees in full-length sparkly dresses!

'Harriet! Oh, Harriet, so lovely to see you. Not changed from work, I see.' Gwen peers over her reading glasses, throwing the chain out of the way like a naughty goose. 'Really, you girls get less feminine by the second. I expect you've been wrestling with crocodiles or the like today. Now you must come in and try my quince marmalade, I've had an absolute bumper crop in my greenhouse. Can you imagine my surprise when the quinces outshone the damsons this year? I know, quite astounding!' Gwen never stops for breath. I see Marissa slumped over a glass in the sturdy country kitchen. She's staring out at the black wet night, fixated by the ricocheting raindrops pelting the wide glass panes.

'Erm … yes, hypnotising … er jam, sounds delicious, Gwen.' She stares at me intently, watching my every eye movement. Gwen is an astute yet detached sort of eccentric who doesn't bother herself with the frailties of the human condition. She concerns herself only with the constant quest for food knowledge, and food facts and statistics. You can talk to her about anything and she would approach the subject as an irritating scientific experiment that interfered with her pickling, gardening and preserving. This mind-set is not without its merits, if you're prepared for a totally uncut honest answer. It drives Marissa crazy; tact is not one of Gwen's virtues, and a teenager prefers tact when blooming from a meadow flower to a summer blossom. Gwen is the embodiment of the mind unplugged, before MTV even thought about it.

'I hope you can shake some sense into that offspring of mine, she's impossibly temperamental.' I nod in agreement, no point arguing, questioning or explaining with Gwen. I've learnt to smile, nod and pass the quizzing Lady of Dartmeet Cottage seamlessly, and with one swift movement bunny hopping into the requisite removal of the outdoor shoes. Being nimble has its advantages. I must see if I can get the move into a scene one day, Marissa will get a kick out of that. It's a practised forward jolty jig of twinned footsteps as if escaping from a vigilant Shylock. Marissa and I have this manoeuvre down to an art, since we discovered the foibles of alcohol at an early age (May Day, behind the haystack, to be precise. Farmer Pottle's cider!). Surprisingly, we grew up quickly … Nature's own catalyst!

Space to express and space for adventure.

'Harry, HARRY!' Marissa jumps out of her seat and apparent trance.

'Marissa.' We hug each other tightly, she feels deprived of affection. I take a look at her face; it's puffed up and tear-stained.

'Marissa, what's going on?'

'I think you'll need a drink for this one. Chardonnay all right?'

I look at her quizzically and nod involuntarily; she's worrying me now.

Marissa walks to the over-sized country dresser, snatches a glass from the shelf and grabs another bottle from the fridge. She must have downed the first. While she pours I study her face. This is not going to be good, her eyes are tired, her skin lacks the usual rosy lustre, no make-up, no spark. Marissa is for once in her life unfocused, not normal in the household of 'DAMN'.

'DO; ACT; MOTIVATE & No Nonsense on the way, please, girls.' Gwen's favourite credo.

'I haven't even told Mum the ins and outs of this one.' Marissa sits down and slugs at the wine glass hard. 'I was right.' My brow crinkles in contemplation and I take a hard swig too.

'No. Not Tim.' I am genuinely shocked.

'Oh, the affair's not all; wait for the sequel.' We both slug in unison.

'Oh, c'mon, you're joking.'

'I really wish I was, that this was a nightmare to wake up from.' Tears form in the corners of her eyes. I reach for her hand and squeeze it; she jumps to her feet, taking the bottle for another refill. She's acting like a woman possessed.

'Ohhhhh yes … the affair I could manage, somehow, maybe … Well, maybe not … but a child? It's a bit much on top. No, he couldn't just have an affair; he had to impregnate the bitch too.'

My mouth drops open. I don't know what to say, how to say it. Wishful thinking makes me imagine Marissa will laugh any minute, it must be a wind-up.

'Put that in your pipe and smoke it, pickle and fucking preserve it, Gwyneth! Mum just thinks I'm having a country break. DON'T, for God's sake, say anything to her. She's never understood why I married him and not some great business oligarch.'

'I don't know what to say. When, and how long's it been going on?'

'Oh, it's been a fact for nine years! Tim has a nine-year-old daughter! That little bit of information somehow – and of COURSE he has his reasons – he forgot to impart, pass on, enlighten … sure, it's a minor detail. Why the hell should I know about it, I'm only his wife!'

Marissa is in a rage, so much so that I'm thinking psychotic, should I get pills, should I get help … No, this revelation needs venting.

'I don't understand!' My mind searches for an explanation but shuts down with information overload. Mine as well as Marissa's world has been tipped on its axis; this is surreal, Tim leading a double life. He's such a nice guy … Why?

'He says it happened at college and he knew nothing about it. Convenient, eh? The inconvenient truth would be better!' I throw another glass of wine down my throat, stunned into silence.

'So that was what all the phone calls were about?'

'Spot on, Harry. He said it was his lawyer sorting out a paternity test. He said he didn't want to worry me unnecessarily. What a joke!'

'But you two weren't an item until his last year in

college.'

Tim is five years older than Marissa. He was doing his masters while she was an undergraduate in design. Marissa needs to talk about this coherently. She drinks as floods of tears roll down her face.

'Listen, Marissa, you're just conjecturing. Have you talked about this calmly?'

'AM I, HARRY? AM I … JUST FUCKING CONJECTURING? AM I … You obviously haven't had your loved ones ripped from beneath your feet, a life that is a lie.' She's intense with rage, then quickly recognises her mistake. She flops down on the seat and grabs my hand. 'Sorry … So sorry, Harry. I didn't mean, you know, I … Look at what that man's done, my best friend taking hurtful insults from a mad woman.'

'Oh for goodness sake, girls, can't you listen to Bach instead of that awful drudging rapture music?'

Marissa and I giggle at the absurdity of the situation; Gwen as ever is a great leveller.

'IT'S CALLED RAP MUSIC, MOTHER DEAREST, NOT RAPTURE.'

The upper-class trill floats again through the hall. 'Yes, I know dear, pap music. Such ineloquent grammar; always shouting double negatives … terrible schooling really! Tut-tut on their mothers. One should know about negation and gloves by the age of twenty … Really, these city-dwellers.'

'I mean, what else is he hiding? Three wives from Persia, a hoard of brothers and sisters for Harrison?' She stews in her misery.

'Look, let's take a step back. Try and imagine it from his point of view. Now don't get angry with me, Marissa,' when I see she is just about to fly at me, 'just hear me out.' She reluctantly sits down like a begrudging teenager.

'What if he didn't know, what would you do? Tell your wife, who has recently given birth, that someone who he had a casual liaison with at college now claims he's the father of her child? Maybe she saw he was successful and went out money-hunting. Wouldn't you wait for the facts to present themselves before spilling that news?'

'I suppose, but it was the secrecy, Harry. How can I ever look at him the same way?'

Harrison's whimpers spill out from the baby monitor.

'Tim's been trying to wangle a meeting with me for weeks. Every day, phone calls, emails, text messages. I think he's trying to butter me up in case of a divorce. Probably protecting his business interests; if it wasn't for me he wouldn't have a business. I'll show him.'

'Hang on, Judge Judy, just hear him out. Go tomorrow with an open mind. Then you can lose it. OK?' I search Marissa's face, looking for sensibility. Where is the rational Marissa I know and love?

'OK.'

She looks forlorn but with a touch more sanity prevailing.

Thank heavens. I thought I'd lost her.

CHAPTER TWENTY-EIGHT

I'm drifting in and out of my own snoring – it always happens after a shared bottle or two of wine. I can see Marissa bobbing Harrison in her arms through the bright sunny window. What a glorious day, compared to the storm of last night.

I must have fallen asleep in the conservatory on the wicker chaise longue; there are indentations all along my arm … its pastry appearance looks like it's been latticed by one of Gwen's baking utensils.

'Café au lait or Earl Grey, Harriet?' I peel the blanket off in embarrassment, blinking into focus.

'Morning, Gwen.' She inspects my eye movement and decides for me.

'I think café au lait. I was heating milk anyway, for the small one. Righto, café au lait it is.' She scuttles away, an army drill in the nicest possible sense. No fussing, no messing, crack on, Sergeant Major Gwyneth.

I signal to Marissa to come in.

'Morning, Snorey!' She springs through the French doors.

'You sound better this morning. Are you a bit more resolved about what's happening today?'

'Suppose so. See, I did listen. I will go and hear his side of the story. But I forgot to tell you that he also said that that wasn't all he wanted to discuss. The plot not only thickens, it's positively bursting. I've decided to put it out of my mind until the time comes.'

'Sounds good, Marissa. Whatever happens I'll be here for you.'

'Thanks, Harry. I think I would try and pummel mum into a fine powder if you weren't. What on earth is that smell?'

I sniff the air – the broiling pots are on the go – and laugh. 'I've never met a woman so engaged with vegetables before!'

'That's not all. Mum's turned the potting shed into the baby-food factory. She's trying out high-nutrient vegetable pulp recipes that are suitable for babies. Harrison's been the guinea pig. Actually, his appetite has grown since we've been down here. Got to wonder at the mad woman's methods – I could make a fortune if she gets this right. There's a plot of land over the hedge that is up for sale. I could invest in some massive greenhouses and make my own business. She doesn't have a clue about marketing. I'll show you some product labels I've designed later.'

Even through crisis she is inventing, creating and bursting with ideas. She is her mother's daughter indeed. I won't dare say it to her. She's positive and vibrant this morning.

'I will be able to support myself if the idiot thinks he's got a legal battle on his hands. I'll put everything in Mum's name, with me as MD.'

'Marissa, Tim won't be like that, please believe me. He would never do anything to hur—' I falter, bad choice of words. She gives it a moment's consideration and plonks her laptop on the table. *Phew!*

'Look at these designs, Harry, pick your favourite one and tell me why when I get back with a fresh new bum.' She sniffs Harrison and pulls a face. 'If only he were a cow we could manure the whole field in a day; those Gwen-Veg-Goulash-Growths have really got him going! Yeah, I'm having trouble with the name – maybe keep it simple like Cottage Cuisine for Kids, or Cuisine for Kids from the Cottage, or Kid's Cottage Cuisine, or Kid's Cuisine lovingly grown for you at the Cottage, or … God, he stinks. I'm off to do the do.'

She's obviously been occupying herself well: Marissa is lightning when it comes to creative ideas, and of course she hasn't been able to do that for a long time, what with supporting Tim's business then Harrison's arrival. Maybe she just needs to do something for herself after all this time. So whatever happens today, something good might come out of it.

'What about something shorter like Kids' Cottage?'

'That's it, Harry. KIDS' COTTAGE! COTTAGE KIDS.'

We're just de-mudding my tyres before the rendezvous and Marissa is yapping away about Cottage Kids, picking out small lumps of clay and mud; she doesn't seem keen to get on the road. Harrison is sleeping in a Sussex trug, Gwen's gardening basket. Cleverly she finds this the most convenient way to look after him while she repots a new breed of tomato she's managed to graft together. Contained in her own excitement she waves us off, or was she merely swatting a fly? You never know with Gwen.

A huge sigh of relief comes out of my passenger.

'Pheeeww – it's good to be out, feel free. I hope she doesn't repot and plant Harrison. I have a terrible image of just his arms swaying about in the cabbage patch.'

I look in the rear mirror and he's nestled nicely under a traditional quilt, propped up by a bonsai growbag as a pillow; you couldn't make this up. Now I'm looking at it a trug seems perfectly suited for a baby's needs. Gwen has triumphed again. What a funny household.

Marissa is quiet as we steam down the track; I leave her to her own thoughts. I still can't imagine Tim being so devious, and I certainly never expected a love child in the equation. My only fear is that Marissa is right. I did wonder whether her hormones were making monkey mischief out of her sanity, that she was being too sensitive. I should have known better, after the phone call I heard. I must keep this in mind when it comes to Alex – realistically, this is a nice shallow fling.

Tim's choice of a venue is odd. I looked it up on Google maps last night and it appears to be in the middle of some old woodland copse, about a mile off a small back road that leads to nowhere. My mind is uncontrollably vivid with images of axes and gruesome burials ... Now I'm away in la-la Land.

Positive focus, Harry, stay within the realms of real life. We turn into the obscured opening by the copse and it starts pouring down with rain. I'm just about to accelerate off-road when I notice a rickety old gate half off its hinges. I brake just in time; the jeep's bull-bars barely touching its mossy wooden bars. *CREEAK.*

I reverse and get out quickly to try to move the wooden wreckage. There are no fresh car tracks and I begin to think it's a wild goose chase. Of course I have the sense not to voice anything out loud. I battle with the gate but it won't budge. Marissa jumps out to join the fun. The ground is getting mushy and we slip and slide all over the place. We're both laughing hard as the gate stubbornly resists our every push and then jolts out of position, sending us flying into the sludge.

Marissa can't contain her mirth. 'Harry ... you ... you ... you look like a grunge version of Morph.'

I'm laughing to the brink of explosion, so much so tears are steamrolling down my face, my breath hardly catching.

'Y-y-yyou ... loooook like you've cacked yourself.'

Marissa turns and glances at her bottom. She's holding her sides, suffering an almighty stitch, her laugh husking on its way out. It sets me off again; the vision of us is chronically comic. *Mud-covered women found by copse possibly asthmatic!*

Finally we both catch our breath. I lift my jumper off and my shirt rides up; it's cold today. I smooth down the collar.

'Harriet!'

I jump in alarm. 'What's the emergency, queen of the mud?'

'Your neck, you have a vampire bite. Are you method acting, Harriet?'

Marissa homes in on my neck like a hungry vulture circling its prey. Shit, must still have the remnants of an Alex night bite. I don't know what came over us that night, teenage passion; we just went mad with biting.

'Harry, I'll give you until I count to three … one … two … three …'

I hate it when she uses toddler tactics.

'All right, all right, I'm sleeping with someone.'

Marissa lets out an almighty scream and I grin at her idiotically.

'Who? Not Brett?'

'No. Not Brett. It's supposed to be a secret.'

'That doesn't include one's best friend.'

That's true and I've been bursting to tell her. Besides, Marissa is getting impatient as she jumps up and down in a murky puddle.

'Alex Canty.'

Again another scream. I giggle.

'WHAT! How … when … wow … Harry!'

I giggle some more.

'I thought you had a glow about you. Oh. My. God!'

'I'll tell you everything but first help me get this gate out the way.'

'Deal.'

By the time we slowly make tracks Marissa has demanded more information than I knew existed.

'You're right. Just keep it casual, for your own sanity. Don't let him have the power, don't let him know anything, especially if you actually like him.'

'Marissa, I'm not under any illusions. He's good company and the sex is amazing!' I'm smiling but feel somewhat melancholic.

'I can't believe you're shafting Alex Canty, you lucky girl.'

'Actually, he's very nice once you get to know him. Not what you imagine at all.'

'Oh, c'mon, Harry, he's a pro at seduction. That doesn't mean he isn't nice but be on your guard.'

'I am, I'm in the driving seat.' I look forward through the misty rain, visibility is growing worse. *No pun intended.*

'I hope you are, otherwise who's driving this?' We start giggling at the dreadful joke.

'Stick to Cottage Kids, woman of the mud!'

I am laughing but I feel slightly annoyed that my shallow affair is being discussed as if it were nothing. Marissa is my best friend – imagine if anyone else knew. People just find him unserious and a serial lad. My heart feels heavy. I'm just going to enjoy it for what it is, join in the laughter, cheer my friend up. On balance, she wasn't going to harp on about love's satisfaction, not in her situation.

'Marissa, have you ever done kinky role play?'

'Noooo … what did you do?' She's animated with curiosity, her mood eager and fun-filled again. She should have guessed that diversion was my toddler tactic.

'Rhett and Scarlet!'

'I bet he has a way with words; he's a convincing actor. Was it electric? Well, frankly, my saucy filly, I can fill your dam.'

'MARISSA! You're so lewd.'

Her words bring out another worry: ACTOR. Alex is a

superb actor. Forget it, concentrate on the mud track in front of you. The lane half exists, it's totally overgrown, nothing's been down here for years. I'm beginning to think we've made the wrong turn.

'Marissa, put on the satnav, this doesn't look right.'

'No, this is the copse. I remember it from a child, mum's favourite elderberry harvesting place. It does look desolate, though, doesn't it?'

'Yeah, let's drive on for ten minutes then turn it on, OK?'

'Yep, Medusa the seducer!'

'Stop … please.'

'Harry the Harlot!'

I would make a jibe back normally but I figure let Marissa have her fun at my expense. It's worth seeing a smile back on her face; this might be the last time for a while, if things take another wrong turn today. Marissa is adamant they will.

'Harriet riding the Alex Chariot!'

'OK, I'll give you that on artistic poetic merit, but it's the last one.'

'Drink some Chianti, bed a Canty!' I shove my mud-caked jumper in her face.

'Mud mask, Mud Arse!'

We've driven more than ten minutes and the track is widening, the rain has come to a dribbling stop.

'Looks like there's a clearing up ahead,' I say, peering through the dirty windscreen.

'This is ridiculous – why we couldn't meet at a place with four walls and a roof is beyond me.'

The car is in second gear as I navigate the potholes carefully; some activity has taken place here recently. Both of us are silent, peering out of the steamy glass. I wind the windows down to clear the condensation then almost by magic to our right is a small clearing with a muddy JCB digger parked up. *Strange.*

We both look at each other in bewilderment. I can just make out a larger opening as the sun's rays engulf the treetops in a dazzling display of light.

'Shall we drive down this bit?'

'Dunno.' Marissa's mood is quiet, indifferent.

'Right, let's give this gravel track a go.' It winds around a few larger oak trees; it's definitely been laid recently. I feel Marissa's pending gloom, the atmosphere is emotive.

'Must be down here.' I'm talking to myself, she's withdrawn into her thoughts, poor girl. The track dissipates into a large green open space. We're just driving to the edge but my tyres are no match to a digger's giant treads, the descent is one of trepidation as I feel the tiny stones sink beneath my wheels.

'There never was a field here. I know because I've combed these woods as a would-be runaway many a time while mum counted her bunches of berries. 'What the—' I hit the brakes; the jeep's barely by the field's boundary. The sun is so bright now I need to put the visors down.

'Oh my God.'

'What is it?' I say, blinking, fearing Tim's put up a crucifix or a dramatic token of his self-loathing; I know how much he loves her. My eyes finally focus. 'Wow!'

'Harry, pinch me.'

'No, you pinch me.'

'I can't move.'

'I can't believe it.'

We both open the jeep's doors in slow motion, not taking our eyes off what stands before us. We both tread in a big pile of mud unconcerned, nothing distracting us from the scene in front of us. Marissa and I walk zombie-like towards the centre of the field. We can't speak, neither of us has any sense of reality; this is the state of the surreal – something that only happens in films. Our mouths drop open in utter astonishment.

'Oh, Marissa …'

Marissa's legs give way and by reflex I catch her.

CHAPTER TWENTY-NINE

Never have two women been rendered so speechless. For what stands before us is truly a vision. The most wonderful wooden structure, a modern architectural marvel, sits nestled in the landscape, magically bursting from the freshly turned brown and sandy ground, a huge pink silken bow fluttering around its roof, caressing the glass-encased façade as the wind ebbs from the surrounding trees.

'Marissa, this is amazing. Tim is amazing.'

'I drew this house once when we were at college. It was late one night and he asked me to picture my ideal world, my ideal home.' Her voice is small, shaky. 'I never knew he kept that ancient scrap of paper. It was part of a coffee-stained envelope that had been rolling around on the floor for weeks in his mess of a room, a silly doodle, childlike ... a stupid pipe dream. How did he ... how ... Oh, Harry, it's beautiful.' She starts crying like a baby. What an emotional rollercoaster she's been on. I must admit this is the most romantic gesture I've ever witnessed. WOW! Far better than the movies.

We tread over the mud mounds and scattered building materials. I'm supporting Marissa's weight, she feels giddy, faint, exulted, confused and any other descriptive adjective that you care to think of. I see Tim emerge apprehensively from behind a scaffold tower.

'Marissa, I'm going to leave you now, go to Tim, he's waiting and remember, he must have been planning this for years, the work he's put into it. His intentions far outweigh whatever mistakes he made in the past. Never once has he lied to you – look at his love without prejudice.' I feel quite proud of my little speech, emotional at my own words, I must be getting soft in my old age. Marissa walks tentatively towards Tim. He moves out of the tower's shadow, his body showing fatigue, his face exhausted from emotion. He runs to her, gathering her into his arms, spinning them both until they fall onto the mud. It's a beautiful mucky sight.

Yep, far better than the movies. I turn away, giving them the privacy they need. I'll just wander around the woods.

'Harry, come on over!' Tim shouts from the distance.

'I'll be back in a while, the blackberries need picking!' I signal the thumbs up and Marissa laughs at the sheer suggestion of me foraging in the woods. They kiss as if Tim has returned from war – which in a sense he has: the war of the hearts. I scoot over to the jeep and grab my even staler bottle of water, perfectly happy to mooch along the green-canopied tracks breathing in fresh untainted air, reaching out at the golden autumn leaves as I stroll by.

I find an old stump bathing in sunlight and sit down with a huge sigh. The knots in my stomach unravel and I feel a huge sense of relief. All is right in the world again. Marissa loves Tim. Tim loves Marissa. I should probably leave the lovebirds to their new wooden cutting-edge aviary and find a country pub somewhere.

I take a look around the copse, forgetting the way I came. Seeing the sun's position I opt for the middle blackberry bush. I walk fast but it takes longer to get back; the marsh I accidentally discovered had something to do with it – I'm encrusted up to my knees.

I climb in the jeep with my muddy boots and turn on the ignition, shifting into reverse. Mud sprays all over the place and the front wheels spin. *Shit!* It's stuck. I leap out, run to the back and retrieve the little shovel. I don't want to disturb the new roost, as it were. Come on, Harry, dig; the wheels sink further.

Dammit!

I kneel down, trying to get the shovel deeper, and it gets stuck. I pull as hard as I can … heave … heave … OH NO!

CRACK! SNAP! The handle breaks straight off and I fly backwards into the mud. Arse, and mud muddy arse. Great, that's all I need.

'Harry, honestly, you can't stay upright or clean for five minutes.'

'What the …' I peer skywards, my focus blurred by the sun's strong rays. A beautiful face swoops down and smothers my lips with lashings of sensual licks and velvet kisses. My muddy predicament seems far removed as I wriggle into his tempting clinch. He makes me forget where I am, what I'm doing, who we are and how we're supposed to behave; everything fades away the moment his touch ignites my skin.

The feeling just intensifies every time I see him. I've never experienced depths of passion like it. My awakening has at long last arrived, despite being stuck in the mud, literally and physically.

'How did you know where to find me?' I ask, after a much-enjoyed grubby grasp.

'I wanted to see you, so I tracked you down. A few questions here and there and it's surprising what a good-looking movie star can find out!'

'The smug vanity of the delusional!' He studies my eyes and his pupils squint in mischievous mystery. He pulls me in and puts his hand over my mouth. 'I missed you and this is the only time I've had in between junkets. Now, shut up. I'm taking you to lunch.'

He masterfully whisks me up in his arms.

This is refreshing, until I detect a dank puddle seeping

onto his clothes.

Surprising or not that surprising we are able to eat our lunch in peace, no whispers, winks or nudges from distant corners, no eyes interrogating our space, our only slice of time. I text Marissa to tell her I'm eating. She knows I hate missing meals, it sends my body into revolt. The pub in its remoteness, both in manner and setting, serves our afternoon well; Alex feels more human to me away from his entourage and trappings.

But back in the car instead of a warm satisfaction filling my body I feel a sense of doom. This isn't going to last. Alex, will move on as soon as the film has wrapped, and me, but what will I do? Will I be able to move on?

The reality hits me: here I am driving towards a real relationship, and Marissa and Tim have been through a hurricane at sea; they are a battered ship that has come out the other side stronger and more resilient than ever. I'm starting to think I must look ridiculous, even to a shallow teenager; a lost, aging, desperate, sex-starved stuntwoman. This is a mere sneeze of an encounter, a liaison of circumstance compared to Marissa and Tim's conquest of the ages!

Oh, shut up, brain, and stop giving me grief. Why does every woman analyse and compare? There's not a lot that you can compare in life, all is unique and, to be totally honest, incomparable! Must be getting my period or something, I am melancholic, trite. Captured by my own thoughts I glance sideways at Alex's head bouncing in time with the track's potholes. He has nodded off and is lightly snoring. I smile; this is an odd day.

I try to force myself to be light-hearted and appeased but shift uncomfortably in my seat. I still feel uneasy, as if I'm in limbo – nothing around me makes sense. Usually I have a clear plan on what proportion of my fee is going towards my next big adventure, this time I haven't even thought where my travels will be. I need to take back control of my head. Alex is a distraction, too much so. Inadvertently, resentment seethes through me onto the steering wheel so by the time Alex wakes up after a deliberate heavy-handed swerve I'm in a rotten mood.

'Steady on, Lewis Hamilton.' Alex's groggy voice pops out, his head cracking backwards. I over-correct the swerve and jolt him sideways. 'Do you want me to drive, Harry?'

'Why should I want that?'

'You just seem a little ... tetchy.'

'Alex, it would have been nice if you'd asked me before you decided to come here.'

His face drops in confusion. 'I didn't think you'd find it a problem.'

'Well, I think that's your problem: you just assume everybody and everything will accommodate you and your demanding presence if and when you feel like it. Not once do you think mere mortals have anything to do away from your plans.' I'm being totally unreasonable but can't seem to stop.

Alex's face tells it all. Not only is it shocked but his eyes are hurt, confusion and anger sweeps across his brow.

'Harry, no need to get spiteful. This is simple – I'll go if my selfish presence annoys you so violently. I merely came to find you because the last weeks haven't allowed us much time together. I see that was a mistake and I read you wrong. You can pull over here and I'll get a cab.'

'You won't get one out here.'

'Not your problem is it?' His tone cuts into my bones. Why do I have to be so horrible?

'Harry, stop the goddamn car, I'll get out here.' His transatlantic accent pierces the air. It seems more pronounced than before. Shit, I've taken my thoughts too far. The fact that Alex found me and came all this way is such a sweet gesture and I've ruined it by looking at the dark side, speculating and unburdening my unfounded anguishes on to a man that was asleep five minutes ago. Why are women so nuts in their subconscious? We find it so difficult to go with the flow unless the flow has been monitored, gauged and tested. I don't know what to do; I can't possibly back down now so with regret I stop the car.

'See you around, Harry.' Alex bolts out of the car, I sit, stunned, unable to utter a single word.

He cuts a fine figure walking down the country track. I just stare at him as his pace quickens. I'm such an irascible lame brain, so much so I'm paralysed to my seat in disgust. He's fading into the mist. Suddenly, I wheel spin into reverse and drive towards his diminutive silhouette.

'Alex, get in,' I order out of the window. He jumps back onto the muddy verge in surprise.

'Jesus, Harry, I thought you were a country lunatic.'

'I am rather today, so just get in and forget what I said.' I muster the conviction of someone who's in control and has no qualms whatsoever.

'That's very accommodating of you, are you certain?' The underlying hint of sarcasm is funny when Alex looks at me with teacher's eyes but I restrain the rising giggle that's bubbling up my gut. It's no good – I relinquish myself to a giggling fit.

'I'm glad you find it funny. There was me, just about to walk to the nearest hill for any bloody 3G signal, my GPS doesn't even know where it is. I could have frozen out here!'

I can't stop laughing. 'I'm surprised the Hollywood studios haven't put a tracker on you – for a start we didn't come that way!'

'How would I know where to go? I was asleep, if you hadn't noticed.

Then I woke to find myself in an argument that I hadn't even participated in. You can at least give a fellow a chance, Harriet! I must be terribly disagreeable in my sleep. I do humbly apologise for my behaviour.'

'Yeah, well, you should watch that.'

'Don't worry, I will. It's a lethal outcome, me the movie star being booted out in the middle of nowhere for something I knew nothing about! What was it – a test of survival?'

'Oh, you movie stars are so dramatic. Let me call make-up for you, I detect a shine on your forehead. A bead of worry, perhaps.'

'Unbelievable. You have the audacity to scorn me even through your berserk Lucifer phase!' I'm still tittering as Alex jumps in, frozen to the bone, cursing under his breath.

'If this is some initiation, I'd gladly bribe the arbiter, just give me the bank details.'

'Theatrical won't build you a shelter, dear!'

'Oh, now I'm theatrical. Well, if I knew it was a survival course with you I'd come prepared. Don't think you can do the outside better than me, missy. Didn't you see my last action piece? Stranded in the Arctic with nothing but a jumper and a small roll of string?'

'With the epidemic of mutated alien bears and their ferocity against humanity as company, yeah I saw it.'

'You don't sound impressed. Well you wait, when you're stuck up in the Arctic and a pack of bears come charging, you'll wish for me and my magic string.'

'Think I'd rather jump into the glacier.'

'You think that now, but beware, feisty one!'

With the tone back to normal sparring Alex soon makes me forget my little bout of episodic madness and we continue in silence.

I feel him turn and stare at my cheek; I ignore it and pretend to be engrossed in the road.

'Harry, I didn't mean to blunder in, I know I should have asked you. I just had the thought and acted on it without any thought, if you know what I mean.'

'It is a nice surprise.'

'Not as nice as I planned it in my head. You're right, I

am a bit self-important. Men don't think further than one idea at a time. There was no ego involved, really there wasn't.' His earnest voice makes me melt into the darkest chocolate, a gooey river of rich emotion.

'It was a really nice thought, really it was. I was out of order. I was such a cow.'

Alex falls to the floor.

'What's wrong? Alex, what is it?'

'Can't compute … Harriet apologising … meltdown.'

'Shut up,' I titter.

'Or you'll what?'

'I'll bruise that ego of yours to kingdom come.' Thinking my witty comeback was the jewel in the tête-à-tête crown.

'Tut, tut, you know I'm the king of the Arctic kingdom.'

'Don't tempt me. I have enough petrol to drive to the Outer Hebrides and test your abhorrent claims, oh Arctic King with a piece of string!' I stick my nose in the air with triumph. 'Why did you do that film, by the way?'

'You're not suggesting it was short of artistic merit and realism, are you, Harriet?'

'No, it was a true masterpiece. Utterly moving.'

'When one wants a nice pad in LA, one must do commercial money-spinners, especially when one has a stake in the merchandising and one's integrity can be seen by one's property portfolio! Plus I secured all the land around my Mum's house – the developers were encroaching so I bought all the land off the National Trust so it will stay a village.'

'Commendable indeed, King of the Arctic.' I smile to myself– he is a real gent beneath the surface. 'I have to go back and check on Marissa.'

'Tim was really anxious.' What??? Did my ears deceive me, how does he know Tim?

'What … you know … how do you know …?' This freaks me out. Is nothing sacred in my life? I think better of it and contain my anger.

'Don't be mad, Harry, please … let me explain. It was the other week and your phone went and I answered it by mistake, you know, when you were in my Winnebago. I know you don't like to attract attention and your stupid ringtone is so recognisable. I pressed the wrong button and it went to loudspeaker and I panicked and answered "Harry's phone can I take a message?" It was sort of automatic, I didn't mean to pry, honest.'

It's a plausible explanation but how does he know about their situation?

'I just got chatting with Tim about architecture and my new house needs remodelling – it's a sixties box. I remembered you'd mentioned he was an architect.'

'Do you think Tim suspects anything about us?'

'Doubt it … he knows we're working together. I told you, blokes don't think like that. Look, we had a common interest and we just got around to talking about houses and he said he was planning something special. What, you don't believe me? He was the one who said you might be down this weekend. I was coming to see his handiwork too, only if the outcome was good, of course and if you didn't mind.'

'Bit of a backward plan.'

'I know, I am totally self-absorbed. You have every right to kick me out.'

'In the future, don't pick up my phone.'

'OK. In that case could you please change your ringtone to less than a thousand decibels?'

'I only have it like that so I can hear it in the country over the diesel engines.'

'If you want privacy, change that bloody awful din.'

'Stop picking up other people's phones.'

'All right, all right … can't a man make a mistake?'

'No, only women!'

He pinches my leg and I punch his arm. Tim must have rung to check up on Marissa, if she wasn't picking up his calls. He would have known we'd been in contact the whole time.

CHAPTER THIRTY

That night we have dinner with Marissa and Tim, and aside from the inherent burst of star struck excitement and googly-eyed staring from Marissa, it turns into a brilliant evening.

The wine flows and laughter ruptures the new home's wooden beams. Alex has an extraordinary ease with people, albeit mostly showmanship. He seems relaxed – not that I ever see him anything but relaxed.

We are essentially in the middle of nowhere so there's no one to spy on him. It must be really nice for him not to be paraded in public and Tim and Marissa are successful people in their own right, quite unconcerned about his fame. After five minutes of drinking games he is fair fodder like the rest of us. Well, Tim is unaffected; Marissa follows me into the toilet like an excited pup, demanding to know how serious things are between us.

'You're reading too much into this,' I say for the billionth time.

'Like hell I am. He followed you across England, now that's not someone who is flinging it!'

'That might be so, but he's bound to make grand gestures – it's the world he lives in. Now, if you don't mind, I'm ready to pee out half a bottle of wine.' She doesn't take the hint and just slams the dusty door shut for even more delving. She sits on a crate and ignores the fact that I'm waiting for her to leave so I can pee in peace.

'It's quite obvious to me he doesn't see it like that. Why involve yourself when you don't have to? I mean, he's making a real effort here, charming the pants off Tim and me. All those nice things he says about you, this is not a casual interest. What about when he poured the wine? He was seeking your approval before reaching for the bottle in case he stepped on Tim's toes. He could see Tim was a bit messy and sloppy. So polite, so caring, oh you must see.'

'Marissa, you're mistaking a well-rehearsed charmer for a boyfriend who's trying to impress his girlfriend's mates.'

'If you choose to ignore it I can't do anything about it. I know what's show and what's not. I haven't taken leave of all my womanly senses.'

'If I just agree will you leave me to pee?'

She rambles on and I can't hold it in any more. Just because she's loved-up again, misguided love euphoria is breaking out more often than a Mills and Boon story in her head.

I continue to sit on the toilet, thinking she might leave me to it, but no, she's as drunk as a skunk.

'Ohhh, shall I go and earwig what they're talking about?'

'Marissa, we're not thirteen!'

'I bet he's too proud to admit his feelings.' She's off having her own conversation again.

'MARISSA! Look at me. I have not a scrap of make-up on, I'm caked in mud, my hair looks like it's having its own Mardi Gras. Alex is not falling for someone that looks like this. He has perfection, which is a world he'll go back to once we've finished filming.'

I'm sardonic enough to grab her attention. She thrusts her hand on mine and squeezes it, even though I have toilet paper ready for the imminent after-task. She squeezes it with such force the paper gets ripped and half of it sticks to her sequinned cardigan. Oblivious to her new white appendage she waves her arms as if she's just discovered the biggest romance in history.

'Marissa, I'm not saying Alex is a bad guy, I am being realistic.'

'Ohhh, poop on you ... This is not someone who just wants to get his oats, far from it. He's made porridge already, now he's in for lunch and dinner!'

'I expect it's a power-kick porridge or muesli ... I'm not knocking it, I mean it's nice to have a brunch occasionally ...' I stop, realising how silly this all sounds – when did food become the great relationship metaphor? We both look at each other and giggle.

'Well, if it's soufflé you want you'd better stop him drinking.'

'Marissa!'

'You can't beat a giant sausage, no chipolatas for you!'

'MARISSA!'

'Is he?'

'Like a donkey,' I yell, just to shut her up. Marissa shrieks with laughter.

'Maybe you should pull your knickers up – you don't want to look too eager.'

She waits for me to finish up and then we head back through the half-finished kitchen. Suddenly she grabs my arm. 'Just don't be too ...' searching for an appropriate word, '*Harry* about it, will you?'

'What's that supposed to mean?'

She opens the doors to avoid answering me. Tim and Alex are standing in front of a roaring fire looking very pleased with themselves, and half a tree appears to be hanging off the massive fireplace.

'Look, my sweet, we've hunted down a tree.' Tim puffs out his chest. Marissa giggles, steps up onto her tiptoes and gives her husband a kiss. 'So I see.'

'Right, time for games.' Alex pipes up after we've

marvelled at their handiwork.

'Games, eh!' Marissa says, blatantly flirting, then hiccups herself down on the sofa.

'Yeah, games, Madam M.'

'This sounds interesting.' Marissa is all over the place. She finally slumps on Tim – they're as far gone as each other now. She necked half a bottle of wine in the toilet, how long were we in there for? Long enough for them to fell a tree, obviously.

'How about truth or dare?' Alex pipes up.

'We're not fourteen!' I sarcastically add, although a bit loudly. I must be squiffy too.

'I thought you weren't thirteen a moment ago – make up your mind, woman. If you're not thirteen you must be fourteen!' Marissa chuckles through a congratulatory nose-in-the-air quip; she's on form.

'What … what were you two doing? I must say, Harry, I like your friend. She doesn't hold back, she's the only one I've seen who isn't slightly scared you'll cripple them with a karate glance.'

'Very funny. Marissa, you might want to take the toilet roll off otherwise you'll ignite!' I raise my eyebrows at her so she'll drop the subject – whatever that subject is.

'Touché, Harry, touché.' Her eyes are beginning to roll.

'What have you been doing?' Alex is desperately curious, wants to know if we've been talking about him, but before I can say anything Marissa butts in.

'Let the carousing begin, and by the way, Mr Canty, not all conversations are for your ears.'

'Anyone for champagne?' Tim says, popping the cork, it goes everywhere.

'We'll have to break open another now.' Marissa swiftly pops open another bottle and soaks Alex and me in the process.

'Looks like I will be having champagne truffles tonight!'

'Don't count on it, Slimy!'

'Harry, you say the nicest things.'

There's a boyish demon look gathering all over his face. Oh, what the hell, and I kiss him like there's no tomorrow.

Tim and Marissa have fallen asleep with the champagne bottles in their hands. I take a photo – it's a comical sight and it is rather a Kodak moment. Their reconciliation!

'Alex, could you move Tim's legs away from the hearth? He's like lead pipe.' I busy myself making them comfortable so they don't wake up stiff and contorted, and put a blanket around them.

I step back, pleased with my handiwork. I grin at Alex and he stares, gormlessly, back at me. 'What is it? You're not about to hurl, are you? Do you want a bucket?'

'What … NO, Harry, I don't want a bucket. I can handle my drink. Marissa means the world to you.'

'Yes, she does. They both do.'

'They're a great couple.'

'They are. I'm just so glad they've worked things out. I just can't imagine them not being together.'

'Do you believe in "the one"?'

This is rather deep. 'I believe in the sanctity of marriage.'

Alex guffaws.

'What?'

'I didn't picture you as the marrying type.'

'My father and stepmother are a great match,' I say, reclining on the sofa. 'They make it look easy.'

'My mother and stepfather are a great match too but my father, on the other hand, has had three wives.'

Like father like son!

'When my mother died it took my dad years before he found love again. Shall we call it a night?' I brush at an invisible thread on my jeans, tears gathering in the corners of my eyes. I blink them back. I'm fine. I think it's the wine that's making me emotional; it's just irrepressibly sad to think I never got to know my real mother.

'I'm sorry.' Alex sits down next to me. 'I didn't know.'

'It was a long time ago.' I shrug. 'I was four. It was a car accident. She was in a coma for days.'

'That must have been tough for you, growing up without a mum.'

'Do you mind if we don't talk about it?'

'OK.'

'The point is, my dad was devastated when my mum died and he grieved for a very long time, and I don't think he ever thought he'd find love again but he did. Ruby came into his life and they have been happily married for ...' I count on my fingers, 'fifteen years. I am so glad he got to love again.'

'He's lucky to have found love a second time.'

'Yes, but I don't think it comes easy for anyone. I think timing has a lot to do with it.'

'Maybe I just haven't met the right woman.'

'You've certainly done extensive research.'

'Low, Harry.'

I grin. 'You'll live.'

But his eyes take on a faraway, hurt look and I think my comment upset him.

CHAPTER THIRTY-ONE

Alex is quiet on the drive back. In fact, he hasn't spoken more than ten words since we left. I feel groggy myself so I don't mind the silence. Two nights of shambled sleep, one night in a wicker chair, and last night with Alex as my bed and a dust blanket as a duvet – I don't think there's a tog count for that. I couldn't believe we actually stayed on the beanbag without rolling off during the night.

It had been fun, like camping out in a wooden lodge. The house is amazing and has Marissa's ambience all over it. We left them both with their heads in buckets of coffee but euphoric smiles on their faces.

I stop for petrol and when I get to the automatic glass doors I glance over to my car and see Alex in a heated conversation on his phone. His face is red and his body posture aggressive. If the phone didn't have its rubber cover I think he might crush it.

I jump back in the car, tossing over a cola can and some fruit pastilles. He ends the call abruptly and picks up the cola can.

'Everything OK?'

Alex just nods at me. He is totally distracted and seems eager to make tracks.

'Have we got very far to go?'

'Not far, another couple of miles or so,' I say. His iPhone keeps buzzing and he keeps hitting the off button.

'Aren't you going to answer that?' He stares at me as though I've just insulted his teetering genius intellect.

'No.'

Excuse me for asking. 'Since when did you have a sense of humour bypass?' Shit, didn't mean to say that out loud.

'What?' His voice is angrier than is reasonable. Maybe it's payback for my nutty episode yesterday.

His iPhone buzzes again and he thrusts his hand over his brow. He doesn't speak to me again until we're driving up the high street. I can see flashing lights and some sort of kerfuffle outside the hotel's modest entrance. On closer inspection it's the paparazzi.

'Harry, can you drop me at the back?'

'Sure.' This is what we normally do but I can't pretend his manner

hasn't pissed me off.

'Not the usual place but by the kitchens, it's around the other side.'

'Er, OK.' I try desperately to sound unconcerned. 'What do you think is going on?'

'Fuck that I know.' His face is thunderous. 'I *said* to go around the back.' He's nearly shouting.

'I am!' Alex is blooming nuts. 'It's the next turn – this one goes to a farm.'

I'm actually counting down the minutes until he gets out my car.

I pull up behind a shed where they make the chocolates and Alex jumps out. I was just about to make a joke to lighten the whole mood but he's gone. I just catch a glimpse of his bag disappearing behind the fire escape. I sit trying to figure out exactly what happened, reeling the non-events back and forth in my mind. Nope, I can't fathom this one at all. Good weekend, small hiccup, hiccup resolved, fun had, more fun had, good rapport between all parties …

Nope, the boy's a loony toon.

I drive out to the high street. It's full of cars and traffic has stopped. Not a typical Sunday evening in rural Buckinghamshire; hundreds of photographers are gathered around the entrance. It can't be for Alex – they've known he's been here for months. My jeep's height gives me a slightly better vantage over the developing frenzy of the crowd but the flashes are disorientating and all I can make out is a woman in a long red dress. It must be a publicity stunt for the film, probably Felicity. I'm just accelerating when I see a mane of cascading blond hair, so long it must be hair extensions. It doesn't look like Felicity – she must be wearing very high heels. The magic of stylists!

CHAPTER THIRTY-TWO

It's four when I bundle through the front door at the B&B. I hear muffled laughter as I peer through the kitchen door. Farmer Toads is outside mending one of Kathy's shed doors, she's got a huge bottle of her homemade cider out there and they are having a whale of a time. I wave furtively through the window, trying to keep my head down before Kathy beckons me out. She signals with her hand but I shake my head and gesture tiredness with mine. She winks and indicates to thc freshly cut cake on the sideboard. I give her a thumbs up and blow her a kiss.

Alex didn't want to stop for lunch and that's not normal for either of us. I feel an uneasiness rumble from my stomach and that's not just hunger, an unsatisfactory end to an extraordinary weekend. Feeling glum I make a quick sandwich and take it, the cake, and a hot chocolate into the cosy den and settle by the fire. Luckily there is an old film on, *The Sandpiper* with Burton and Taylor. Brilliant … one of my guilty girly pleasures. The couple are intriguing to watch, their passion so obviously raw, even though both were excellent at their acting craft. That's where I come to the conclusion that Alex can't be acting – passion is hard to disguise. I watch the beauty of the performances, the obvious fascination that they both had with each other; I'm

transported into their chemistry, my eyelids are heavy …
zzzzzzzz.

'Harry, HARRY!'

I snort awake. 'Er … what … er … yes …' I must have
dozed off. Kathy is hanging over me with excitement. 'We
better be watching the six o'clock news, it's all over the
village, you know, the hotel where your *friend* is staying …'
Her voice topples out quicker than marbles in a school
playground.

'What's going on?' I stretch, bleary-eyed, but before I
have a chance to bring my senses together there she is,
standing outside the hotel, all cameras flashing and
reporters shouting. It wasn't Felicity at all but someone
called

Kimberly. I have a vague sense I've seen her somewhere
before – I think she was on a soap opera or something in
the US.

Kathy is gripped by the footage. Actually, I start
wondering if Kimberly is in the film at the end; there is a
mystery cameo role that is being kept hush-hush for PR –
some vixen comes to corrupt Alex's character when he's
fighting against his vampire morals, how ridiculous does
that sound? Give me Christopher Lee's depiction any day. I
think nothing of it until I hear one reporter shout, 'Are you
and Canty still an item?'

I peer intently at the screen, my heart in my mouth,
waiting for her response. She is deliberately ambiguous with
her eyebrows … As much as one can be with that much
Botox and filler – she looks like an overstressed puffer fish.
It's so unearthly, unholy, unwholesome, unreal.

'Kathy, it's just a PR stunt,' I say groggily, nestling down
under my blanket.

'To be sure, but it's not every day we see one of those
Hollywood creations down here.'

'You see quite a few, you had one under your roof the
other day.'

'No, Harry, tis not that. What I mean is those Frankenstein creations, the ones that have been sculpted under a hot burning flame, dat's what it looks like to me, anyway. You stay natural, my girl, you're far prettier than all this eyelash and hair additions, you'd tink they were pantomime cows with those long peculiarities.'

I laugh. Thank heavens most people don't mistake trickery for anything to do with beauty. I watch the screen; the woman looks like a vampire already. She's brazen in front of the camera. I lean forward, there is a fascination about her. I'm studying her every movement now then boiingg … it hits me colder and harder than a raw slimy kipper – what did that reporter say?

Still involved? Now I am on the verge of exploding, my guts are somersaulting. I feel sick, disorientated, but Kathy is perched on the edge of her comfy armchair, hanging on every word gushing out from the square box. I stare powerlessly at the box too, it's eating all my hope.

Alex never mentioned a thing, why should he? CLANG … the proverbial bell finally chimes. That's what all the SMSs were about – it was probably her.

I shake the green-eyed monster from my head and think rationally about the surreal situation unravelling in front of my eyes. The press will make up anything to sell papers; it could be a deliberate PR stunt to create interest. My mind replays every detail of the weekend; Saturday was good, Sunday feckless. It must have been his agent informing him about the PR spectacle, that's what it was. I unwillingly grab my laptop and type Kimberly's name in. Straight away it comes up with photographs of her with Alex on set in that silly doctor soap opera. A snake looks less constricting than her body language towards him. It's obvious there is some history, why didn't he tell me? I flick through pages and pages of them at events, premieres, there are pictures of them kissing. SLAM! Right in the gut.

I pick up my iPhone with every intention of shouting

my mind down the unsuspecting line to Alex's ear but then I think better of it. I knew he was a cad and, just as I thought, I was the gullible filler until the real glamour – as putrid as that might look – came along. Or back, as it seems in this case. How idiotic to think I thought we were turning a corner. I thought I'd been let into the real Alex, I thought we had a ... connection ... huh ... Oh yeah, there was a connection all right. His sexual appetite with his notion of conquest, getting the resistor into bed. I'm angrier with myself than him now.

I rush out into the open-air feeling ... I don't know what to do with myself. It's raining, I'm cold, I have no feeling, just numbness. I try to rationalise ... RATIONALISE!

I jump in my jeep and drive like a mad woman down the country lanes and somehow land up at Alex's hotel. I sit parked around the back staring up at his window. Shit, I've become a jealous deranged stalker. I'm possessed. This won't do. I go to turn on the ignition and just see a hint of a waif-like female silhouette gliding swiftly across his blinds. Alex's suite has been specially modelled to the back of the hotel so no one would know where to look. He paid for a few suites to ensure privacy – looks like he needs it now. I drive without sensation: I drive just to drive. I'm in the middle of a common when the engine starts coughing. Shit, there's steam coming out the bonnet. I've been in a total daze. I just hope there is water left in that old stagnant bottle of mine. I stop the car; the temperature gauge is off the scale. At least it diverts my mind out of its current status of gloom and mounting incredulous anger. I pop the lid and steam burns my face. I jump back, fall over and start crying. I don't know how long I sit there in my own misery, it must be a while, then there's a flash of headlights and a car slows up. Oh no, I hope it's not a crazed person. Hang on; I'm the crazed person. I stand up and look as aggressive as I can. A burly man jumps out from an Alfa Romeo, the lights blur my vision, and I pick up a spanner in preparation of an attack. Of course I can karate chop them into dust but you can still feel vulnerable in this type of predicament. Wake up, Harry, you are not a helpless woman!

Shielding my eyes from the glare I can make out the familiar swagger: bloody hell, it's Paul the rigger.

'Thought that was your car, Harry, what's the problem?' Immediately he puts himself to work under the bonnet. I don't know why but I feel like crying all over again.

'It's your good fortune that I have this blooming Italian car – that way you're forced to bring your tools out with you,' he says jovially. 'You know you're gonna have to get this car to a mechanic? The head gasket is blown as well as a hole in your radiator. I can get it ticking over ...' Everything he says is real, true and tangible ... a cold slap of reality compared to what was racing through my mind five minutes ago.

'Thanks, Paul, I'll ring the hire people, they can do it. Bloody stupid thing.' I kick the wheel.

'Shall I follow you home just in case?'

'Do you want to get a drink? Maybe the Snapping Turtle or the Fox and Pheasant?' Paul looks at me in surprise.

'I mean, it is still early and the weekend isn't over yet.'

'Sure,' he smiles, and gathers his tools up.

The Snapping Turtle is adjacent to the hotel, tucked around a corner of the medieval town's square. Paul doesn't know what's hit him. I storm straight ahead, nearly busting the old wooden door off its hinges, and order a large brandy. I hate brandy. Paul scuttles after me, poor guy; I immediately order another.

Somehow he manages to sit me down by the roaring fire. Not knowing quite what to do, he offers up the menu. 'You hungry?'

'No, just thirsty.' He does a double-take, trying to check my mood, but my eyes are fixed on the flames. In a flash he's back with wine, olives, peanuts, crisps, taking no chances of me getting too soaked too quickly. A sensible move.

I'm impressed. Paul takes control, pushing the various snacks directly under my nose. He has the good sense not to ask what's up. It's apparent he's not oblivious to my demented rage, rather he is in possession of emotional tact that I wasn't expecting; a rare quality indeed, especially in a man.

I know Paul pretty well in a one-dimensional sort of way: in work, in a pub, but I've never spent time alone with him. I eat an olive and slug back a glass of wine.

'Whatever has happened, it's not worth it.' His words spin in my head. 'I was married once,' he suddenly says, resting his glass on the table in front of me. I look at him in shock. 'Surprised? Most people are. She was gorgeous, a real beauty … personality of a street rat and morals … well the morals were the problem. She was only happy when two or three men were after her. Only concerned about her pulling power, her looks, nothing else. Needless to say it didn't make for a lasting relationship.' I sit, stunned, and I don't know how to reply.

'Sorry, Paul.'

'Don't be – she was a manipulative tart. The best thing I ever did was divorcing her skinny arse.'

I nod with a smile but I still can't believe he was married.

'It's best to just get on with your own things, Harry, and let nature take its course. Don't succumb to the glamour; these situations we get into at work are all just that … making up the pretend. Their footing has no basis, a bit like a building, the blocks have to be on level ground first.'

After I have made so much effort to conceal everything Paul has spotted the smallest tell. He peers at me, intrepid with his eyes.

'Don't worry, your secret's safe.'

The release I feel across my body oozes out and my appetite returns. I pinpoint the peanuts. Who would have thought Paul would be my emotional flying buttress, my solace in a time like this?

'Is it obvious?'

'You were distracted every time he came near.'

'Shit, did anyone else notice?'

'No, you were the consummate professional. My ex-wife was an actress; a desirable one too. You can't compete with the constant competition their egos naturally seek, the reinforcement needed when they're satisfied their spell has worked on you. I'm not saying he's like that but it is the downfall of stardom, the convenience of getting what they want.'

I dare to mention the commotion of today's events. 'Do you know what happened this afternoon?'

'It was madness. No one really knows why she turned up. The paparazzi were there before she was so it looks like the whole thing was staged. That guy, you know, the one who's always on the phone hanging off Alex's every move, we've nicknamed him the waiting pariah, he was there on his phone all day. I was reading my newspaper at breakfast and the man just sat there, incessantly pressing the little keys.' He pokes a few olives onto a cocktail stick. 'From where I was sitting I could hear a raised voice on the other end.'

Of course it was Alex – he was probably furious his little frolic was on the verge of being found out, a boy's lollipop snatched away mid lick. The shift of power makes a monster of men.

In sullenness I eat the rest of the olives. Finding a decent man is no more complicated than flushing a harvest mouse out whilst he's flossing his teeth. My head slumps down and Paul pours the wine. He's cleverly silent while I reflect over how stupid I've been.

CHAPTER THIRTY-THREE

Kathy clatters about the kitchen, she's brought me two racks of toast and she's literally bouncing off the walls trying to occupy my mind. She's a wise woman. The paper's headline screams out, there's no avoiding it.

True Love Bites.

A sleepy village got a surprise visit by one of Hollywood's most talked about TV stars, Kimberly Roberts, twenty-six. The beautiful starlet descended upon the sleeping village of Little Brumble after much speculation over Canty's private life in recent months. The visit has fortified gossip surrounding the screen stars' on–off relationship after they met and fell in love on the set of The Doctor's Shifts, *the popular TV medic-drama. According to an inside source, the romance was never off. Our source, reportedly from Kimberly's inner circle of friends, said it was the love affair of the century ...*

I've read enough. I lift my coffee cup and drink the last dregs.

A lyrical voice bursts out from the hall. 'You can't be believing all these tings they write in papers these days, full of rubbish ... full of it.'

'Thanks, Kathy, got to go.' I rush out, forgetting my jeep is probably en route to the workshop. I hear gravel squashing beneath tyres and for a moment I think of Alex and turn with a surprised smile on my face. Paul pulls up the driveway with his Alfa Romeo.

'Thought you might need a lift this morning.' I smile, jump in and fight back the tears. I will only have this one journey to recollect, contain, and compose myself. I will rise above his seedy conduct.

'Press still hanging around then?' I'm trying my best at normal conversation.

'No, that's the weird thing. As soon as they got that shot they were off, and no one's seen Alex since yesterday afternoon.'

'They must have a lot of catching up to do.' I try to joke but my lip quivers.

'Apparently that Kimberly's gone psycho,' Paul says eagerly.

'How can you tell? I mean, nothing moves from the neck up!'

He chuckles. 'She went totally bananas at the breakfast staff because she ordered an egg-white omelette and they just did a normal one.'

'Surprised they didn't have breakfast in bed.'

'Harry, as I said, no one has seen Alex since yesterday afternoon, only his publicist has been allowed in the room.'

'Well, it keeps the media guessing, doesn't it?'

'No ... something's up. The woman is a nightmare, highly strung. I think she's doped up as well. She reminds me of Janice Dickinson on crack!'

I laugh at the very notion. Paul is a tonic, a breath of fresh air.

We have to drive through the village to reach this morning's location. I avert my gaze, but we are caught at the roadworks. My eyes wander towards the hotel – what bad timing: Alex is running to his car, dark shades on. It looks like a woman is in tow but he slams the door in her face. I peer over, blinking at the scene that just happened;

maybe she got tired of waiting to go public too. If she's been waiting since Alex's soap opera days, no wonder she's gone mad.

'Paul, go, GO, Paul it's green!' I desperately want to get there before Alex.

I gulp down a double espresso, wanting to seem sprightly on set but feeling anything but. My nerves are frayed to the point of ragged so caffeine really isn't helping. It's the second time the director has called cut.

'Harry, you're too quick,' Sam whispers from aside.

'Harry, you nearly clipped my eyebrow with that heel!' Luke scowls at me.

Breathe, Harry, breathe. I can't believe I'm fucking up on my timing. It's one of my greatest skills, one I've honed for years; I can shut my eyes and react to a kick before my opponent has even thought about it. Damn that man.

With many disgruntled huffs the director picks up his megaphone: 'Let's go again.'

We do many takes before anyone is satisfied. When the director calls a wrap I can't face anyone so I slump off to the tea van. Tentatively, I look around – business is pretty much as usual, nothing abnormal. A few people are peering over towards the Winnebagos. There is a muffled shrill voice piercing the low mumbles of the riggers; must be one of the make-up girls having another trying session with the evil vampire who thinks his make-up is unflattering, ACTORS – who do they think they are?

I spy Pepé le Pew, the French cinematographer shouting a barrage of French profanities at Paul and some other crew-members before stampeding off. A small round of applause erupts from the crew-members and Paul takes a bow before catching my eye and giving me a wink. I wonder what that was all about? After the laughter dies down a horrendous crash is heard, like someone throwing metal against metal, next thing Alex is storming out of his

Winnebago. He roars past everyone, ripping his vampire cloak off. Not far behind him is Kimberly, red-faced, teetering in stilettos that are sinking into the mud; she looks ridiculous. We all stand there motionless.

'Get security,' Alex snaps at anyone close by.

'Alex, you'd better listen, your career is all down to me. If I hadn't gotten you that part with Daddy you'd be nothing, no one.'

My mouth hangs open. She's scarier in real life than the purposely blurred, soft, up-lit television shots. Alex's face is harrowing as he grabs her hands and leads her off behind the tents.

The day is a hard, long slog, and cold. I can't feel my feet or my left buttock. Alex disappeared three hours ago, apparently nursing some migraine ... all bullshit. Kimberly wasn't removed from set but held up in Alex's Winnebago all afternoon.

Her presence has tilted the natural balance; Sam's been noble, calming the team in their resented overtime. I feel somewhat responsible but it was only one scene I retook three times, nothing compared to cancelling a whole afternoon's filming schedule.

I'm bored waiting for the next shot so I wander restlessly, meandering around the many vans and Winnebagos, just to get feeling back in my buttock. I can hear a heated conversation bouncing off soft furnishing. Shit, I'm outside Alex's. I duck down, not knowing what to do. I press my ear closer but it's still muffled, Kimberly is definitely in there with Alex. My knees lock and, oh damn, the door handle is rattling. What to do? What to do? Oh no, they're walking in my direction. I can't move, they'll look around, so I decide the best plan of action is to do nothing, stand still, and hope for obscurity.

'Oh yeah, your precious Jane, who can forget.' Her voice is livid, bitter and chilling.

'Leave Jane out of this, you don't know anything.' Alex sounds exasperated. Who is Jane?

'Who is it then? What's the tart's name?' Her menacing words travel like electric shocks about my stomach. 'You don't care about her, Alex, stop being ridiculous and take your place next to me at the Globes.'

I shouldn't be here. I don't want to be caught listening. I carefully retreat and trudge back to set, melancholy squeezing itself around my heart like fog encroaching lonely ships at sea.

The next week drags. I spend most of my time avoiding Alex. Fortunately he has a film to make and all his spare time is preoccupied with controlling Kimberly's outrageous threats. By all accounts she hounds him day and night, trying to wear him down. He must have made a pact with the devil, judging by her relentless persecution. I've been spending a bit of time with Paul, the odd after-work drink, nothing romantic, just hanging out, and it's been easy. I don't think he fancies me anyway, I just think we understand each other and mutually enjoy the company. I've spoken to my parents and Marissa and promised to visit as soon as filming finishes, which is only a week away for me. I did have Marissa rising to Alex's defence and so I hung up on her; she soon got the message I don't want to talk about him.

CHAPTER THIRTY-FOUR

Whack! That's the sound of a fist slamming against my cheekbone …

Thud!

That's the sound of my body slamming against the wall.

Crack!

That's the sound of my head as it smashes against a concrete post … and then darkness. I am falling down a tunnel, my hearing and sight fading in and out as I float gently out of consciousness. My mind is still … at last … ah, so peaceful—

'Harry! HARRY!'

Noise crashes into my sub-consciousness. I try to block it out but it persists until I can no longer ignore it. Eurgh, my head.

I come around to a burst of activity. Recognisable voices shouting at each other but I can't quite focus on what is being said as I'm having trouble … eh, focusing. Everything is too bright and blurry, I think I'm going to throw up.

'Harry! Harry!'

There's that noise again but it's not noise, it's a male voice, a warm, familiar male voice and it's caressing my left ear. My eyelids flutter open, savouring the soothing voice and gentle touch.

'Harry. Can you hear me?'

I lift my head and squint with my good eye, and there he is, the man I hate, crouching down beside me, his face just inches from mine.

My head is spinning. I try and jerk away and a gag bellows out of my mouth.

He brushes my hair from my face and forehead.

'Eurghhh … mmm,' I murmur. I close my good eye. I just need a moment of silence …

'Harry! Please answer me.' Alex's voice grows more urgent.

I jerk awake. 'I'm fff-fine.' The fog in my head starts to clear and I force myself to focus. I look up and Alex's gaze bores into me.

'You're bleeding.'

'Am I?' I say blankly. I touch my forehead and there's blood on my fingers.

As I start to focus on where I am I'm aware that I have become the centre of attention. I'm going to hurl, not a girl's best moment, and certainly not one for an ever-multiplying audience. Donald Mann has called cut, Sam and Luke have come over.

'Harry, you OK?' Sam kneels beside me.

'You fucking idiot, Luke, you could have killed her.' Alex has more fury than a petrol-laden bonfire.

'Now calm down, Alex, this doesn't help,' Sam intervenes.

'You're supposed to miss!'

'It was an accident.' Luke's voice is full of remorse. I know he'll be

hating himself right now.

'I'm OK, Luke,' I reassure him.

'No you're not.' Alex seems like a man possessed.

'Luke. Go. Harry will be fine,' Sam commands, then rounds on Alex. 'Now, Alex, get a grip and calm down.'

'Did we get the shot?' I ask Sam.

'Yes,' Sam reassures me.

'I'm very happy.' I look up and Donald is smiling.

'That's good.' At least I'm finished for the day. I go to pick myself off the floor but my legs wobble. I sit back down. 'I'll be fine in a minute. I'll just sit here for a second.' I smile, desperate to defuse the tense atmosphere.

'No, you are not fine,' and before I or anyone else can say anything Alex drags me to my feet, lifts me up in his arms and carries me off set in front of the entire crew.

What the fff-uck!

'Alex!' I hiss angrily. 'You're not Richard Gere, and this is not an Officer and a Gentleman moment.'

But he isn't listening. I'm aware that everyone is watching us, the faces alive with curiosity. I try to look for Sam and Donald but my focus is sluggish and I feel the warm slime dripping down my throat, my mini vomit has arrived.

I want to struggle to fight and break away but at the same time I want to cling to nestle into his strength. The conflicting sensations swirl around me, colliding with the dizzying awareness of the heat generated by his body and the coiled power of the arms that grip me. He doesn't let me go until he has lifted me into his trailer and propped me up against the table.

'For God's sake, Kimberly, would you go and infect someone else's life for once!' he shouts at the skeleton on the sofa. She looks like a skeleton in my eyes. 'This isn't a spectator sport, you know.' All I hear is a mumble of insults and the door slamming.

Alex starts rummaging in the cupboard. 'I can't understand why you do this,' he mutters half to himself.

I'm only now beginning to realise the implications of what has just happened. I will be humiliated as another notch on Canty's bedpost. 'Alex, people are going to talk.'

'Let them. Oh, Harriet, why do you have to put yourself in a vulnerable position where you can get hurt? I don't understand. We all know you're tough – you don't have to prove it.'

'You're over-reacting.' I choke out over another bit of mini sick. Oops, there goes his Armani shirt that was lying pristine on the sofa.

Alex ignores it. 'Just be still and quiet, I'm going to call an ambulance.'

'Don't be ridiculous.' But Alex isn't listening. 'For goodness sake, I've had worse!' I can really taste bile now. This doesn't seem to be what he wants to hear. I have a strange impulse to laugh.

'Why are you laughing? This isn't funny.' Even through all this dizzy, nauseated fuzziness I can find irony quicker than dogs on the trail of bacon. It is strange – we haven't spoken for days and now he bulldozers his way back into my life and behaves like he cares.

He steps towards me; there is so much menace in his slow advance that I start to retreat and wriggle down the end of the table. Alex doesn't stop until his face is inches from mine. 'What are you doing?'

'I'm going to attend to your wound.'

'There's a set nurse for this. You were only a TV doctor, don't let it go to your head.'

The reference is double-edged – he reacts to neither implication. No explanation of Kimberly or his fake heroics.

'You could have internal bleeding.' I have an impulse to giggle again. Alex is just panicking. 'I promised myself I wouldn't drag you into this circus that's my life and I can't seem to help myself,' he says.

Is that all he has to say? I'm tired of his dramatics. Maybe in la-la land they live like this but not me, and especially not in rural Buckinghamshire.

A deep-seated feeling of retaliation springs to my legs.

'Harry, please just lie up – you shouldn't move. Not until you've had a brain scan.'

'For God's sake, Alex, this isn't a film. I've been knocked out and been sick – that's the sign of recovery in my business.' I force my arms underneath and push my body up with all my might, only to fall straight back down.

I mumble under my breath. His Florence Nightingale role won't wash with me. He rushes over with a flannel and mops my brow and wipes my bile-encrusted face.

'We need to talk.'

'I was wondering when you'd finally get around to that,' I say, sarcastically, ready for the lies and excuses.

He is tender, reaching for iodine to wipe my head wound; it stings ever so slightly. Every time I wince his body shudders. I suppose his next line will be 'your pain is my pain' or some crap like that.

He leans in and he smells delicious – well, anything would smell better than me at the moment. I breathe in all of him and involuntarily part my lips in an expectant kiss; it feels so natural for him to be close. Alex looks down and panics. 'Harry, don't go to sleep, DON'T GO TO SLEEP!' He shakes me slightly and my moment of weakness passes, emulating some poorly written coma scene in a medical drama.

'I need to explain something about Kimberly. She's sick, she needs …' There's a knock at the door and whatever Alex wants to tell me about Kimberly has to wait.

'Alex, open the door!'

Sam steps into the Winnebago, followed by the set nurse.

I don't know what Alex thinks he can tell me that will make a difference as to how our relationship meets its end. When a relationship dissolves, one party always ends up slightly more de-elevated than the other: usually the one more smitten or left with diminished dignity after begging and bribery has failed. I could see this fairy tale getting miserably unfavourable as soon as I let my coupling thoughts take the driver's seat. I did imagine what it would be like to journey to India with Alex. It would have been nice to have a travel companion for once; someone who I could just turn to, point and say, 'Wow, look at that.' I mean, it's nice to share experiences sometimes.

Alex is pushed aside as the set nurse checks my pupils. His hand reaches out in one last attempt to keep control and brushes my wrist. Sparks fly out of my palpitating chest and in my giddiness, you've guessed it, I'm a little bit sick on the nurse.

'That's good, but I need to keep you under observation. You're concussed and we need to monitor this vomiting.'

'Does she need the hospital?' Alex asks.

'She will go to my trailer – I'll watch her,' Sam insists. If there is any risk, any risk at all, Sam will make me go to hospital; you become a better diagnostic than a medic after thirty years in the stunt business – unconsciousness is your second state of being.

Sam helps me to my feet. He has the power grip of a transformer, freaky chi strength mastered in the mountains of China for ten years – one touch and you're begging for mercy.

The last thing I see as my head swings low is a tremulous look descending upon Alex's face, most likely in regret of his reactions showcasing the connection that had taken place between us.

CHAPTER THIRTY-FIVE

Hours pass and Sam lulls me into going to a private hospital just for safety. All checked out with a clean bill of health, no brain swelling or internal bleeding, and I'm homebound to the B&B.

'You know, Alex was right about getting you checked out.' Sam

looks at me for a response but I keep silent. 'Lucky he acted so fast in keeping you awake, eh?' Again he waits for a response.

'Yes, very valiant … yes, yes, yes … he was very attentive.' What is Sam getting at? He knows, doesn't he? Oh God, who else has put two and two together?

'Harry, the last few weeks you were happy, this week you're off balance. Whatever is going on with you, you can control it.'

I think Sam is trying to tell me something, not outright but suggesting an answer that relates both to work and life. As always, he's my Yoda.

'OK, Sam, thanks.' I slam the door in controlled defiance. I wink, wave and waggle my hand at him.

He speeds away, beeping the horn a couple of times.

It's my last day on set and all eyes greet me with silence

and then there's an urgent flurry of 'How are you?', huge irises anticipating, searching for a bigger answer, so I duly reply with a curt succinct,

'Fine, thanks.' And totally blank them out. I feel like a sideshow. If this is what it's like to be famous, you can keep it. It's freaking me out. I feel distressingly paranoid; everywhere I turn eyes are peering back. Luckily Paul charges over with a coffee and diverts their attentions perfectly.

Karumph … swing … thud and it's over.

A crescendo of applause ripples around the cast and crew.

After months of hard work and lots of coffee it's now over to post-production.

I always feel a bit sad, a little bit empty, when filming ends. You work so closely with everyone it just feels strange not to be seeing them again tomorrow.

But I suppose there is the wrap party to look forward to …

Alex is edging towards me when Sam, Luke, and the stunt team decide to rush me with a huge bouquet of weeds, drowning out his approaching figure.

'Really you shouldn't have,' I say, furtively peeking over the top of the wilting buds. They do this every time.

Everyone is celebrating; their voices subside into a low buzzing sound.

I'm not really concentrating on what is being said, just nod and smile intermittently. I feel tired, which is only to be expected after my concussion, I suppose, although I suspect my emotions may be the culprit of this spaced-out, sedated stuntwoman. Oh yeah, I was really het up by the hospital trip so they gave me Valium to make me lie still in the scanner. Valium has dulled my anger towards Alex; actually, it's dulled and diluted most of the feelings I have.

Paul keeps filling my glass but I'm unaware that my

wrist is positioned at a forty-five-degree angle so most of it is landing on the ground. I decide to slink away, taking a few stealthy steps backwards, slowly, slowly.

'You can't help yourself, can you?' What, what the hell? I nearly trip over the shadowed body in the twilight.

'Excuse me,' I say harshly, as the question posed was aggressive.

'You honestly think you hold up to me?' My eyes blink at the shrouded character, trying to make out its face.

'Very funny, Felicity, I know you're fond of the costumes.' I turn to go but a thin arm thrusts itself in my chosen path. 'Looks like you could do with eating a few more victims, oh vampy one!' thinking the arm was a trick of the light with the dark skeletal costume.

'What?' The voice is too high, too nasal, for Felicity; maybe she's putting it on. I don't know how many times she's done that to everyone's phones. On set she placed bets and ran a book. She loves practical jokes; the best one was when she got Luke with his triplet love children. She pretended to be Caroline Benton from Social Services, and had his DNA graph. But Luke just panicked and wasn't listening to the ludicrous paternity methods. So I suppose it was my turn, as she hasn't managed to get me yet.

'How did you get that arm to look so bony?' I'm curious now.

'What?' She's staying in character admirably. I giggle. 'Good voice, though you sound ridiculous!'

'What?' She can go on like this for hours so I mosey onwards to my car. All the floodlights crash on, illuminating the whole location for packing up, and in the stark reality of near daylight I fling a 'cheerio see you later' look back at Felicity. Momentarily my eyes deceive me and I do a double-take: there, standing rigid in between vehicles, is Kimberly, looking at her arm in bewilderment.

Shit … I had no idea. What a weirdo though. What is she doing sneaking around the set in a hooded cloak, waiting to throw out dramatic statements at someone she doesn't know or has even met? She is definitely delusional.

Unhinged, must be a case of mistaken identity. I hurry with my keys and make a break for it – she's scary. Maybe I won't have to go to the wrap party if I sneak out without anyone noticing.

'Oh, hello, Luke.' Damn, he's standing by my jeep with a bottle, slightly the worse for wear already.

'She hasn't phoned, Harry. I only looked at another woman, OK, stared at her chest but …'

'Welcome to the girls' world, Luke! Get in, I'll drive you back.'

CHAPTER THIRTY-SIX

The wrap party is looming over me and I'm still dithering over whether to attend. Luke has more or less coaxed me into going as his plus one, out of sympathy for him since Isabel is refusing to answer his calls. Boot on the other foot springs to mind. It might teach him to tread more carefully when dealing with the ladies in future. I've never seen him so distraught so I guiltily half promised to go with him for moral support.

I slip into my Selfridges purchase, a long, backless, shimmering black dress by Diane von Furstenberg. The material glides over my body. It is the most elegant dress I own. I lift up the hem and wrestle my flat, heavy-duty, footwear off – this is a dress for heels – and replace them with fierce-looking Manolos.

BBBBBBBEEEEEPPPPPPPP

Luke obviously carried on drinking. From my bedroom window I can see he's strewn all over the embarrassed taxi driver. I open the window and shout down, 'Give me a minute.' The taxi driver looks up, thankful, and Luke slumps down on the back seat waiting restlessly.

I don't even notice or have time to think on the journey to the wrap-party venue, which happens to be in a vast mansion house about a mile away from the village. Luke is twittering on about love lost, love found in a repetitive loop.

'For goodness sake, Luke, phone her and apologise!'

He looks at me, stunned by my brusque tone.

'OK, OK, anyone would think I was irritating you.'

We both laugh and Luke humbly picks up the phone and confesses his immense idiocy on her voicemail with the panache that only a real idiot-in-love can.

Thank goodness we arrive because I can't bear hearing it for another minute. Feeling a bit heartless I grab Luke's arm as we stumble towards the imposing doors.

'Luke.'

'Yes, ma'am?'

'Cut it out!'

'OK, ma'am!'

I roll my eyes. 'The weirdest thing happened to me.'

'Oh yeah?'

'Just as I was leaving, Kimberly accosted me, saying some weird stuff.'

'What? Alex's Kimberly?'

I wince. 'Yeah, that one.'

'She's a loon,' he says.

'They're an item then?' I ask searchingly.

'No, but that's not what she thinks.'

'Really?'

'She's a number-one nut job. Alex has a restraining order against her in the States. There's some confusion of its jurisdiction over here. He's had lawyers on this since last Sunday. She's totally obsessed with him and her father has asked Alex out of kindness to keep the real circumstances quiet until he can get her a head doctor over here. Poor bloke, he's been a prisoner all week. Shit, I wasn't supposed to say anything!' He clamps a hand over his mouth.

Too late! I wasn't expecting that. Real life can be stranger than fiction.

'I think he slept with her years ago ...' Well, that's not

surprising. Immediately my eyes dart around looking for Alex. They come to rest upon Paul who's animated in some rock-climbing story. Then I spy Alex sitting on a chesterfield in the far corner surrounded by women, seemingly enjoying himself. A blonde has draped herself over his left side like a dribbling brooch; the women actually look like vampires ready for the kill.

Luke chats with the bartender and orders a most complicated cocktail. Every time he thinks he said all the ingredients he starts again counting them off on his fingers. The bartender is very polite, letting him ramble on. I hang around the edge of the room, hidden somewhat by a pre-Raphaelite statue on a column, thinking I'm safe from prying eyes. Felicity spots me and brings over a tray of nibbles.

'Where did you get to earlier?'

'Oh, I took Luke home – he was on the fast track with drink.'

'Not avoiding someone are you, Harry?'

'No, why would you think that?'

She arches a brow at me.

'I don't know what you're talking about.'

'Fair enough. Paul is nice, though, isn't he?'

'Felicity, just give me a canapé and shut up.'

'Not for you, for me.'

She's not serious? Shit. She is.

'I'm not sure actresses are his thing,' I add carefully.

'Oh, look at that French idiot!' she says, changing the subject, and we both duck our heads out from the column.

'He might go into another hissy fit if the pâté is bad,' I joke.

'Harry, passion in a man is a quality I deeply admire. '

She says it so seriously that at first I'm not sure if she's joking. Then I see her smirk and I snort out a laugh, really loudly. Everyone stops in their midst and stares towards the statue. We both duck behind like little girls giggling our heads off. We can't stop, tears flow down my face – it's a while since I've laughed.

'Nearly had you, didn't I?'

I laugh. 'You crazy girl.'

Felicity grins delightedly. 'Don't be angry at Alex.' And with that low parting shot she glides off to wind up the cinematographer.

I stand, woefully stunned, then, needing the toilet, I skirt the edges of the room, attempting to go unnoticed. I walk delicately backwards, amused by watching Luke ordering another concoction that the bartender has never heard of.

CRASH. A glass falls to the floor.

'Oh, um … sorry.' I offer an apology immediately to the unfortunate bumpee. My eyes follow the legs up as I try and clear the glass from the floor.

I meet his eyes – and it's like an electric shock all over my body.

'Finally, Harry!'

'Alex … oops! Excuse me,' I say and somehow force myself to walk on, grimacing slightly. He grabs my arm, intense electrical sparks fly, making my heart palpitate.

'You look …' Words seem to fail him and sadness floods his blue eyes. 'You look … er … incredible.'

A short humourless laugh escapes me. 'Umm, I was just going … to …' I lamely point towards the bathroom sign.

Then we fall silent. Alex tries reaching for my hand but I swiftly move back, averting my eyes to the nearest wall.

'Please, please, Harry, just two minutes, that's all I ask …' I consider it only for a moment and shake my head, continuing to pass him. Not here.

'Just one minute then …' He forcibly grabs my arm and I'm just about to punch him when another hand grabs my other arm, pulling me in the opposite direction.

'Sorry, Alex, I need Harry.'

'Sam!' I glance up, gratefully. He ushers me away by putting a protective arm around me and leading me to the entrance. Everyone continues to party inside the great hall, dancing figures stream into a colourful blur through my peripheral vision as Sam quickens his steps, immediately sensing something is wrong.

'Sam, what is it?'

His face is grave and a cold chill runs up and down my spine. 'I've just got a call from the hospital.'

Cries of delight echo in the background and the music fades to a mere thudding beat. Everything has suddenly become very still and quiet, adrenalin kicks my chest out and my breathing becomes shallow.

Sam's eyes don't falter. 'Harry, your dad's been taken to …'

I say nothing, I feel sick. My vision slips away in a tide of drifting hazy pictures rolling out to sea.

'HARRY, HARRY!' Sam shakes me as tears crash down my face. I need to see him. I need to get to the hospital. Sam is already one step ahead of me.

'I have my car outside. I only have sketchy details – Ruby's phone had really bad reception and she couldn't get any connection to yours at all.' I check all my coat pockets; it must be in my other jacket back at Kathy's, how stupid, how thoughtless, I'm the world's worst daughter.

'Before you start beating yourself up, mine barely works out here. It just so happens I was on the roof terrace talking with Donald so he could smoke his blasted cigar that I got any at all. Now don't panic and try and keep calm. I know he was rushed in with a suspected heart attack. Ruby found him in the garden.'

I have so many ugly images forming in my head that I'm barely holding it together.

Sam squeezes my shoulder. 'Now let's see what Paul's Alfa can do!'

With all the confusion I never realised we weren't in Sam's car.

'Paul gave me the keys. You are a popular girl.' Sam's

attempting to cheer me up but it falls on deaf ears.

CHAPTER THIRTY-SEVEN

We pull up outside the hospital and I'm frozen to my seat. We've driven for three hours straight and I spent the whole-time fidgeting. Now we are here I feel so sick, so fearful of what awaits me behind those doors, that I don't budge.

Sam opens the doors and then I'm on my feet being guided through the many corridors, the never-ending lifts up to the cardiac ward. I feel as if I'm four years old again, being led to see Mum. It's as if history might repeat itself. My legs give way but Sam catches me.

'Harry, remember you can control this too.' He looks at me with all the love in the world, tears forming quietly in his gentle eyes. I stand up straight and march towards the sister who shows us to the intensive care unit. I bravely walk passed the heavily sedated bodies in the other beds, unnerved by the periodic pips and bleeps of the equipment. Some are breathing but it's an unearthly sound, a mechanical breath. My body shivers from head to toe. One curtain flickers to reveal a glimpse of a visiting priest. I ignore the macabre scene by shutting my eyes as if I was a little girl escaping monsters under my bed. I reach a private room and peer through the window; countless tubes and machines are wired up all over him. I want to rip them off;

they are invaders, they have stolen his colour, his rosy cheeks. The hope I conjured up momentarily seeps out of my body in an almighty wave. I walk over to his frail body. My dad the tough guy. Tears are engulfing me; I place a kiss on his forehead and sit holding his hand. I don't know how long I've been there when a doctor pops her head around the curtain corner.

'Harry?'

'Er …' I wipe my face dry. 'Yes.'

'He told us not to call you Harriet!' She smiles warmly. 'When we took him down for surgery,' she adds quickly, seeing my confused face.

'Surgery?'

'Oh, you haven't spoken to—'

'No, I ha—' Anger rushes in and my fists clench. The doctor immediately holds her palms out, signalling me to calm down. Any more flapping and she'll be a fledgling taking off. *Shit, Harry, control.*

'Calm dow-n … I can call you Harry … can't …' My God I must be scary, the woman is visibly shaking. Alex has borne the brunt of this a few times; I wonder why he stuck around at all, I'm horrible.

'Er … um … yes … well, as I was saying we took him down for an emergency triple-bypass. We're keeping him sedated for now as we had a ventricular leak. We replaced the valve too …'

A heavy feeling washes over me, my arms and legs are just phantom limbs uselessly hanging. Peering over her reading glasses she ruffles the notes on her clipboard chaotically. 'No, no … you misunderstand. The operation went well, the heart attack served him well. Like a warning. He's like a brand-new man, or he will be. He has to rest for a few weeks …' Her voice fades away and relief sweeps into my outer extremities which regain some feeling. I collapse back into the chair elated.

I see Ruby's head bob past the double doors. She's

talking to Sam outside. I walk, blinkered, towards them.

'Ruby!'

I rush into her arms, nearly knocking her to the floor. Her arms come around me. 'Harry … easy, sweetheart, he's going to be fine.'

We all sit under the grey fluorescent light with cheap coffee scalding our hands in its thin plastic cup. Two hours pass until the sister allows another visit. As it's the middle of the night she lets all of us in under the strict instructions of being quiet and respectful of other patients.

Not more than ten minutes go by and finally Dad opens his eyes. The release of tension is bigger than a bungee jumper falling from the moon.

His eyes, at least, are exactly the same; full of warmth and humour.

'Now you didn't all have to dress up on my account.' His voice sounds dry and even more gravelly than usual. I completely forgot I was still wearing my floor-sweeping gown.

I smile uncertainly. 'How are you, Dad?' I can barely get my words out.

'I have had better days.' His eyes mock. 'You didn't have to leave the wrap party on my account. I hear the canapés stink here.'

'Even a heart attack can't put a stop to your dry wit, eh, David,' Sam says.

'If I'd known you were visiting I would have got the whisky in!' He winks at one of the ICU nurses.

Then he coughs, clutching his chest, crumpling the sheet up. It's obvious he's in tremendous pain; he waves his hand, horrified at all the wide-eyed faces desperately looking for help.

'Do I look worried?' A young authoritative Irish accent spills out from the darkness. All eyes turn to the efficient-sounding nurse seated in the middle of the room at her desk. 'Now if I don't look worried, nor should you. You got that? Any more jumping out of your skins and you're out of my ward, have I made myself clear?' In the easiness of her humour the whole world is put to rights and we all nod and smile dutifully.

After heaving some oxygen into his lungs Dad asks for a cup of tea. Ruby and Sam volunteer as I think they're both a bit scared of Nurse McNabb and besides, it is the middle of the night. Sam seems to have taken a particular shine to the confident nurse, offering to bring her a cuppa too.

'Come and sit down,' Dad whispers as he pushes the oxygen mask aside. He puts his hand over mine. 'How are you? You look a little peaky.'

'You're hardly an advert for a holiday brochure either!'

We both giggle and Dad shoves the oxygen mask back on, steaming it up.

'That's enough excitement over there, David. Now be good or I'll be over there reassessing where to put that catheter.'

I sit back while Dad dozes after his ordeal. My mind drifts off, lost in the unfamiliar rhythmic beats of the surrounding machines, contemplating how insignificant my grumbles have been recently. When I look at how tenuous life can be I ask myself to show more clemency to those who partake in mine. I have been wretched and self-absorbed and it has to stop.

Nurse McNabb gently rocks me awake; emotional tiredness got the better of me.

'Now, would you go home and let me get on? It's four in the morning and that dress needs hanging!' I look around, dazed. 'And yes, all his vital signs are perfect. Now be off and come back when you've slept. I'll be having no grouchy visitors on this ward tomorrow!' She takes me to the door where I'm tickled to see Sam barricaded by girls' feet, legs, hair and bags, propped up in the waiting room. Ruby has been here for hours – she must be exhausted. I push the girls down on a porter's trolley and Sam effortlessly lifts Ruby without waking her. I grab her bag, find the keys for the four by four and drive back to the farm where we settle everyone in the lounge and promptly fall asleep for the whole day and night.

CHAPTER THIRTY-EIGHT

I wake to the smell of coffee. The sofa has been vacated and all that remains are the fluffy refuse of disturbed sleep.

'Where's Ruby?' I ask in the direction of the kitchen.

'She and the girls went to the hospital. She wanted you to sleep on just so you're fresh for visiting this afternoon. Remember, Nurse McNabb said not too many visitors at once, it will tire your dad out and he needs rest.'

'He looked well, considering, didn't he?' I search for reassurance.

'Amazing, considering he'd had a heart attack and major surgery all on the same night.'

I unravel the duvet cocoon, stand up and stretch. I pick up the coffee, which Sam has already milked and sugared, and blow. Looking above the steaming cup into the garden I see the overturned wheelbarrow, soil scattered all over the lawn. My heart winces at the thought of my father collapsing onto the cold ground. Luckily Ruby was making a casserole and called the ambulance immediately, otherwise the story might have had a different ending.

'Eat this, Harry.' It's a bacon sandwich.

Sam's phone beeps. 'See who that is.'

'It's Ruby, Dad's been moved to the cardiac ward, he's

out of the ICU.' I look up and grin.

Thank goodness, today has started with the best news, the greatest hope. I'm transported into happiness.

The doctors and nurses are astounded at Dad's recovery.

'I can recommend it to anyone. McNabb runs a spa, it's not ICU!' Dad winks over to her as she hangs his case notes at the bottom of the bed.

'Don't you go thinking Sister Blackford is a walk in the park. Her beady eyes note an irregular bowel movement before you've even had it!' We all laugh and sentiment is good, relief conquering the fears of yesterday.

'Jeeze, David, trust you to outshine medical science,' Sam says as he gently slaps Dad on the shoulder.

'Don't think you'll be running around at home. Nurse McNabb has given me a strict list of what you can and can't do.' Ruby flings the recovery booklet up in the air for all to see, especially Nurse McNabb who's chatting with Sister Blackford at the end of the ward. The two women are of the yesteryear, strict, quick-witted and professional, with that ever-so-matronly presence exuding from their uniforms despite their young years. It's incredibly reassuring to have such committed souls tend to your only blood parent.

After an hour I go to stretch my legs, wandering around the many corridors, looking for the little shop I swore was on the second floor. Eventually, after a couple of wrong turns resulting in a slight panic attack, I reach it.

'Can I still buy—'

'No chocolate no flowers,' The little old Chinese lady says as she busies herself climbing a makeshift stepladder of crates to reach the door's lock.

'Excuse me?' I'm slightly puzzled and must look that way to her also.

'All gifts gone,' she repeats with annoyance.

'But I just—'

'Fruit, you can have fruit.'

The little shop is half empty. Great, I love being in the country, nothing is where you want it when you want it. I toy with the idea of a fruit basket but the fruit looks more battered than a computer programmer in a rugby scrum. One pineapple sitting proudly against a sea of second-rate chocolate bars later, I leave with the tacky over-sized basket rearranged into the strangest possible offering for Dad's bedside table.

I lug the monstrosity up the relentless hospital-smelling corridors and into the lift. It stops seven times before I reach the cardiac ward, bustling groups of nurses and porters entering and exiting the small grey box, each politely shocked at the extent of manoeuvring it requires to fit around me and my extravaganza. I'm sure I'm blushing but who can see behind this lugging great pineapple? Wholly regretting my gift choice as it spears out from its enormous basket, I waddle back to the nurses' station to plonk it down. Any minute now the feeble handle will de-wicker itself and I'll be left with a pineapple explosion, looking like a poor excuse for the Easter bunny.

'Thank goodness,' I say to myself, offloading my barmy basket in the middle of the counter.

None of the nurses are about – all is quiet; I hear muffled voices and laughter coming from a distance. I check the little change I have left in my pocket for the drinks machine – after Mrs-I'm-gonna-make-up-exorbitant-prices-I-shut-now – and promptly drop it all over the floor. Scrambling for the last ten pence, which has slid awkwardly under the machine, I hear raucous laughter wafting down the corridor again. I think to myself, *well, OK, I know doctors have a warped sense of humour, probably comes with the territory. I mean, dealing with people's inner plumbing on a daily basis you would have a somewhat macabre viewpoint … but really, it is a cardiac ward and some sense of decorum should be expected.*

I compose myself after a swift cola and release all the little burps delicately behind my hand. I stare at the pineapple and, believe me, it stares back. Chuckling to myself I pick it up for the last leg of its journey and proceed to the unveiling of Fruit Basket Extraordinaire.

As I struggle to pull the door open, carefully balancing the basket of forgotten beauty, I see there is a crowd of people surrounding Dad's bed. On closer inspection, it seems all the nurses and doctors from other wards have besieged the space. They don't look concerned – they're all laughing energetically. Surely Dad isn't telling his Sumo wrestling story already? I labour with my peculiar offering to reach as near to his crowded bedside as I can, two nurses running past me as I struggle to walk in a straight line. Trying to peer through the crowd I edge to the end of the bed, pineapple first, so people realign by necessity. Who would want to get in the way of a recovering man with a penchant for pineapples!

I smell something in the air and it's not hospital – I can't place it but it's a bit like musky vanilla.

Now I'm only three rows back from the front and steady the demonic arrangement with both hands for a momentary rest to see what all the fuss is about. The doctor before me is a burly man blocking my view. I gently elbow through with an 'excuse me' here and 'pardon me' there, sweat beads generating on my brow, more through embarrassment than physical effort, mind you.

I drop the pineapple right on Sam's foot.

'OWW.' But I'm not even concerned, for what stands before me is a sight that I couldn't imagine. The flowers, the chocolates, the balloons are overwhelming the walls, they are so big and sprawling. The eyes of the entertainer look up and stop, reading my flabbergasted expression.

'Alex?' I blink. The view is unexpected, the scene is ridiculous, there is a pineapple on Sam's foot and, to top it all, an audience.

'Harry, I couldn't reach you, then I heard ... um, then I ... er, came to see you were all right.'

'Alex was just telling me of your rough initiation of him.' Dad looks at me and I glance back and forth at the two then turn my attentions to Sam who merely shrugs his shoulders. I narrow my eyes at him and he smiles innocently at me.

I'm livid but have the sense to realise the entire hospital staff are watching our exchange more avidly than Wimbledon's final. Nurses are eyeing me intensely, doctors admiringly and Alex hopefully. All eyes would be an understatement, in other words.

A timid smile starts on Alex's face; a pleading look for forgiveness.

I hurriedly observe all the medical notes with autographs inked on the top page. A doctor breaks the stalemate situation unintentionally.

'So, shall we say paediatrics at three then, Mr Canty? That will give our nurses a chance to take control of their own temperatures.'

The ever-growing medical crowd laugh and there is such good feeling in the room I decide to bite down on my tongue hard.

'In fact, Mr Canty, there is one particular boy who has your action figures strewn across every possible surface, and I'm afraid he's not responding to the chemo as we hoped. If you wouldn't mind ...?'

'No, not at all, it would be my pleasure. But if you don't mind I prefer to keep this visit private. I mean, no press, if that's OK?'

'But of course, we fully understand.' The doctor points at all the nurses who hurriedly hide their phones.

The doctor turns and in the slipstream of his white jacket tails everyone resumes hospital business, and hastily at that. He must be the CEO, top dog or whatever they have at hospitals.

'Well, that's just splendid of you, Alex, helping the children.' Ruby pipes up.

My lips twist in rage – how can I show anger and annoyance now? Now that he's all pally-pally with my family and charitable with the hospital staff.

'Yes, jolly decent of you to check on Harry, and the gifts, it really is too much. Why don't you take them to the children?' Dad adds to his never-ending feat of selflessness. I swear my face looks like it's being electrocuted. *I'm fuming.*

Of course, everyone is oblivious to the tense situation, apart from Sam who blatantly continues to ignore my evil stares.

'Look, Harry, I never meant to—'

'Alex, just in time. Everyone for coffee, tea?'

The orders are taken and I purposely shove Alex's beautiful handmade chocolates away and replace them with the atomic pineapple.

I look at it, sitting overpowering everything in the room, and start to laugh.

'It's all she had – some idiot had bought the whole shop!' Everyone giggles at the bizarre collection and at Alex.

Dad coughs up over a pained chortled, 'It's an unexpected pineapple surprise, Harry, that's all, *unexpected.*' He hangs on the last word, deliberately engaging me, knowing there is more than meets the eye here.

I ignore everyone and go to get the beverages. Anything to get out of there.

'Harry, wait up I'll help you.' Oh bugger. Like a forlorn puppy he follows my quick pace to the vending machine.

'Er ... I know what you must think ... I would never intrude on ... I did phone Sam to ask if you were—'

'Intrude, INTRUDE! You don't know the meaning of the word. Now that you've got everyone onside, would you please leave?'

'Please, I tried your phone a hundred times.'

'You tried … TRIED. You didn't try very hard last week, did you?'

'You have every right—'

'Yes, Alex, I have every right to ask you to go. Who do you think you are?'

He hangs on the side of the vending machine, desperate for eye contact. I don't give in.

'I need to explain …'

'And you think the best place for your silly boyish explanations is at the hospital where I'm with my father who's recovering from a heart attack and a triple bypass? You think … the great Alex thinks this is the most opportune time to give some vague and useless excuse as to why he is such a prick? You do, do you?' I've never been this angry in my life. If I had a weapon I'd fear for what I might do, what my anger could tempt me to do.

He looks to the floor. I force the coins in the machine with might. 'You can't buy into someone's life and drop it at your convenience. You can't buy acceptance. You can't buy affections. How dare you come here.'

Feeling this is my last and final statement and he would go, I take the cardboard tray and turn my back on him. Luckily, he does not pursue the matter and I hear slow footsteps in the opposite direction.

CHAPTER THIRTY-NINE

For the second time today I waddle into the ward trying to balance a cumbersome array of offerings, this time off-balance in more ways than one.

'Alex will be with the children now, how charitable,' Ruby says as she examines her wristwatch. 'You never told us you and he were friends.'

Ruby inspects my face with a curiously excited look, only shared by expectant journalists.

'Er … well, we were friendly on set, I suppose.' I hope this is the end of her line of questioning. Ruby sits down gently on Dad's bed and both of them look at me as if I was hiding the crown jewels.

'It's very thoughtful of him to rush out to come here. According to Sam

he's cancelled his flight home and a BBC interview.' Sam has conveniently gone to look out the window. Oh no, they're both looking at me now; not so much journalist but hungry paparazzi. I can't lie to them.

'We went out a few times socially.' I start sugaring and fighting with the little milk capsules so I won't be asked to elaborate on the details.

My dad calms my shaking hands. 'Harry, that's not the behaviour of a man who's had a nice pint down the pub …

you know what I mean!' I hate it when he refers to sex like that. I screw my eyes up and make a strange sound of frustration.

'I think my girl's in love, Ruby!' He seems jovial, and a tad condescending. 'Look, she's getting angry again. Harry, I've never seen you so angry at one person – it must be love!'

'I'm glad my love life entertains you all so much!' I snap.

'So it's love life now.' Dad starts nudging Ruby who's beaming at the very thought of a superstar coming to eat her low-fat high-fibre cuisine. Damn it, poor choice of words, Harriet. Dad looks like he's been given the all-clear to eat as much cholesterol as he can. Sam wisely sticks to his window spot.

'I meant love life in the general sense, not with that ...' I refrain from over-reacting. 'I mean, not with Alex ... er ... and yes, that's very sweet he came to see if I all was all right. I will send him, or his assistant, a thank-you e-mail.'

This doesn't go down well. Ruby and Dad are whispering amongst themselves then both turn their heads to assassinate my feeble attempt at closing the subject down.

'Harry, pick up on the scent, will you!' Ruby is animated with frustration. 'The boy adores you, look at the actions of a man, not what he does or doesn't say!' Oh brother, this is going to be tricky, I don't want to divulge anything much but I will have to put them straight on wonderful Mr Canty.

Again I stand on ceremony, trying to explain my life. But I can't explain it. Dumbfounded by my own dumbfoundedness, I turn and gently lower myself onto the edge of the bed next to Ruby and Dad.

'I can't explain it.' I hear the words come out but I don't feel remotely in control of what I'm saying. I sit there in a haze. Ruby nuzzles up beside me, placing her arm around me.

'Harry, no love fought, no love lost, whatever he's done

he really wants your approval, your acceptance, otherwise why all the effort? He was ever so embarrassed coming in here. He got the whole hospital frantically searching for you when you couldn't be found. He sat down and said as much, he was very humble. Talk to him, *listen* to him, and then decide if you want to hate him forever, but don't decide on anything until you've talked, OK?' I look at my pillar of wisdom stepmother with the love of a biological child. Usually I'm so private but I can't contain my emotions this time.

'It's not that simple.'

'It never is,' Dad says after a puff on the oxygen.

'OK, if I agree to listen to him will you all stop talking about me?'

'Oh yes, definitely,' they say in unison, smiling broadly. I walk out of the ward, not with the intention of talking to Alex, just to get outside for some fresh air. My life being discussed is my own form of open-heart surgery, just with a more jaded prospect.

I sit down with a heavy heart and a thumping headache in the hexagonal courtyard garden. This place must have been built in the seventies. Some people in wheelchairs are convalescing in the early sun. I am tucked away in a quiet spot by a willow tree – it reminds me of Kathy's garden, that one moment in the last few months where I felt in harmony despite my sprained ankle: it was blissful. As I ponder over Alex and his grand gestures I think better of succumbing to a man who can't just be straight up and honest. As exciting as it was with him I'm not prepared for so much heart wrenching. All he had to do was phone, that's all. At least I could have been given the chance to understand his situation, not hear about it third-hand from everybody else. My arms grow cold and goose pimples erupt over my skin. I check the time; it's nearly four o'clock so I'd better go back up, visiting time will be over soon. I languidly stand up, getting a strong whiff of fresh paint. I look over at the people on the other side of the garden being tended and nurtured by their beloveds. Love must be about the same needs and wants.

I walk steadily towards the cardiac building and the paint smell gets stronger and stronger. I look around for activity but see none with a paintbrush. Then, just as I go to open a little side door, I hear my name.

'Harry … pssst … Harry.' I look around me, nothing. I reach for the door handle.

'Harry, up here.'

I look up and there, on the second floor, with face paint that makes him look like a chipmunk, is the topic of all the conversations. I burst out laughing.

'Harry, you've got to come up and help me, I'm exhausted. These small people are making a meal out of me. They think I'm a magician or a wizard. They were so disappointed I wasn't Harry Potter! Please, Harry.'

The look of terror on his face is priceless. I couldn't have been more pleased.

'Alex, you always said what a fantastic actor you are. Siberian alien bear hunter that you are, you can hone your expertise, play to your strengths!'

'Harriet!' He looks terrified.

'Bye, Alex.' I turn the door handle and let him stew for another twenty minutes before rescuing him from fifty children.

By the time the last little toddler has been removed from his back and chocolate cake from his neck, Alex's nerves are starting to materialise over his strong features. It's not obvious to those who don't know him – I suppose I know him a little better now. We say our goodbyes to the children and Alex signs a few more autographs for the nurses who have all pushed up their bras and undone their top buttons. Last time I saw a paediatric nurse she didn't try imitating the attire of *Baywatch*. But this doesn't bother me.

We walk down the corridor in comparative silence, each

not knowing what to say or when to say it. He takes a long stride and I start giggling.

'Alex, your hair is encrusted with chocolate and you've got a chewy sweet stuck on your back. Stop a minute, I'll get it off.' I brush him down, smelling the musky vanilla that seems to seep from his pores. This is the last time so I breathe it in deeply. My hands feel electrified at the touch so I stop and pat him on the back in a matter-of-fact way.

'Thanks, it seems you have something on your back too.'

'Don't worry about that, I'll change when I get home.'

'No, I mean you have …' Alex laughs. It's a short laugh at first, trembling into a fit of giggles.

'It's just that … Oh, it's just a little something!' He can't contain his mirth.

'What? What is it?' I'm visibly annoyed with him now. He pulls me over to a window and turns me around. I can't believe it. My reflection is stripy white; I have the shadow of the garden bench on my back.

'No wonder the kids thought we were clowns!' Alex and his ruffled chocolate hair and me and my bench paint stumble down the corridor in hysterics – we look ridiculous.

'Shhh, Alex, there's sick people here.'

'You're looking a little peaky yourself. A little pale!' He snorts back his tears and we both go out of the nearest exit, which happens to take us right back to the garden.

'The sign fell off – it's in the crocuses!'

'Shut up, chocolate head.'

'Is this the latest London has to offer in fashion?'

'Better than pink chewy earmuffs.'

'You sure about that?'

'Oh yes, it was quite deliberate.'

'It's that half-finished look. Shall we make it a complete design?' He picks me up and drops me back down on the bench. I pull him down and his jeans get covered in paint.

'You look like a convicted M&M.' I pull him over as he

sits on me, making sure the paint rubs in.

'You'll pay for that.'

'What with, jelly? You have quite a collection going on.' Before I can break away he kisses me. My first reaction is to push him off but it feels glorious, natural and exciting.

'Sorry,' he says, pulling himself back.

'No, I'm sorry,' I say. 'We should probably be friends. We can be friends, can't we?' This is harder than I thought; of course I don't want to be friends. Why do women tell such lies?

'Can I just say one last thing then?' His eyes fix firmly on my face. 'The problem is Harriet -,'

'Harry,' I reply.

He sighs. '… just ssh for a minute.'

'I don't like being called —' But I don't get to finish my sentence – he sucks the words from my mouth, kissing me with a violent hunger, his usual control for elegant passion gone with the feeling of wanton lust.

After a few seconds he pulls away and adjusts his position on the wet paint. He looks at me and gives me the biggest grin. 'Harriet, Harriet, HARRIET, I will say the name of the woman I love and you can't do anything about it, stripy.'

My heart does a pole vault jump and my mouth flops open like an iron gate against gravity. I have lost the power of speech.

'Kimberly is a dark horrible thing that I wanted to shield you from. I didn't want you caught up in her spiderweb of lies. If she knew how much I cared for you she would do everything in her power to ruin it.' He clears his throat. 'She's an awful, vindictive, twisted person and I didn't want you to have that ugliness near you … you're too beautiful for that.'

He just called me beautiful. And he loves me.

'Who knows what she would have done?' He continues. 'She picked up scissors the other day to go and stab you.

So, Harry,' he implores. 'My dilemma was very real. And I promised her father I would keep her with me until he could get to England. He's a nice man and I owe him a great deal. So there you have it. The truth.'

For a moment we just stare at each other; I can't believe I got it so wrong. So totally wrong. His eyes meet mine and all I can do is stare back. He hands me an envelope, his face long and sombre.

I hesitate then rip the envelope open. Inside are two first-class air tickets to India peeking out from their paper pouches. For a moment it feels like the oxygen has been sucked out of the air and I struggle to breathe. I could really do with a puff on Dad's oxygen mask right now. I stare, blinking, at the tickets in my hand. I still can't find the words, which is so unlike me. But this is it, now or never.

'I love you with all my being, all my soul,' he says, his voice cracking slightly.

I look back at the man I love, and a huge smile engulfs my face.

'Is that a yes?' Alex asks, cautiously.

EPILOGUE

I wake, bolt upright, my body clammy, my heart beating double time. Then I remember where I am and my heart slows down and I smile. Through the mosquito net I watch the shirtless figure drinking coffee out on the veranda. Now that's a sight you don't see on TripAdvisor!

I fight to get out of the net; it tangles up so I end up pulling the whole thing down on my head. Alex turns around when he hears the enormous clang.

He strolls towards me, a sexy smile on his lips. 'Harry, do you have to fight with everything you see?'

'Shut up, sexy, and get me out of this.'

'You're really going to cost me in these spa hotels; karate chopping the fixtures, attacking room service every time they open a door. Goodness knows what you're going to cook up for the masseur I booked for you later.'

'You can always visit me in my tent and save me from the alien arctic bears?'

Alex peers up at the hole I've caused in the ceiling. A worried frown is etched across his face as the iron bars swing limply, and plaster dust falls over my hair. 'You, my girl, need calming down.'

I sigh happily as he pulls me into his arms.

'I love you,' I say, as he carries me onto the veranda.

'I love you too,' Alex says, and we kiss then kiss some more. Did I mention how much I love travelling? India is so far my favourite country. It is hot and I have seriously hot company!

ABOUT THE AUTHOR

Nina Whyle is writing duo - Nina Bradley and Clare Whyle. They have been finishing each other's sentences since 2010 - but have been friends a lot longer.

You can follow them on Facebook, Twitter and Instagram.

Want to read more books from Nina Whyle?
Moving Up On Manolos
Fighting Love
When Life Goes Pop!
My DisOrganised Life

www.ninawhyle.weebly.com

Printed in Great Britain
by Amazon